From Rags to Kisses
The Survivors: Book XI

Shana Galen

FROM RAGS TO KISSES
Copyright © 2021 by Shana Galen

Cover Design by The Killion Group, Inc.

Also by Shana Galen

Dedication and Acknowledgments

This book is dedicated to my BFF from childhood—Laura Faulkenberry.

Thank you to Abby Saul for all her suggestions and revisions and editing advice.

Part One

I

She should have jumped over the body lying in the street. Everyone else was stepping over it, and she was in a hurry. That Charley had spotted her, and he was sure to remember her from last week when she'd managed to escape him after stealing that crust of bread. Jenny didn't want to be dragged before a magistrate or clapped in the stocks.

Again.

The body was barefoot and dressed in coat and trousers. It lay face down in a mud puddle, the wetness on the ground left over from the rain the night before. If horses and carriages ever passed through this dirty, narrow street in Spitalfields, the body would have been trampled. But no one with enough blunt for a horse and carriage ever ventured to this corner of London. There were no gaming hells or painted women or gin houses here. Just hunger, poverty, and despair.

Jenny slowed and looked over her shoulder. The Charley wasn't behind her. She might have lost him. Or he might have been too much of a coward to come this way alone. A few rough-looking men leaned against buildings, spoiling for a fight, and a Charley would make a nice target for their foul moods.

A couple walking in front of her stepped over the body as if it were a piece of trash. Nearby, a woman hung once-white sheets on a clothesline while a small child—Jenny couldn't tell if it was a boy or girl—clung to her ragged skirts. Jenny figured the body's pockets had already been picked clean, but she was starving. No harm in giving them another once-over. She patted it down then rolled it over.

She jumped back in shock and crossed herself when its eyes fluttered open. It was a boy, and he looked up at her with dark eyes, made darker still by large, black pupils. He gazed at her, unseeing, then closed his eyes again. Her heart slowed enough that she stopped fearing it would burst. He wasn't dead. She hadn't disturbed his eternal rest. Jenny glanced over at the woman, still hanging her laundry. She hadn't seen Jenny, but her child was watching. Jenny told herself the child had nothing to do with why she didn't walk away. It wasn't up to her to teach that kid some semblance of humanity, but she couldn't abandon this boy all together.

What if he died and haunted her because she didn't try to help him?

She stood and wiped her hands on her rough trousers. "Oy," she said and nudged the boy with the toe of her too-small shoe. "Ye better get up now."

The boy moaned something and didn't move.

"Oy!" Jenny said louder. "Yer lying in the street. Get up."

When he still didn't move, she swore then got an arm around his shoulders, his *wet* shoulders, and dragged him to the side of the street. She propped him up against a wall and sat down beside him. It annoyed her that her shirt was wet again. She'd been drenched in the downpours the night before. Though it was spring—or so she supposed because green buds had started appearing on the trees again—the morning was still cold enough that she moved closer to him, hoping to steal some of his body heat. Not that he had much of that. He didn't seem to have much of anything.

A cursory glance at his clothing told her it had once been good quality. It was little more than rags now. He had a black eye, bruises on his jaw, and scraped knuckles. "Looks like ye got into a bit of a tousle," she said.

He rolled his head to look at her out of his one good eye. "You might say that."

The way he spoke surprised her. It wasn't like the people she knew. It sounded like the gentlemen who came to Spitalfields half drunk and stumbled about with their friends looking for cheap gin and whores. They slapped each other on the back for their bravery when everyone could see they carried walking sticks and were followed by burly footmen, keeping anyone with nefarious intentions away.

" 'Ave to learn to run faster," she said. "Me. I can run fast as the wind. Were it the Watch or a group of rogues?"

"I tried to run," he said, raking a hand through his dark hair. "But two of them were behind me and then two stepped out in front."

"Oldest trick in the book," she said. "Two of them 'erd ye where the others lie in wait."

He held out a hand. "Aidan Sterling."

She looked down at his hand.

"You shake it," he said. "Like this." He took her hand and pumped it up and down.

"I know wot to do," she said, pulling her hand back. "I don't know why ye'd want to do it. I'm Jenny Tate."

His eyes widened slightly. "Yer a girl?"

"That's right." She always felt a little defensive when boys looked at her like that. She was thirteen and skinny and flat as a boy, and she dressed in boys' clothing to keep anyone from getting ideas—most especially arch rogues who ran the gangs in this part of London. But she still didn't like when people looked at her like being a girl was a liability. "And I could knock ye down quick as any boy."

"I don't doubt it," he said. "But then that little child over there could knock me down."

"Ye don't belong 'ere," she said. "Where do ye belong? I'll make sure ye get 'ome." And she might just get a big reward for it too.

"Unfortunately," he said, "I do belong here. I have nowhere else to go."

"Yer an orphan?"

"Yes. My mother died…what day is it now?"

Jenny shrugged. She didn't even know what month it was.

"I suppose it was a month ago now. My father died before that and *his lordship* hadn't thought to provide for us."

His lordship. There was blunt in those words. Jenny knew it. "Who was yer father?" she asked.

"You wouldn't believe me if I told you," the boy said. Some color had returned to his face, and he looked almost human, except for that swollen eye.

"Try me."

"The Earl of Cranbourne."

She laughed. "Yer right. I don't believe ye."

"I'm not his legitimate offspring," he said.

"Wot's that mean?"

"To be blunt, Jenny—may I call you Jenny?"

She shrugged.

"To be blunt, I'm a bastard. My mother was a chambermaid in the earl's service. When she bore me, the earl recognized me and gave my mother money for a house and for my schooling, but it seems he made no provision for me in his will."

"Ye got a lot of fancy words."

He nodded but didn't behave as though she were stupid. "It means, once he died, my mother and I received nothing. I'm sure she had a plan. I know she went to the new earl's chief of staff and his solicitor. But neither of them liked her very much, always thought she was a grasping—well, they wouldn't help her. Without any money, I couldn't go to school, we couldn't pay the rent. My mother became ill, and we couldn't afford a doctor."

Jenny knew a hundred stories like this. Half the children on the street had stories of parents who'd become ill and died because there was no blunt for doctors or medicine. The charity hospitals weren't much better than the street. But not everyone's story included an earl. Jenny wouldn't have believed it except the way the boy talked was definitely unusual.

She moved to tell him good-bye and continue her search for something to eat. It wasn't as though he could help her, and she couldn't help him. She could take care of herself, and that was it. If she started getting all soft-hearted and trying to save every street rat, she'd be buried under a pile of needy kids in two minutes.

"What about you? Are you an orphan?"

Jenny didn't move. No one had ever asked about her before. No one had ever cared.

"No," she said, even though she rarely talked about her family. "I can only wish I were an orphan." Her parents clung stubbornly to life, despite having every disadvantage.

"That bad, eh?" He scratched his head. Jenny imagined he probably had fleas or worse. "Perhaps we could be friends."

Jenny would have laughed, except he looked serious. She sat straight. She'd never had a friend before. The idea was intriguing. "Alright then. Wot do I get out of it?"

He gave her a puzzled look. "You'd rather our relationship be transactional? A business partnership?"

"Wot ye just said. Business. I do my part, and ye do yer part." Jenny didn't know why she was even suggesting such a thing. She knew enough of people to know that you couldn't trust them. Someone promised to give you half the loaf of bread they pinched, but then they disappeared with the whole thing. She'd been no older than four when she realized she had to hide any money she earned begging. Her parents would steal it while she slept if she wasn't careful. At first, she'd hid her half pennies under her pillow, but as she got older and wiser, she found a hiding place outside the dingy room where the two of them—sometimes three if her father remembered to come home—lived. A few years before her father had reached under her pillow while she was asleep, thinking she might still keep her coin there. She'd pulled a knife on him and threatened to slit his throat.

The next day, when she'd been making her way through Spitalfields, he'd ambushed her and beat her bloody.

Jenny no longer slept at home if her father was there.

The boy held out his hand, and Jenny looked at it. There wasn't any coin in his palm. "You shake it," he reminded her. "That seals the deal."

"Wot deal?" Jenny asked.

"We look out for each other. I share what I have, and you share what you have."

She squinted at him. "Ye don't 'ave nothing."

He tapped his temple. "I have an education."

"Book learning." She spat.

"I can teach you to read."

Jenny looked up at him.

"If you could read, you'd know what all the pamphlets nailed to the posts say. Then you'd know where to go to pick pockets."

"I'm not a pickpocket." She looked about to make sure no one was listening. "I'm a 'ouse breaker."

"Then you'll know if what you steal from houses has any real value."

" 'Ow does reading 'elp with that?"

He gave her a surprised look. "Books are everything. They have all the information in the world. Let's say you steal an old coin. How do you know if it's a hundred years old or five hundred years old? You look it up in a book."

She looked him up and down. "All yer book learning 'asn't kept ye from being beaten and 'aving yer shoes pinched."

"Then I can learn from you and you from me." He offered his hand again. "What do you say?"

She put her hand in his, surprised at how warm his flesh was. He moved her hand up and down and smiled. "So," he said, releasing her hand. "What do we do first?"

"First, we steal something to eat." She rose and took his hand, pulling him up. As they started for the market and the food stalls, it occurred to her that having a partner might have benefits. When they neared the market, she pulled him aside and pointed to the stalls. "Wot do ye fancy?"

"Bread and soup would be lovely."

She elbowed him then pulled out her pockets. She always wore trousers. Dresses made it too hard to run fast and climb when a quick escape was necessary. "No blunt for bread and soup. We 'ave to steal wot we want, and I can't run off with a bowl of soup."

The boy, Aidan, nodded thoughtfully. "Why don't we try and earn our coin?"

She put her hands on her hips and glared at him. "Ye think I 'aven't tried that?" She pointed to his black eye and then to herself. "Who would 'ire us?"

"Fine. Do we just grab an apple and run?" he asked.

"Only if we want to be chased. I usually wait for a distraction or try to cause one. Then while everyone is looking, I causally pocket a loaf of bread or a couple of onions."

"I can cause a distraction."

Jenny gave him a skeptical look. "If ye make a muck of this, we'll both be 'ungry tonight."

"I won't."

"If ye do, then ye can forget about our deal."

His eyes widened with shock. "You would go back on a handshake?"

She wanted to grab his shoulders, shake them, and scream, *Look around ye! No one cares about a 'andshake!* But the look of surprise on his face only made her feel more protective of him. "Just make sure ye distract them," she said.

He gave her a nod, squared those skinny shoulders again, and marched back toward the stalls. Instead of going to the costermongers, he made his way to a pedestal with a statue of some man she didn't know. He climbed up beside the statue and cleared his throat. "Ladies and gentlemen," he said. A few people glanced at him, but most paid him no heed. Mentally, she prepared herself for another long night with a protesting belly.

"Ladies and gentlemen," Aidan said, this time his voice carrying. He raised a hand and turned to the side dramatically. Jenny would have laughed at this posture if her meal hadn't depended on it.

"To be, or not to be, that is the question," he said. A few more heads turned toward him. That seemed to be the encouragement he needed because he continued in a deeper voice. "Whether 'tis nobler in the mind to suffer the slings and arrows of outrageous fortune—"

Jenny slid out of her spot and walked casually toward the costermonger selling fruit. He was watching with some interest, and she'd been eyeing those plums all afternoon.

"Or to take arms against a sea of troubles and by opposing end them. To die!" His voice rose with emotion as Jenny neared the wheelbarrow the man had lowered to watch.

"To sleep, no more; and by a sleep to say we end the heart-ache." He clenched his chest dramatically and Jenny reached out, grasped the fruit, and sidled away. She could still hear him as she continued on her way. She thought about walking on. She thought about leaving him behind and feasting on the two plums herself. But she thought about that shocked look on his face, and how he'd seemed to believe that a handshake meant something. And so when he finally finished his flowery words and bowed to a smattering of applause, she was waiting when he joined her.

"Did you get something?" he asked, holding out a hand.

"Not 'ere," she hissed. She motioned for him to follow and led him to a dusty yard behind a tavern. Horses had once been stabled here, but the stable was gone, and no one came out this way except to toss out rubbish. They found a place and sat with their backs up against the back of the tavern. The sound of laughter washed over them as she handed him a plum. He nodded at her as though expecting more. She produced the second plum. "That's it."

"That's it?"

"Eat it and shut yer potato 'ole."

He seemed to know enough not to argue. He bit into the plum, and for a time there was silence as they savored the fruit. But it was gone all too quickly. Jenny licked the juice from her fingers. "Wot was that ye were saying up there?" she asked. "Did ye make it up?"

"It was Shakespeare."

"Shakes a spear?"

He laughed. "No. Shakespeare. He wrote plays. I was quoting one of his more famous ones."

"I didn't understand a word ye said."

He leaned close to her, smelling of dirt, boy, and plum juice. "Can I tell you a secret?"

She lifted one shoulder in a shrug.

"I don't understand it either." He laughed, and his laugh was so infectious, she laughed too. And before long they were both laughing so hard tears streamed from their eyes. She leaned her head against his shoulder as she wiped away the tears, and he said, "I like you, Jenny Tate."

And though she didn't say it back, she liked Aidan Sterling too.

***

"Well, well, wot do we 'ave 'ere?"

Aidan opened his eyes and looked up at a boy. The lad looked to be close to his own age of twelve, maybe a year older. Though Aidan had been running with Jenny for two months now and looked and smelled every day of those two months on the street, this boy was so dirty, Aidan doubted he'd ever seen a bathtub. His face was hard, his skin raw from dirt and the weather, and his clothes hung on his lanky frame like a scarecrow Aidan had seen once when he and his mother had traveled to a fair in Richmond.

Aidan pushed up on one elbow. Behind him, he felt Jenny push up too. She swore under her breath.

"We don't have any food or blunt," Aidan said, which was a lie. They had a little of both, but he'd risk injury and death to protect them. He had only three priorities these days—food, blunt, and Jenny. "You're wasting your time with us."

"I'll decide that," the boy said, his gaze flitting across the dim room. "Gideon!" he called over his shoulder. "I found something."

"Let me do the talking," Jenny said as another boy, this one a little older, taller, and better fed, stepped through the doorway. Jenny and Aidan had slept in this room for the past three nights. The building had once been some sort of shop, but it hadn't had any residents other than rodents for years. There were other signs of occasional habitation, but those didn't look recent. Aidan had just been happy to find a place to shelter from the frequent spring rainstorms, even if it meant sharing that space with rats.

Jenny always wanted to do the talking, and Aidan had no arguments in this case. She was better at lying than him and better at negotiating with boys like these, who were bent on doing them harm. When it came to negotiating with shopkeepers or businessmen for a quick job or blunt, that was when Aidan stepped in.

The boy called Gideon swept his eyes over them and looked decidedly unimpressed. "They're just kids."

"Satin is always looking for more cubs. Ye watch them while I fetch 'im."

"Sure," Gideon said as the other boy hurried out. Gideon crossed his arms and leaned on the doorjamb. Jenny stood up.

"Wot gang are ye from?"

"Covent Garden Cubs."

"Covent Garden? Wot are ye doing in this part of London?"

"We 'ave places all over the city in case we need to lie low."

"Listen," Aidan said. "We don't want any trouble. If this is your place, we'll leave."

Jenny elbowed him. " 'E won't let us just leave. 'Is arch rogue is coming. But it's two against one." She gave Gideon a menacing look.

Aidan stared at her to make certain she hadn't gone insane overnight. This Gideon was much bigger than either of them. It had taken weeks for the swelling in Aidan's face to go down. He didn't relish another black eye.

"Ye might as well go," Gideon said. "If ye don't and Satin wants ye, there's no getting away."

"Ye'd risk a beating for us?"

Gideon shrugged. "Spry is the one who's leading Satin 'ere. 'E'll most likely get the beating. Now get out before I change me mind."

Jenny grabbed Aidan's arm and pulled him away. Aidan tried to shake the older lad's hand to thank him, but he had to call out his thanks instead as Jenny yanked at him harder. Once outside, she released him but walked quickly until they reached the edge of the Spitalfields market. It was crowded with shoppers, and they would not be easy to find among the throngs of people. They ducked behind a cart and crouched down.

The next thing Aidan knew, her hand was around his throat. "What are you doing?" he croaked.

"Did ye think ye could make some extra blunt by selling me?" she asked, squeezing his throat harder.

"What?" Aidan wheezed.

"When did they approach ye? Yesterday when I went to the river or maybe it was a couple of days ago when I went to Mayfair?"

"I've never seen any of them before in my life."

She squeezed harder, and Aidan grasped her hand and pried it away. She was stronger than she looked but then so was he now. "What's wrong with you?" Aidan gasped, rubbing his throat. "We're friends. Even if we weren't, I wouldn't sell a dog to those thugs."

"How can I believe ye?" she asked, hands on hips.

"We made a deal," Aidan said. "We shook on it."

Jenny spat. "Those are just words."

"Not to me." Aidan stared at her. How could she say those were just words? A deal was a deal. "When I say something, I mean it. I thought you did too."

Gingerly, he sat down behind the cart again. He didn't know what had happened to her to make her so hard and suspicious. He didn't think there was anything he could do to help her either. Two months of being by her side almost constantly, working together to survive, hadn't convinced her. He lived in constant fear that she'd desert him, and he'd be alone again. Without Jenny, he'd starve. And worse than the fear of death was the fact that even though she'd given him no encouragement, he rather liked her. Underneath her hard outer shell, he suspected she was good and kind. He'd told himself not to get attached to anyone. He'd lost his mother, and he didn't want the pain of losing anyone else. But he'd become fond of Jenny regardless.

So instead of walking away, he gave her yet another chance,

"I can't make you trust me, but if we're going to work together, you have to try a little."

She didn't speak, but she sat down beside him. "That was too close."

Apparently, they were pretending she hadn't just tried to kill him and going on as though everything were normal. Not that Aidan knew what *normal* was any longer. A quarter of a year ago, he'd been safe and cozy, living with his mother, attending school, eating when he was hungry. They hadn't had much, but they'd always had enough.

When his father died, they'd had to do what his mother called *economize*. It meant no more sweets or new shoes, even though his hurt his toes and were too small. She said she would figure something out, and Aidan believed her. He never once doubted.

He hadn't even been very worried when his mother became sick with fever. She stayed in bed for the day while he went to school. But when he'd come home that afternoon, she'd been barely coherent. And when he fetched the doctor, the man had demanded payment in advance. Aidan hadn't been able to find more than a few shillings, and the doctor left without a backward look. Aidan had asked the neighbors for help, but they'd never liked him or his mother much. They said she put on airs. And so in the end, his mother had died, and he'd been the only one with her, the only one who cared. He didn't have the funds for a burial, so the city had taken her away. And then the rent had come due, and he'd been out on the street.

He'd considered going to his father's family, but they had refused to help his mother. Why would they care about him? He pushed thoughts of his mother away. It still hurt to think of her, and he'd cried enough tears to fill the Thames.

He tried to cry late at night, when Jenny was asleep, but sometimes she reached over and held his hand, so he knew she heard him.

But they didn't talk about it. Just like they weren't going to talk about how she'd just tried to strangle him.

"Who were those boys?" he asked now.

"Part of a gang. The arch rogue is the leader. They steal for 'im. In return, 'e gives them safety. 'E also beats them regularly and sells the girls as whores. Last thing I want is to be part of a gang."

She'd talked about gangs before and taught Aidan to avoid them whenever possible. Once they'd hidden in a cellar for two hours to wait for a gang to move on. Aidan asked the question he'd wanted to ask then. "Why don't the children go to the magistrate and report the arch rogue? It's not legal to sell people or force them to steal."

She gave him a look he was beginning to recognize. It was her are-you-completely-daft look. "Wot does the magistrate care? No one cares wot 'appens to a child around 'ere."

Aidan was beginning to learn that.

"And them magistrates don't want to deal with the arch rogues. Everyone stays out of their way."

Aidan closed his eyes. Surviving was exhausting most of the time. "We'll have to find another place to sleep."

"Another month or so and we can sleep outside."

"We also need something to eat." His stomach was always reminding him of that fact.

"Wot we really need," she said, looking about, "is blunt."

Aidan straightened at what was, perhaps, his favorite word. She was right, of course. They did need coin. But he'd tried many times over the past couple of months to secure some form of employment, and at best he was ignored and at worst he was kicked or otherwise assaulted. "We've tried that."

"It's time I taught ye a new skill," she said. " 'Ousebreaking."

"I don't like stealing."

" 'Ow do ye like starving to death?"

Aidan had to admit, he liked that even less.

Jenny led him halfway around London until they stopped in a park across from several enormous houses. "Why are we in Mayfair?" he asked. His father had lived in this part of London. He didn't know where precisely that house was, but his mother had pointed it out to him when he'd been younger. He scrutinized these houses, but none looked like the Earl of Cranbourne's.

She stopped under a tree whose branches were heavy with green leaves and pulled him into the shade with her. "Before I met ye, I'd been watching this 'ouse. The people who live 'ere are so rich they 'ave another 'ouse in the country. Right now they're still away and only a 'andful of servants are 'ere to keep this 'ouse. And ye know wot that means."

Aidan tried to think what it could mean.

"When the master is away, the servants play."

"I think it's when the cat is away, the mice—"

"I don't care. When they're out or asleep tonight, I'll break in and take a few silver candlesticks or plates to sell. They won't even know it's gone."

"What do I do?" Aidan said.

"Ye keep watch. Make sure no one sees me go in or out. Ye think ye can do that?"

"Yes, but what if they catch you inside?" Fear roiled in his belly. This was why he hadn't wanted to become attached to Jenny. He could so easily lose her. He tried to tell himself it was just because he'd probably be dead without her. He reminded himself that most of the time she acted as though she could hardly stand him. But it was hard not to like her anyway. She was clever and resourceful and almost always shared with him.

"I can take care of myself," she said, and Aidan believed it.

They went to the river to watch the ships pass while they waited for dark. "I don't like you taking such a big risk," Aidan said, dangling his legs over the bridge.

"I've done it a 'undred times," she said. "Ye do yer part, and we'll be fine. The Watch will be out, and if they walk by when I'm going in or out, ye 'ave to distract them. I'm trusting ye to do yer part." She gave him a long look.

Aidan wanted to ask who had betrayed her and made her so suspicious, but he knew he wouldn't get an answer. "Who taught you to break into houses?"

"My father. 'E didn't teach me so much as take me with 'im. I could squeeze through small windows and little openings then go to the front door and let 'im in. 'E's a big man and not so steady on 'is feet when 'e drinks. And 'e always drinks."

She'd mentioned her parents only once or twice before. "Where is your father now?"

"Who cares?" she said with a shrug. "Probably passed out on the floor of a gin 'ouse. I stopped working with 'im when I was six or seven after 'e—"

Aidan waited, but she didn't finish. "After he?"

"A woman came upon us one night when we were pilfering. My father wasn't being very quiet, and the noise probably woke 'er. I wanted to run, but my father, 'e seemed to like being caught. 'E took a candlestick and beat 'er until it seemed like the whole room was spattered in red. 'E said 'e 'ad to kill 'er or she'd tell the magistrate. But it were dark, and she wouldn't 'ave recognized us."

Aidan stared at her. "Then why did he kill her? Why did he do it?"

She looked at him, her eyes gray and hard, but her face was almost beautiful. He could see that with a bit more food and a bath, she'd be striking. "Because 'e likes to 'urt and 'e likes to kill. I stay away from 'im," she said.

"Then we'll both keep away from him, and I'll watch your back."

She gave him a look laced with doubt, but he knew he'd prove himself in time. His life was tied to Jenny's now. He'd protect her with his life.

II

"I like it up here," Aidan said. They'd climbed to the top of one of the roofs and his gaze roved over what he could see of London. This roof was higher than some others, and he could make out St. Paul's in the distance as well as the trestles of London Bridge. Jenny sat beside him, and she gave him a grin.

"Which 'alf do ye want?" she asked.

"Hmm." He considered. This was a game they often played. It didn't have a name, but he thought of it as Emperors of All They Surveyed. He pointed and made a slicing motion with his arm. "I'll take this half."

"Ye always take the Tower."

"I can't let it fall into the wrong hands. I left you Vauxhall Gardens, and there's plenty of entertainment there."

"We should go," she said. "To celebrate."

He glanced at her. "Celebrate what?"

33

"It's spring again." She gestured to some trees in the distance. They were beginning to bud with green. "We've been friends for a year now."

Aidan didn't quite know that he wanted to celebrate the fact that he'd been an orphan for a year. But it was a year he'd survived. He supposed that was something to honor.

"Wot would ye buy if ye 'ad all the blunt in the world?" she asked as the shadows grew longer and the sun dipped below St. Paul's spire.

He was hungry—he was always hungry at thirteen—and he began listing all the food he could think of. The food his mother had made him when she was alive. "Meat pies and hot cross buns and apple tart and buttered turnip mash and—"

She waved a hand. "All ye ever think about is stuffing yer potato 'ole."

Aidan didn't understand how she *couldn't* think about food. They'd split a rotten apple this morning and had nothing else the entire day. Hunger seemed to gnaw at him like a beast with insomnia living in his belly. But Aidan had learned that the more he thought about food, the worse it was. Jenny was right to move the topic away from all the food they didn't have. "Very well, what would you buy?"

"I'd buy me a ticket."

"A ticket? To Vauxhall Gardens?"

"Maybe. Or maybe I'd buy me a ticket to that big museum. The one with all the dead people."

He had to translate that. "The British Museum and the mummies?"

She looked at him. " 'Ave ye been?"

He shook his head. "No, but I read about it in the papers, and we learned about the Egyptians at school."

"I wish I could go to school," she said.

Aidan rolled his eyes. They'd had this conversation before, and Aidan had assured her she would hate school. "You'd have to sit still all day," he reminded her. "No talking, hands folded before you. And you'd have to wear a dress."

"I like dresses," she said, which was obviously a lie. He'd never seen her wear one.

Aidan thought harder. "You'd have to be inside all day."

Jenny sighed, and he knew he'd made his point. He couldn't picture her in school. She was like a bird who would die if caged. She loved her freedom. But he hated to think of her despondent. "I taught you how to read a little," he said. "And do simple sums. Once you know that, you can teach yourself the rest, anyway."

"I suppose yer right, but if I 'ad some schooling, maybe I'd know wot this was." She pulled a small silver piece from her pocket and held it out to him. Aidan took it and immediately placed the opening on his pinky finger. It fit just over the tip like a small cover.

"It feels too heavy for silver," he said.

"It's pewter," she said. "Not as valuable."

"The scrollwork is nice." He admired the vines teched on the outside of the metal. "Is it a thimble?"

She shook her head. "Too long and thin. I thought it might be the top part of a long case."

Aidan nodded. It would have been a small case to hold small items. It looked like the sort of thing a lady might own, but his mother had not been a lady. "Where did you find it?"

She shrugged. "Around."

He gave her a long look.

"All right then. One of the mudlarks gave it to me."

Aidan jumped up and almost lost his balance. Jenny quickly pulled him back down.

"Ye'll fall off, ye will, and then wot will I do!"

"I wouldn't fall off if you didn't lie to me. No one gives away anything for free." If he'd learned anything in a year, he'd learned that.

She sighed and held out her hand. He dropped the pewter piece back into it. "I shouldn't 'ave done it, but I couldn't seem to stop myself. Billy said he thought it was a 'undred years old."

Aidan snorted. "Not likely."

"They do find old things. Billy showed me an old coin once."

"Billy would tell you anything if he thought he might get the chance to kiss you or feel under your shirt." Heat flashed through him at the thought of anyone touching Jenny. Not that Aidan wanted to kiss her or touch her. He didn't think about her that way. He'd really only started to look at girls differently. Just started to notice that Jenny didn't look as much like a boy as she used to now that she was fourteen. But he told himself to stop noticing. Jenny was his friend, like a sister to him. But when he thought of Billy kissing her, Aidan felt more jealous than the urge to protect.

"Fat chance of that," she said with a laugh. " 'e smells like a sewer."

Aidan wondered if he smelled any better. "Then how did you get that pewter bauble?" he asked. Billy might have a soft spot for a pretty girl—and Jenny with her blue-gray eyes and black hair was indisputably pretty—but he had a boss who oversaw his work, and he couldn't come home empty-handed unless he wanted a beating. But one of the other boys might give him one of their finds if…

Aidan's belly rumbled. "You didn't."

"It was all I 'ad besides the apple," she said.

"You told me the baker was out of day-old bread!"

"No, I didn't. Ye assumed that."

It was true. When they'd met up—he with the apple and she without the bread—he'd immediately said how disappointed he was that the baker was out of the bread he'd give them in exchange for lugging sacks of flour or sweeping his shop floor. "You didn't correct me."

"I'm correcting ye now."

"You traded our food for"—he gestured to the useless piece of pewter—"this!"

She stood up and swiped at her face. If Aidan didn't know her better, he'd think she was crying. "Ye don't understand," she said. And then with an agility Aidan could only dream about, she'd jumped to another roof and then another, and he was left in the burnt orange of the setting sun alone.

He went after her a half hour later. There were only two places she could be. One was her parents' house. She sometimes stopped in to see if her ma had any food or coin. But what her ma earned on her back, she spent on gin. And if she didn't spend it, Jenny's father took it and disappeared for days. But she wouldn't go home with the pewter trinket. Aidan knew exactly where she'd take it. He made his way through Spitalfields, careful not to attract the attention of any of a number of groups of boys and men looking for an easy target. Aidan didn't have any coin, but they'd beat him for the fun of it or to take his shoes or his coat. And Aidan didn't relish going without.

It took almost an hour of sneaking through shadows and taking detours before he reached the abandoned building. It was one of any number of abandoned buildings in the area, but this one was almost always empty. It was so decrepit, the wooden beams so rotten, that only the most desperate slept here. One side had caved in, and Aidan climbed in through a window on the side still standing. The building creaked and groaned when he stepped on the floor, and it always made him nervous. The whole place could fall at any moment. The stairway had already collapsed as had part of the first floor. Water dripped in a continual *plop plop*, and it smelled as though something died.

"Jenny!" he hissed.

No answer.

"Are you here? I'm sorry. Jenny!"

Still no answer. Aidan clenched his fists and plucked up his bravery and walked carefully across the uneven floorboards. He reached a door wedged half open and squeezed through. It might have been his imagination, but he'd been able to fit through it easier the last time he'd been here. Inside, he moved along one wall, trusting his sense of touch more than anything as it was pitch black, until he felt where the floor took a steep shift down. Aidan moved to his hands and knees and peered into the hole in the floor. "Jenny?"

"Wot?" came the response. A moment later a small flickering light illuminated the hole in the floor and what might have once been a cellar underneath. Using the light, he wriggled into the hole, holding onto the edge until his feet dangled just a foot or two from the floor. Then he let go and turned to face Jenny. She didn't say anything, just retreated into a small antechamber in the back. Aidan had speculated it might have been a wine cellar at one time as it had any number of shelves lining the small space. But the wine was gone, and Jenny had made use of the shelves to store her treasures. Aidan's gaze roved over one shelf that held a scrap of lace, a broken mirror, and a ladies' brush for cosmetics. Another shelf held part of an earring, whose jewel made of paste glittered in the candlelight. There were other bits and bobs, nothing of any real value, just trinkets that interested her. Aidan noted that she'd placed the new find on the last shelf.

"Listen, I'm sorry I got upset."

She shrugged. "Yer 'ungry. I shouldn't 'ave traded the bread."

He wanted to say, no, she shouldn't have traded the bread, but how could he ask her to deny herself the only beauty in the world she possessed? These useless pieces of rubbish were beautiful treasures to her. They gave her a comfort he couldn't understand, and if that was something she needed, how could he take it away?

"I'm not so hungry anymore," he said and glanced at her.

A slow smile spread over her face. "Liar."

He settled back against a wall of the cellar and slid down to sit, hands wrapped around his knees. "Maybe you can help me forget."

"How?"

But she knew how. Whenever she was sad or he missed his mother, they'd come here and she'd pretend she was a famous explorer who had unearthed these priceless objects. She'd make up stories about her adventures and the pieces she'd found. "This is my newest find," she said, picking up the pewter piece. "I found it while exploring the jungles of Greece."

He didn't bother to tell her that Greece didn't have jungles. He just let her talk about how it was the cap to a bottle that held a magical potion, a gift from the gods of Olympus. After a while, she blew out the candle and came to sit beside him. He lay down, his head in her lap, and she stroked his hair and made up more stories about fabulous places they'd never go. And a long time

later, she lay down too, and he wrapped his arms around her, and he thought he was almost happy.

III

He was following her. He'd been following her for the last quarter hour, and no matter what she did, she couldn't lose him. She was late meeting Aidan behind the Brown Bear, and she'd be later still because she didn't want to lead *him* there. It was bad enough he was after her. She didn't want Aidan in any danger.

"Oh, Jenny, my love!" he called, his voice sickly sweet and thick with drink. Sometimes he was in a good mood when he was drunk. And sometimes not. She couldn't predict what he'd do or whose side he'd be on from one moment to the next. And she didn't want to try.

A couple of years ago, Jenny had made the mistake of stopping in to see her ma. She told her to stay away. Her father planned to do her in.

It didn't matter why. The trespass was probably something in his mind. But he'd do it if given half a chance.

She started down a dark alley, made more shadowy because of the stone supports built to shore up the buildings

43

on either side. It was either the alley or emerge into the open, where her father could easily catch her. At the end of this short lane was a wall she could climb that led to another warren of alleys and her best hope for losing him. Drunk and a good sixteen years her senior, she didn't think he'd be able to manage the climb.

"There ye are!" came his voice, and Jenny jumped at how close he was. She turned and moved sideways toward the wall.

"I can't talk right now, pa. I 'ave to be somewhere."

"Looking for yer fancy man, are ye?"

" "E's not a fancy man. 'E's as poor as the rest of us."

"Talks like a fancy man." Her father stumbled toward her, and Jenny resisted the urge to run. If she ran, he'd start running too. "Did 'e put a babe in yer belly yet?"

"No."

"And 'e won't neither. Not after I'm done with ye. Little ungrateful bitch." He lunged for her, and Jenny couldn't resist any longer. She ran, reaching the wall in a matter of seconds and scrambling up it.

But she wasn't fast enough. Richard Tate's hand clamped on her ankle, and he yanked her down. Before she could punch or scratch at him, his fist slammed into her shoulder. He only missed her face because she dodged to the side. She went down like a sack of flour and looked up as he raised his booted foot to bring it down on her face.

But a blur flashed over her and whatever it was—a giant bird?—landed on her father and they both crashed to the ground. It took Jenny a moment to realize it wasn't a bird but Aidan. She'd stolen a long black greatcoat, which he'd taken to wearing in all sorts of weather, and it had flapped out behind him like a great crow's wings when he'd jumped from the wall. Why had he been on the other side? How had he known she needed him?

She pushed up and winced at the sharp pain in her shoulder. Aidan had the advantage for the moment, since he'd landed on top of her father and taken him down. Aidan could definitely defend himself in a fight, but most of the ruffians about had some sense of self-preservation. They'd run if they were outmatched. Richard Tate would fight to the death.

Even as she thought it, her father kicked out, and Aidan doubled over, clutching his belly. Her father rose to his feet. "Good. Now I 'ave both of ye." He grasped Aidan's hair and yanked his head up.

"No!" Jenny yelled.

Aidan's fist darted out from his midsection and plowed into her father's face. He stumbled back and Aidan planted a booted foot in the center of his chest, pushing him over. Jenny felt a rush of excitement run through her. They were winning. Aidan had her father down. She stood, and Aidan looked back at her. "Want me to kill him?" he asked, breathing heavily. She noticed he'd withdrawn the dagger he always kept with him from his boot.

He would do it, too. She knew it. Aidan would do anything for her. But as much as she wanted her father dead, she would also do anything for Aidan. And she wasn't about to let him live with a murder on his soul.

"No," she said, moving gingerly toward her father who was groaning and trying to sit up. "But we can't 'ave 'im coming for us again."

She placed her own boot on her father's chest, holding him down. He looked up at her with eyes the same blue gray as her own. "Kill me, why don't ye? Always were a coward."

Jenny lifted her foot and brought it down as hard as she could on his right hand. He screamed as the sound of crunching bones echoed in the dark alley. Aidan stepped back, and Jenny wasn't sure if he was repulsed or just giving her the space to do as she wanted. She ground the heel of her foot into his hand then bent over him until she was close enough for him to hear her whisper. "That's for all the times I felt the back of that 'and," she said. "That's for all the times

I couldn't talk because ye split my lip or sleep because my 'ead 'urt so bad from yer blows. The next time ye try and take a piss or 'old a cup, ye think of me. And if ye come for me or 'im ever again, next time, we won't be so forgiving."

She gave him a hard kick in the ribs and walked away. Aidan was already at the wall. At sixteen, he was tall enough that he could just reach up and pull himself over. Jenny had to jump and grab onto the top. Her shoulder screamed in pain, but she pulled herself up and jumped down on the other side.

"You're hurt," Aidan said as soon as she landed. "I can see it in your face."

"Just a bruise on my shoulder," she said. "Let's go."

He took her hand and they walked quickly away. The commotion might attract the Watch, and they didn't want to look suspicious. Instead of going to the Brown Bear as planned, they climbed to the roof of a building where they stayed some nights when the weather was mild. They'd hidden a blanket and a bit of food up there, and Aidan laid out the blanket and handed her a half-empty bottle of wine. She took a long swig.

"How bad is it?" he asked.

" 'Urts like the devil," she said. "But it would 'ave been a lot worse if ye 'adn't come. 'Ow'd ye know I was in trouble?"

"One of the boys you give scraps to spotted you and came running to tell me."

"I don't give scraps to anyone!" she protested.

"Sure you don't. Anyway, he told me the direction he'd seen you go, and I figured you'd head for the alley. I went around the long way or I'd have been there sooner."

"I told ye 'e'd kill me some day."

"Not today," Aidan said. "Not any day I'm here. Let me see your shoulder."

She unfastened the buttons at the neck and drew the shirt up and over one side of her body, leaving the other side in place. Her breasts were bound so there was nothing to see. Aidan wouldn't have looked anyway. He never looked at her, and she was ashamed to admit she sometimes wished he would. There was a feeling she sometimes got between her legs, and it had only grown since she'd turned seventeen. Sometimes it was hard to lay beside Aidan and not want to touch him or kiss him. She found small ways to do it—an arm on his shoulder, moving closer to him when it was cold, or brushing against him in a narrow passage. But he was always respectful. Even when she was careless about changing in front of him, he turned his back to give her privacy. He obviously wouldn't ever think of her as anything more than a friend.

And she was his friend. She just wanted to be his friend and then some.

Aidan moved so he could see her shoulder, keeping his gaze above the area of her chest. "You'll have a bruise there," he said. "It's already turning purple."

She looked down and swore at the mottled skin. "I'm lucky 'e didn't 'it me in the face, or I'd be in a lot worse shape," she said.

"It wasn't luck." He put two fingers on her shoulder, right near the bruise, and slid them over her skin. "You don't need luck."

Jenny couldn't stop a shiver as his fingers trailed down her bare arm, pausing at her elbow. She looked up and away from his hand and saw his gaze was on her face. His eyes were so dark, and he hadn't been able to shave in a week or so and there was a shadow on his jaw.

"I was scared," he said, sounding a bit like the boy he'd been when they'd met four years ago.

"I'm not that easy to be rid of," she said.

"Good." His tongue darted out, wetting his lips, and her breath hitched. He wanted to kiss her. She knew him, and though she'd never done that with him, she knew what he wanted. She wanted the same thing.

"Jenny, may I—"

"Yes," she said, her voice little more than a whisper. "I've been wanting ye to do it for ages now."

He cocked his head to the side, his fingers lightly grasping her bare forearm. "Why didn't you say so?"

"Why didn't ye?"

"I didn't think you wanted me like that." His free hand went to her face and cupped her jaw. His touch was so gentle, so sweet. She was shivering all over now, trembling like a newborn kitten.

"I thought ye didn't want me. Like that."

He let out a small laugh. "Jenny, I've never wanted anyone but you." He leaned forward, his lips brushing over hers in the sweetest kiss she'd ever had. Warmth shot through her, and she kissed him back, wrapping her hand around his neck and moving closer until they were pressed against each other and breathing hard. Aidan pulled back first. "You'd better put your shirt back on," he said. "You'll get cold."

"I'm plenty warm," she said, but she moved back and tugged her sleeve back, wincing only slightly at the discomfort.

"I'll keep you warm," he said, taking the bottle from her hand and lowering her to the blanket.

***

He loved her. Aidan loved Jenny, despite the fact that he'd never wanted to love anyone again after losing his mother. He did love Jenny.

But he didn't dare tell her. He didn't know how she'd react. Her own parents hadn't loved her. That much was clear. He didn't know how she'd react to such a confession. Over the years he'd noticed she always argued when he gave her any kind of compliment. She never thought she deserved praise or kindness. Aidan didn't think she thought she deserved love.

He considered how to tell her for months until one night they were laying together under London Bridge. For some reason that day he had been thinking about his own mother, and how she always told him how much she loved him, and how much that had meant to him. And so that night, as they lay on their sides, looking into the other's eyes, arms around the other, he said, "I love you, Jenny."

She'd stiffened. "Wot'd ye say?"

"I said, I love you. You know that, don't you?" He'd lifted himself onto his elbow and looked down at her face. "Why are you crying?"

"No reason," she said with a sniff. "Course I knew ye loved me."

He swiped at one of her tears with his thumb. She cried so rarely that it was a novelty to see tears like this.

"Ye took me by surprise is all. That and—"

He didn't speak, waited for her to go on. But she didn't need to say anything. He knew her so well that he understood without hearing the words. "No one has ever said that to you before. Christ, Jenny, I should have said it before."

"I didn't know I needed ye to say it," she answered, her voice low. "Now I feel like I should say it."

He smiled. "Only if you want to." But he suddenly needed the words too. He needed them more than he ever might have believed.

"Oy, well, in that case."

"Jenny," he groaned, and she laughed, though it came out as something of a sob.

"I love ye, Aidan. I love ye with all my 'eart and soul." She began to sob, and he held her tighter.

"Why are you crying now?"

"Because I love ye and ye'll leave me."

He laughed. "Don't be ridiculous. I'll never leave you." But the back of his neck prickled as he spoke because he was always thinking of ways to get out of here. He wanted to take Jenny with him, but he didn't know if she'd go.

She looked up at him. "Promise?"

"Promise." He bent to kiss her lightly, to seal the promise, but when her mouth met his, there was more there than sweetness. There was a sensuality that made his blood heat and his heart pound. His breathing quickened, but he didn't rush to grasp at her breast or use his tongue. He felt differently about her, about this act, tonight. They'd finally figured out how to copulate successfully, and they both enjoyed it now. Tonight, was different, though.

He loved her, and she loved him. He wanted to show her how much he loved her. Show her that he was hers forever.

Their kisses seemed to go on and on, their hands exploring even as their mouths did the same. He couldn't undress her, not here in the open, but he revealed and then covered until he had explored all of her and left her panting for more. She was as eager to touch him, but for once he was able to control his desire, so he did not come as soon as her hand slid into his trousers. He sought the heat of her hand and then of her body, and when he'd slid into her, the pleasure was dark and lovely. He didn't race to climax this time, but savored the feel of her, the taste of her mouth on his, the way she moved beneath him. When she gasped, he repeated the action until she gasped again.

"That," she said, her voice sounding so unlike the Jenny he knew. "Do that again."

He'd complied, feeling her muscles clench as she began to soar. He soared with her, following her up, finding a little slice of heaven in the hell on earth that was their daily lives. He pulled out at the last minute, of course. It was painful to do so as her body was clenching him tightly and she was making such delicious sounds of contentment, but they couldn't risk a child.

Afterward, Aidan had gathered her in his arms and held her tightly. "No wonder men pay for that," she said after a while. "I never understood before."

"Neither did I."

His belly rumbled and she patted his back. "Try to forget it and sleep."

She fell asleep a few minutes later. She could always sleep, but the hunger and the mixture of emotions he felt kept Aidan awake. He listened to her soft, even breaths and knew that he should be happy. He had everything he needed. But like Jenny who was always collecting small treasures, Aidan wanted something more. He didn't want to spend the rest of his nights sleeping on roofs or under bridges or in abandoned buildings. He wanted to know when his next meal would be. He wanted coin in his pocket.

He wasn't a child any longer, at the mercy of others. He was sixteen and a grown man. He had to find a way to get out of Spitalfields. He'd do whatever it took.

IV

"Oy!" Jenny spun around, leaving the rotting produce in the bin behind her and crouching, ready for battle. "I 'ave a message for ye."

Jenny pointed to her chest.

"No. 'Im." The publican pointed to Aidan. She glanced at Aidan, tall and lanky with a mop of dark hair and eyes so dark sometimes even she had trouble reading his expression. But she had no trouble now. He looked wary.

"We're just looking for scraps," he said defensively. "If we don't take it, the dogs will."

"This isn't about the rubbish," the publican said. "I got a message for ye. From a nob."

Aidan's brow lowered, and he glanced at Jenny. She shrugged. She didn't know any nobs. But Aidan always said his father was a lord. The Earl of Cranbourne, he said. She didn't doubt him, but she didn't exactly believe him either.

"Wot's the message?" Jenny asked because Aidan seemed frozen, and the silence had gone on too long.

"The nob says come to Cranbourne 'Ouse. Yer uncle wants to see ye." The publican went back inside, leaving Aidan and Jenny alone in the stinking yard with the rubbish.

"Yer uncle?" she said, finally. "Is that the earl now?"

He nodded. "When my father died, my mother tried to reach him, but he wouldn't see her. We went to the house, but his servants turned us away. She even went to his solicitor's office, but..." His cheeks colored, and she knew whatever had happened had mortified the young boy.

"Why does 'e want to see ye now?" she asked.

"I don't know."

"Are ye going?"

"I don't know."

Fear gripped her. She didn't want him to go. If he went to this Cranbourne House, she'd lose him. She knew that without any doubt whatsoever. Aidan had never belonged in the rookeries. He'd always been destined for more. Now was his chance. She should be happy for him. But she was selfish. She didn't want to lose him.

For days, he said nothing of the message, and the two of them went on as they always did. But she should have known that wasn't the end of it. She wasn't the kind of girl who got happy endings.

Two or three weeks after that night under the bridge—
the night when he'd told her he loved her, when he'd said he
would never leave—Aidan had looked at her, and she knew
what he would say. "I have to go see my uncle," he said.

"No, ye don't," she argued. "Ye can stay 'ere. 'E'll
never find ye. If 'e could, 'e wouldn't 'ave left word at the
pub." He'd left word at several pubs and a number of
publicans had passed on the message now.

"Jenny," Aidan said softly. "I want to see my uncle."

It was dark and they were lying on the banks of the
Thames, looking up at the few stars they could see. The night
was warm, but they'd been lying close together, listening to
the lapping water and the distant sounds of taverns and ships
on the river.

She turned her head sharply. "Why? All those years ago,
'e didn't want to see ye."

"He wants to now. Maybe he wants to take me in.
Maybe he'll give me money."

"Yer that eager to leave me?" She sat and hugged her
knees.

"I'm not leaving you." Aidan wrapped his arms around
her from behind. "This is for both of us. Jenny, I love you."
He kissed her neck, sending ripples of sensation down her
skin. "I'll never leave you."

She looked back at him, and he took her face and kissed her gently. The kiss turned deeper and then they were lying together, hands under clothes, Aidan touching her in that way that made her gasp and cry out. When he fell asleep afterward, she turned her head away and cried. She knew this was the end.

The next day, he went to see his uncle. It hurt to watch him try and slick his hair back and out of his eyes, to tug his too-short trousers down so his ankles weren't visible. It hurt to know he wanted to make a good impression for someone other than she. When he left, she didn't tell him good-bye or wish him good luck. She went to her treasure room and sat there all day, but even her trinkets hadn't made her feel better.

He found her there that evening, coming in to sit beside her. Wordlessly, he handed her bread and cheese. "That's for you," he said. "I already ate my fill at Cranbourne House."

But suddenly Jenny didn't feel hungry. She placed the food down beside her and wrapped her arms around her knees. " 'E saw ye then?"

"He did. He was…kind."

She glanced at him because his voice was different somehow. It was full of wonder.

"He said he hadn't known about me or my mother until recently. My father's solicitor never told him. But that man died, and when he hired another, that new man went through the ledgers and papers and informed him he had a nephew. Me." Aidan looked up at the dark ceiling. "He's been looking for me for months now."

"So yer leaving then," she said.

"Jenny." He put his hand on her shoulder. "I didn't say that."

"Ye don't 'ave to."

"He told me he wants to help me—help us."

"Ye told 'im about me?"

"Yes. I told him all about life here, and he said he wants to buy me a commission in the army."

She jerked her head to look at him. "The army? A redcoat?"

He nodded. "I would be an officer. I'd be trained and be given food, lodging, and a monthly salary."

"Ye'd have to go to France and kill Frenchies."

He sighed. "I might, but he also said to start I'd be quartered in England. I could travel the country. Soldiers are welcomed in most towns. They're invited to balls and dinners—"

"Dinners? Sounds like yer mind is made up. When do ye leave?"

"My mind isn't made up. I don't want to leave you, Jenny."

She shrugged, causing his hand to slide off her shoulder. "I can't join the army. They don't allow women."

"I asked my uncle about that. I told him I couldn't leave you here alone."

"Rubbish." She stood. "Ye 'ave to look out for yerself. 'Ave I taught ye nothing all these years?"

"Jenny!" Aidan grasped her hand and held her in place. "He offered to help you too."

She stilled, willing her heart to stop pounding with hope. "Why would 'e want to 'elp me?"

"Because I asked him to."

"And wot did 'e say?"

Aidan didn't answer right away. He paused a long time, and then he took in a breath. "He said he would find a place for you in his household. You could work for him, for my family. You'd be safe and well-paid and—"

"A place in the 'ouse'old? A servant?"

"Yes, a maid. You could work your way up from scullery maid to—"

"Ye want me to scrub floors and privies for yer uncle?"

Aidan stood, ducking slightly because the ceiling here was low. "It's a start, and it's only for a few years. Once I make my name in the army, I'll come back and marry you. You can set up your own house and—"

Jenny pushed Aidan back while he called her name, she crawled out of the old wine cellar and ran out into the night.

***

She hid from him that night and the next day. Anger burned inside her. Anger and shame. She had taken him in when he was all but dead on the street. And now he wanted her to scrub floors for him, to bow and scrape and say, *yes, my lord.* He'd never loved her. He looked down on her. She was beneath him. She knew it, had always known it. Maybe being his servant was her rightful place, but she couldn't do it. She couldn't bear it.

He finally found her on the roof when she decided to let him find her because she wasn't a coward. She could face him. As soon as he stepped into view, she said, "I won't do it."

His shoulders slumped. "Then I won't go. I'm not leaving you." He came to sit beside her, their feet dangling over the edge of the roof.

"Ye'll go," she said, not looking at him. "Ye were always meant to go."

"So were you!"

"No. I was born 'ere, and I'll die 'ere."

"Jenny—"

She jumped to her feet. "Aidan, I don't want yer pity or to be yer servant. From the day ye arrived, ye were looking for a way out. I was only looking to get through each day, but ye—" She shook her head. "Ye wanted a job. Ye wanted to save yer blunt. Ye wanted security and something better out of life. Ye taught me 'ow to read and do sums and then take the numbers away again—"

"Subtract."

"Yes! And ye get up and spout poetry to distract people when I snatch goods from their stalls."

"It was a soliloquy actually, not poetry."

"Yer just proving my point."

His shoulders slumped again, and she sat beside him and put a hand on his shoulder.

"I promised I'd never leave you."

"It's not the first lie I've been told."

He looked at her, his gaze pleading. "Please come with me."

"Or ye can stay 'ere. With me," she said.

He blew out a breath. "I'm offering you a chance—"

"To scrub floors and empty chamber pots? No. Just go. I'm better off without ye. My life will be easier without 'aving to look after ye and listen to ye whine about yer empty belly."

He flinched back, and she knew she'd hurt him. Good. Because he was tearing her heart out.

"You don't mean that."

She rose and stalked toward the chimney where he'd once kissed her so passionately. "I do. I felt sorry for ye all these years, but I've been thinking I'd be better off on my own for a while now."

"Jenny, don't do this. I love you."

"That's yer loss. Ye'll find another chit to love. One who doesn't 'ave to steal and beg and sleep under bridges. Will ye go already? I told ye, I'm done with ye."

He stared at her. "I know you don't mean this."

She rolled her eyes. "Think wot ye want."

"I'll be back for you. When I make a name for myself. I'll come back with fame and fortune, and I'll take you out of here."

"Ye'll be shot and die on a battlefield in France," she said, voice hard and cold. "Think I care?"

"I'll leave you everything," he said. "I'm taking only what's on my back."

She shrugged, pretending tears weren't stinging her eyes. She couldn't let him see her cry, couldn't let him know she cared. There would be time for that later. Plenty of time to curse him and herself for ever believing he loved her.

"Good-bye, Jenny," he said. She flicked a wrist at him and went back to sitting on the edge of the roof. After a time, he came out of the door below and walked away, toward Mayfair.

He never even once looked back.

$\mathcal{V}$

London 1806

"The thief is back again, my lord."

"Oh, excellent, Quinnell!" Viscount Chamberlayne rose from the chair in his bed chamber and rubbed his hands together. "My ruse worked."

"Yes, my lord. The house is dark, and all the servants have been instructed to stay quiet and in their rooms."

His valet brought his dressing robe, and Roland donned it. "Is he entering the parlor again?"

"He is dawdling under that window, my lord. Are you certain you do not want to call the magistrate?"

"Quite certain."

"The Bow Street Runners?"

"Not yet, Quinnell. Last time he was here, he took that Egyptian pendant, the one from the Middle Kingdom. I want to see if that was luck or if this thief knows what he is about."

"Of course, my lord." The butler stood straight as an arrow, his black hair swept back from his forehead. With his long nose, Quinnell had always struck Roland as looking rather like a crow.

"Slippers," he told his valet. The valet brought them, and in a few moments, Roland was making his way soundlessly downstairs toward the parlor. He heard a faint thud and knew the thief had entered. How very exciting. The door had been left open just a crack, and he took his place now and peered inside.

To his surprise, the thief was not a boy at all, but a girl. It was easy to see why he'd made that mistake. She wore male clothing, but he could see the tail of her hair and the silhouette of slight curves.

She stood by the window she'd come in and silently lowered the pack she carried on her back to the carpeted floor then crouched to feel inside. A moment later she produced a long, flat piece of metal. Roland wondered what it might be. It looked rather deadly, and he hoped he hadn't been mistaken and the thief was actually a murderer.

She inserted the tool into a loop on her black trousers and moved around the perimeter of the room. She was in no hurry. She obviously thought he was out and would not return until the wee hours of the morning. It was barely midnight now. Still, she was silent. She moved like a shadow across the room, and Roland was impressed.

She stopped in front of a vase on a pedestal and studied it. Roland held his breath. It was valuable but she had to realize it would be hard to transport without breaking. She seemed to decide against the paintings on the walls as well as she gave them only a cursory glance. Or perhaps she did not know much about art and didn't realize their value. The thief moved to a glass display case with a variety of perfume bottles and pieces of jewelry. She pulled the metal piece from the loop and jammed it between the crack in the door. Roland winced at the damage that would do but watched with interest as she gave the tool a swift upward thrust. The cabinet lock sprang free, and the glass door swung silently open.

She admired several of the pieces then closed the door again. Roland was surprised. He had been certain she would take a piece from the cabinet. Why else would she open it? It amazed him she didn't just empty the entire contents into her sack. Why didn't she take it all?

She crossed to his bookshelf where several books were laid out. She ignored those standing upright and lifted at those lying flat. Could she read? She lifted one book, opened it to reveal an illustrated page, then nodded and continued her perusal. Finally, she tucked a book in her sack and then glanced back at the jewelry. Roland could almost hear her weighing the risks and benefits. Jewelry was hard to pawn. Anyone who knew the real value of the piece would ask too many questions. But she could pawn a piece to someone who didn't know the value for pocket change. The thought appalled him, but then he'd often found treasure among junk.

She glanced out the window, and Roland almost moved forward to show himself. He didn't want her leaving yet. But then she started back across the room. She eased the display case door open again and reached for one of the rings, her hand hesitating as she debated between two rings.

This was his chance. Roland eased the oiled door open and stepped into the parlor. Slowly, she turned her head to the side and met his gaze. Her face showed a moment of shock, but her hand held steady.

"Ye must be the viscount," she said, her accent making an absolute wreck of the English language. But she hadn't screamed or fought or ran. She stood there as though his appearance was not unexpected.

"Which will you choose?" he asked, trying to sound less interested than he was. She looked momentarily confused, so he clarified. "The rings."

"The signet ring," she said, lowering her finger to stroke it. "Not the ruby?"

"It's right fetching," she said, "but the signet ring is worth more."

"Right you are," he said. "Clever girl. Quinnell, check her rucksack, will you?"

The door opened further to admit Quinnell, who set a lamp on the table. In the light, Roland could see her more clearly. She was barely more than a child. He would eat the ring she was eyeing if she'd yet reached twenty. She was pretty in a rough sort of way. She had pale gray eyes and dark hair. She was just a bit shorter than average and slim of build. He looked into her eyes again. They were hard as flint, and he felt them assessing him.

Quinnell walked across the room, lifted the sack she'd left by the window and pulled out the book. And still the thief didn't move, hand still poised above the signet ring, though it shook slightly now.

"It's the Gutenberg, my lord."

Roland gave her an approving look. "Very clever girl."

The thief looked from him to Quinnell, obviously unhappy to have her escape routes blocked. "I suppose ye'll call the magistrate now," she said.

"That would be a waste."

She stared at him, brows lowering. "Then I can go?"

"That would also be a waste." He stepped into the room and closed the door behind him. "I have a better idea."

"I'm not taking me clothes off," she said, stepping back from the display case.

He jerked back in shock. The very idea! "Why would I want you to disrobe? This is purely a business meeting. Quinnell, would you bring tea? And sandwiches as well, I think. You're hungry, I take it?"

"Ye think I'll let ye roger me for a sandwich?"

He sat in his favorite chair, which was upholstered in gold and royal blue fabric, and crossed his legs. He was careful to move slowly so as not to startle her. She was like a bird. Ready to fly away at the slightest sound. "I don't want to roger you. No offense. I'm sure under that dirt you're a pretty girl, but I'm more interested in your mind, you see. Why did you take the book and not, say, the vase? It's from the Han dynasty and very valuable."

Quinnell slipped out of the room, and her gaze went back to the window. She was already planning her escape. He didn't have much time left. She edged toward the window. "Easy to break," she answered. "And 'ard to pawn."

"But surely you have a confederate who would buy it from you."

"A wot?"

"A confederate. A partner, so to speak."

"I 'ad a partner until about a year ago. Now I work alone. Wot's it to ye?"

"Suspicious sort, aren't you? I suppose you have to be." He waved a hand. "We have a lot in common, you know."

He laughed at the disbelief on her face. "What I mean, dear girl, is we are both collectors."

The thief glanced around the room and Roland knew he saw appreciation on her face.

"You have an eye for the rare and valuable, and that is not something that can be taught. Believe you me, I have tried." He uncrossed his legs and leaned forward. "How old are you?"

"Old enough. 'Ow old are ye?"

"Three and twenty," he said. "I've been collecting since I was younger than you. Have you ever thought what you would do with these antiquities if you did not have to steal them?"

She shrugged. "That's the sort of question a man with soft 'ands and wearing a silk dress asks."

"It's a banyan, and I suppose it is a question you've not considered before."

"I don't believe in fairy tales."

"No time for them, I'm sure." He considered. He'd intrigued her, but now to harness that interest. "What if I told you I have other rooms like this with items just as valuable, if not more valuable? What if I said I need someone to catalogue and appraise them?"

"I'd ask where they were."

He laughed again. "So you could steal the items. Yes, I see."

She curled her lip, clearly confused as to why he found her answer so amusing.

"But what if I paid you to study the artifacts? What if I paid you to travel with me and buy others even more valuable?"

The thief stared at him. Hope bloomed on her face but she just as quickly snuffed it out. "Why would ye do that?"

"Because you have a rare talent." He gestured to her hand inside her trouser pocket. "Take the ring out of your pocket," he said.

She started. She obviously didn't think he'd seen her palm it.

"Go on, take it out. Then bring it close to the light." He rose and lit a lamp on a long table then unrolled a deep blue strip of velvet. "Lay it here and take a look."

The thief didn't move.

Roland frowned at her. "Humor me. If my proposal doesn't appeal, you can keep the ring for hearing me out."

"I can keep the ring?" she said.

"If you hear me out."

"That's the only catch?"

"That is my sole condition. I give you my word as a gentleman."

That didn't seem to reassure her, but after a brief internal battle, she brought him the ring.

"Place it here." He indicated the velvet. She placed the ring on the fabric, and the viscount moved the lamp closer. The ring looked lovely against the deep blue background and in the warm lamplight.

Roland pulled two items from a velvet bag and laid them beside the ring. One looked like some sort of medical instrument while the other was round and looked like a lens from spectacles.

"This is a loupe," he said, holding up the lens. "It magnifies the item so you might see details invisible or too small to be seen clearly by the naked eye." He held it out to her, and she took it and reached for the ring. His hand stayed hers. "These are pincers," he said, holding up the metal medical-looking instrument. "They allow you to hold the item still and without dirtying it with your hands. May I show you?"

He held his hand out for the loupe back. Reluctantly, she handed it over and watched as he held the ring with the end of the pincers and used the loupe to examine the inside band. "Ah, yes. There it is." He handed the pincers and the loupe back to her. "Have a look."

She did so, and he watched as she squinted then drew back then looked again.

"That's the maker's mark," he said quietly, almost reverently. "I have books and books of those marks. That one is from the 1600s and a jeweler in France. He served the Bourbon family—the royal family."

She looked up at him. "This was the ring of a king?"

"It was. This ring belonged to Louis le Juste. That was Louis XIII."

She looked at the ring through the loupe again.

"So you see, when you chose the signet ring, you unknowingly chose one of the most valuable items I possess. Think what you could do with some training."

"Training?" She looked up at him.

"Like an apprenticeship," he said, stepping back. "I will teach you what I know. In return, you help me find the great treasures of the world."

"The world?"

"Have you ever even been outside of London, dear girl? Would you like to go to Paris? Constantinople? Berlin?"

She stared at him. "Wot's the catch?"

"You will have to bathe regularly, for one. And you'll have to learn to read—in several languages. You'll have to study for years to be good enough. And in return…"

"Yes?" she asked. He heard eagerness in her voice, though she tried to muffle it.

"I will provide you with a salary as well as room and board—not here. This is a purely professional partnership. You'll be my apprentice and one day, if you are good enough, my partner."

"I'm good enough," she said.

"Then we have a deal?" He held out his hand, and she stared at it.

"You shake it," he said. She looked at him sharply, and something changed in her expression. He saw it soften. Then she put her hand in his and he squeezed it warmly, hoping he was right about her. Hoping she didn't rob him blind and murder him in his sleep.

Part II

One

Aidan hoped he hadn't made a colossal mistake. He'd come to Lady Birtwistle's ball to speak with the prime minister. Having just acquired a new shipping venture, Aidan hoped to discuss a bill that would ease tariffs with the prime minister. But he'd either come too early or too late. The prime minister was not in attendance.

He didn't regret making an appearance. He'd fought with Lady Birtwistle's younger brother Rafe during the war. Several of his former comrades-in-arms were in attendance, including the Duke of Mayne and Colin FitzRoy. At least FitzRoy's wife was here, which meant Colin must be about somewhere. But where was the prime minister?

"You could at least pretend to enjoy yourself," Lady Birtwistle said, coming to stand beside him, glass of champagne in hand.

"I'm having a wonderful evening," Aidan said, raising his own untouched glass in a salute. "This is surely the best ball of the Season."

"Liar." She said it with a grin. "This is not the best ball of the Season, and you are not having a wonderful evening." Her blue eyes shone with humor. "You are looking for someone because you have business to attend to. Do you never take an evening off?"

Only someone who had never known a day of hunger or faced a night sleeping under a bridge in the cold would think of taking an evening off for leisure. "I'll take an evening off when I'm dead," he said. "Have you seen Lord Liverpool?"

She frowned at him then her countenance brightened as she spotted someone she knew. "Lord Chamberlayne, do bring your lovely betrothed over here." A handsome man with blond hair, bright blue eyes, and a long angular face approached. He wore a sleepy expression and had a woman on his arm.

Aidan began to move away, but Lady Birtwistle grasped his elbow in a vice-like grip. "Lord Chamberlayne, might I present Mr. Sterling?"

Aidan bowed and Chamberlayne's eyes widened slightly. "Sterling! I was hoping to meet you. I heard you uncovered some interesting items in a ground floor room that had been walled over in your town house. But where are my manners? Lady Birtwistle, Mr. Sterling, might I present my bride to be, Miss Tate."

Aidan bowed to her, glancing at her briefly and then straightening as though he'd been hit by lightning.

And perhaps he had. The last decade faded away, and he stared at his past. She'd been staring at him as well—those same gray eyes that had always been so cool and assessing were scrutinizing him now. When their gazes met, he saw not surprise but curiosity. She was waiting to see what he'd do. He wanted to shout her name and pull her into his arms.

He knew he'd hurt her. Still, he knew Jenny and when she was done with someone or something, she was done. She'd given him his marching orders, and he'd known as he walked out of Spitalfields that he'd never see her again.

He'd missed her terribly. He'd felt like half a person for months, like the other half of him had been cut off. But as the years passed, he also told himself not to think of her. People in Spitalfields didn't live long lives. If sickness didn't kill them, poverty would. When he'd returned from the war, he'd spent weeks looking for her to no avail. He'd told himself she was dead and in a better place now. He didn't want to know how she'd died—hanging or murder or sickness. It was better not to know.

But now he realized it hadn't been better, only easier. Because here she was, and his elation at seeing her was almost as fierce as the pain.

One look at her face certainly helped Aidan control his surprise. She didn't look any happier to see him than she'd been that last night together.

"A pleasure," Aidan murmured belatedly as their hostess complimented Jenny's ivory gown and diamond parure. Aidan wondered if she'd stolen them.

"Have you set a date?" Lady Birtwistle asked.

"Not yet," Jenny said, her voice a rich alto. "We were thinking of late summer, weren't we, darling?" She looked at the viscount who smiled and nodded.

Her voice was familiar and yet novel. She spoke slower than he remembered, her words chosen carefully. It took him a moment to realize she was masking her accent. She'd done a good job of it too. He could hardly hear the rookeries at all.

"But I've been reading about your discovery," Chamberlayne said, obviously much more interested in the first floor of Aidan's town house than his impending nuptials. "The papers were vague, but they mentioned items from the seventeenth century. Perhaps some even older."

Aidan was having trouble concentrating on the conversation. Jenny Tate was here, in Lady Birtwistle's ballroom. And she was engaged to be married to Viscount Chamberlayne. Was it a swindle? Was it part of a plan to steal Lady Birtwistle's…what? Jenny's parure looked more expensive than the one Lady Birtwistle wore, and the more he looked at the diamonds, the more he was certain they were not paste but every bit as valuable as they looked.

Aidan forced his eyes away from the jewelry set. "I'm not an expert, but the items do look quite old. I'll have them appraised before I sell them, of course. Miss Tate—"

"Ah, you need an appraiser then," the viscount interrupted.

Aidan glanced at him. "I suppose I do. Do you have one you recommend?"

"Oh, absolutely. I recommend myself, if that's not too gauche. I'm the best there is—well, perhaps Miss Tate is better." He smiled at her. "Do call on me if you are interested in having me take a look, Sterling. I'd be honored." He seemed to spot someone behind Aidan and nodded at whoever it was. "Excuse me for a moment, would you?" he said to Jenny.

"Of course."

He left her side and Lady Birtwistle drew Jenny away to introduce her to some other friends. Aidan watched her go, but Jenny never looked back at him. He supposed he deserved that. He hadn't looked back when he'd left her all those years ago.

Part of him wanted to go after her, but he needed to think of someone besides himself. Seeking her out would only cause her betrothed to ask questions and could ruin the new life she'd built for herself. He couldn't be the person responsible for destroying her happiness. Not again.

A selfless man would put her out of his mind. He'd done it before, but that was when he thought she was dead. Not when she was in the same room as him and very much alive.

He spent a quarter hour wandering in a daze before he was finally able to remind himself he was no longer a boy, but a man. With a supreme effort, he fixed his thoughts on business and kept them there.

Aidan made a circuit of the ball once again, checking the card room for the prime minister, and, not finding him, decided to try other venues. He'd left the damn discussion for the bill too late. The vote was tomorrow. He should have sought out the prime minister before now. He paused to check his pocket watch and the next thing he knew he was hauled backward into a curtained alcove.

He would have defended himself if he hadn't known who'd cornered—er, alcoved him.

"Wot are ye doing 'ere?" Jenny hissed in her real accent, the one he remembered. The urge to take her in his arms rose again, and he pushed it down. She'd probably punch him if he dared touch her. He would have to be content with being close to her, and the alcove was small.

"I think the better question is what are you doing here," he said, his first instinct to defend himself.

She drew back, as though offended. "I know wot ye think. I'm 'ere to pinch the nobs?"

"I admit the thought had crossed my mind. Jenny, I haven't seen you in ten years—"

"Thirteen."

"—thirteen years and you show up here claiming to be engaged to a viscount."

"I *am* engaged to Roland, and I don't need you mucking it up."

His heart fell. He didn't know why. He should be happy for her.

"So will ye keep yer potato 'ole shut or no?"

Aidan stared at her. He'd always thought she was pretty, even dirty and smelling like the rubbish pile she'd slept in the previous night. She had those gray eyes that could look cold and hard when she was angry but also very blue when she smiled and her cheeks pinkened. But he'd had no idea she could look like she looked now. She was still small and slim, but there was no doubt she was a woman. All that dark, dark hair was lifted off her face and shoulders to reveal a graceful neck and alabaster skin. The white gown was simple but expensive and delicate. The gauzy sleeves fluttered over rounded shoulders and arms and the scalloped bodice curved over rounded breasts. The high waist meant he couldn't see much of her waist or legs, but he remembered her wearing trousers often enough. She'd had a small waist and shapely legs.

"Wot are ye staring at? Surprised I look like one of yer ladies?"

"I tried to help you," he said, voice lowering.

She shook her head. "I didn't want yer pity then and I don't want it now."

He'd been such a fool to ever suggest she become a servant in his uncle's house. Even then he'd known she would never do it, and if she had, she would have been sacked in a week. Jenny was no one's lackey, and she didn't abide by anyone's rules but her own. He'd just been so desperate to save her. Clearly, she had saved herself—as usual. "I didn't offer pity, and you know it," he said because he had never pitied her.

"Charity." She made a face that brought him right back to the streets again. "But it was my fault for thinking we were friends. Ye always thought ye were better than me. Walked away and never came back."

"I did come back. I looked for you."

Her eyes widened in what he thought was genuine surprise. And then they narrowed again. "Sure ye did. No matter. It was too late."

"I came as soon as I could." Aidan reminded himself to lower his voice. "I spent years in the army. I was risking life and limb—"

She waved a hand. "Will ye keep yer potato 'ole shut or no?"

He gave her a long look. "I'll keep my potato hole shut."

She nodded and straightened. "Thank you, sir," she said, her façade back in place. "And might I suggest we avoid each other if we're ever in company again?"

"You sound ridiculous," he said.

"Must be a bit like hearing yourself." She began to move past him, but he caught her arm. He didn't grasp it tightly. She could easily shake him off, but she paused, turned her head, and looked at him. He saw the challenge in her eyes, and God knew he'd always liked a challenge. He leaned forward, anticipating the feel of her lips under his, the way she kissed as though it might be the last thing she ever did. The way she did everything as though it were the last time wrecked him. But just as his mouth brushed hers, she put a hand on his chest, staying him.

"I told you, sir. I am betrothed to Lord Chamberlayne." And she parted the curtains and disappeared back into the ball.

Aidan didn't move, partly because he didn't want to be seen emerging right after her. Partly because his erection would have made his appearance even more scandalous. Instead, he leaned a shoulder against the wall and took a breath and then another.

It wasn't until he arrived home an hour later that he realized he'd forgotten all about the prime minister.

***

Roland sat down in the chair across from Jenny and buttered a piece of toast. They often breakfasted together at his town house. They worked there together as well when they weren't called away to the countryside to paw through the contents of an old castle or a newly discovered trunk in the attic of a deceased great-grandmother. Jenny was aware most men of the upper class would have disdained work of any sort, but Roland was obsessed with antiquities, especially anything Roman. He'd dragged Jenny to the middle of more than one windswept field in the interior of England to inspect an item a farmer found that might be a Roman coin or a piece of pottery.

Jenny hadn't minded. For a woman who'd never been out of London, she had traveled a great deal these past twelve years and seen much of the world. It was a big world, much bigger than she'd ever supposed, and yet she liked her little corner of it best.

"You didn't tell me you knew Aidan Sterling," Roland said, nibbling his toast.

She shrugged and tried to ignore the old anger that welled up in her whenever she thought about him. "Didn't realize the Aidan Sterling I knew was the same one in all the papers." The Aidan Sterling she'd known would have starved to death or been killed by one gang or other if she hadn't stepped in to help him. Who would have thought he would one day emerge as one of the wealthiest men in England?

"You almost jumped out of your skin when Lady Birtwistle introduced you last night. How do you know him, dear girl?"

She would have answered, but the door opened then and Mr. Oscar Lexum strolled in, wearing Roland's banyan and a sleepy smile. His light brown hair was tousled, and he looked as though he'd spent a thoroughly enjoyable night. He leaned down, kissed Roland on the cheek, and then moved to Jenny to do the same. "Am I interrupting?" he asked.

"Always," Roland said, "but you're so pretty we tolerate it."

Oscar Lexum *was* pretty. He had unruly curls and green eyes and full lips. He was the son of a nobody, like she, but his nobody earned a bit more blunt, and Oscar had an education. He fancied himself an artist, and Roland had met him at a museum in Paris. Like any reputable artist, Lexum suffered for his art. He'd been poor and hungry, traits immensely appealing to Roland, who liked to save people. Jenny knew that from first-hand experience. But while Roland had wanted her for a business partner, his intentions toward Oscar had been wholly different. Jenny had watched as Oscar and Roland entered dining rooms or drawing rooms. Every woman's eye was instantly drawn to one or both of the men. Little did the women know, the men only had eyes for each other.

"I heard you were brilliant at the ball last night," Oscar told her. He hadn't attended, having not been invited and unable to attend as Roland's betrothed, though he fit that role more than Jenny ever would.

"I think we fooled them," she said, sipping her tea.

"She didn't drop a single H," Roland said. "She was flawless. The only problem might be Sterling. Will he keep your secret, do you think?"

"Sterling?" Oscar asked, filling his plate and taking it to his usual place beside Roland. "Who is Sterling?"

"Aidan Sterling," Roland told him. "The man who owns most of London and half the rest of the world. Apparently, our Miss Tate knows the man and never even breathed a word. And she knows how much I want to get my hands on those antiquities found buried away in his town house."

"I told ye I didn't know they were the same man. When I knew 'im, 'e were so thin a breeze would have blown 'im over and even the beggars felt sorry for 'im." And that was as much as she wanted to say about the man.

Roland lifted his brows. "Are you saying he owes you a debt?"

"Did you save his life?" Oscar asked.

"I wouldn't say that, exactly." They'd saved each other, and in the end, he'd saved himself—and only himself. But in the early days, she had done more saving than he, to be sure.

"You must have known him during the lost years," Roland said. "That's what the newspaper men call them, at any rate. The years after his father died, and he disappeared. Then his uncle found him, and he went into the army."

She nodded. " 'E didn't talk about 'is father much, but 'e mentioned 'is father was one of the nobs. Not that I was surprised. 'E talked like one of them."

"You should be practicing your dialect too," Roland chided. Jenny refrained from rolling her eyes, but just barely. "His father was indeed one of the nobs, as you say. He was the Earl of Cranbourne. Sterling was said to be a bastard he got off a pretty chambermaid, but the earl acknowledged the baby. I never knew his father, but I've seen his uncle a time or two, and Sterling is definitely a Cranbourne."

"Whoever he is," Jenny said in her best upper-class accent, "I had a word with him last night and 'e—*he*— promised to keep his potato—"

Roland raised a brow and Oscar smiled.

"He promised never to breathe a word of our former acquaintance."

Oscar clapped. "Oh, well done!"

"With only a month left in the Season," she said, "I doubt we will see him again." But she knew it wouldn't be so easy.

"Never say so," Roland chided her. "I want a look in those trunks of his. Quinnell!" Roland raised his voice, and a moment later, the butler entered.

"Yes, my lord?"

"Send for my solicitor, posthaste, will you? There's a good man." He looked back at Jenny and Oscar. "I want to know what clubs Sterling belongs to, what invitations he's accepted, and who he keeps for a mistress. We absolutely must see him again, and this time we need him to agree to let us appraise those treasures of his."

"He might let *her* see his treasures," Oscar said with a smile.

Jenny did roll her eyes now. "I've already seen his treasures."

"Really?" Roland's eyes went wide. "You were lovers."

"I was seventeen and he was sixteen. Calling us lovers is putting a sheen on it."

"Was he your first?" Oscar asked.

"Oscar!" Roland chided him then looked at Jenny. "Was he?"

"A lady never kisses and tells," she said.

"*Now* she wants to be a lady."

Roland nodded his agreement. "This does make things more interesting." He tapped his chin. "I don't see Sterling as a particularly sentimental man, but he's loyal. He's always in the company of that troop he fought with in the war. Perhaps we can use loyalty to secure access to the find."

"Roland," Jenny said, "there are other jobs we can take. There's a stack of correspondence on your desk, all of it from people who will pay for you to appraise their jewelry or paintings."

He waved a hand. "Trinkets. I want Sterling's find. I have a good feeling about it. Quinnell!"

Jenny rose and left Roland to his machinations. She wanted no more talk of Aidan Sterling. Although she didn't reside at Roland's town house—she had a flat not far away—she felt at home there. Judging by the gleam in Roland's eye, it would be at least an hour before any real work for the day would begin. So she started up a set of marble stairs that gradually narrowed and became merely serviceable and wooden. They ended at an unpainted wood door. She took the key from the hook on the wall beside the door and unlocked it, stepping out into the midday sun shining down on the town house roof.

Unlike most town houses, the roof of Roland's was flat and encircled by a brick wall painted white, like the outside of the house. Plants and small trees circled the perimeter and flower boxes added pinks and purples and whites to the green. In one corner stood a large aviary, well shaded by several trees and an awning. Jenny could hear the pigeons cooing almost as soon as she stepped onto the rooftop. She made her way to the aviary, opened the door, and stepped back as several of the homing pigeons flew down from their boxes and hopped out onto the rooftop. She watched the gray-and-black birds peck around the flowers and trees for insects, the iridescent feathers on their neck gleaming in the sun. Until she had met Roland, she had not known people kept pigeons. She had seen them as scavengers, like herself.

But Roland had trained his pigeons to return home, and whenever he traveled, he took several pigeons with him so he could send messages to her or his solicitor in London. It was much faster than the mail. Jenny even took pigeons home with her some evenings when she was working on an artifact so she could send her findings back quickly.

The door to the roof opened and Oscar stepped out. He immediately shielded his eyes. "It's too bright," he complained. "How do you stand it?"

"I like the daylight," she said. "It's easier to stomach if ye go to bed before dawn."

"So says the belle of the ball." He sat in one of the groupings of chairs and a pigeon flew up to his knee. He stroked the bird gently, keeping his eyes on the bird as he spoke. "So Aidan Sterling. I hear he's handsome."

"If ye like that sort," she said.

"He's tall with dark hair, dark eyes, and millions of pounds. Who doesn't like that sort?"

"Ye forget that 'e only cares about blunt. For four years we were mates and then one day 'e 'as the opportunity to get out, and it's like 'e never knew me." She lifted a metal watering can and strolled to one of the trees, tipping the can to the soil. "Ye can't trust a man like that."

"Rollie isn't asking you to trust him, just appraise his artifacts."

She moved to the next tree. "I'd rather stay away. Don't want to get mixed up with 'im. No one knows my past, and I don't want nobody to know."

"Darling, no one has more invested in keeping your past a secret than I do. The sooner you are wedded to Rollie the better. Already your betrothal has quashed all the whispers that he's a sodomite. Once he marries you, we'll all breathe easier."

Jenny set the empty watering can down and went to fetch another. "The nobs last night licked the betrothal up like it were cream," she said. "Ye 'ave nothing to worry about."

"Jenny," Oscar said, his voice so serious that she looked up from the flowers she was watering. "I'm not worried about myself. I'm worried about you. You know I never wanted Rollie to agree to marry you."

She hadn't actually known that. She had gone to the two men together to propose—so to speak—that she marry Roland and become Viscountess Chamberlayne. Jenny had thought it hilarious at first. Her, a viscountess?

But Roland had taken her seriously. A few weeks before he'd shown her a story in the paper that didn't mention him by name, but which gave enough hints to indicate it was him. The story implied Roland had a preference for bedding men. That was true, but Jenny didn't see how it was anyone's business. Roland had explained that buggery was a hanging offense. Of course, as a nobleman his punishment was less severe, but Oscar could be hung if they were caught. Roland didn't think he and Oscar would be safe unless he married. Other men with his preferences had done so and continued on much as they had done before, albeit with caution and discretion.

Jenny had decided then and there to marry him. Roland promised if she did so, she would become the viscountess and be well provided for, even if he should die before her. Jenny had learned never to depend on anyone else, and she didn't depend on Viscount Chamberlayne. But if she were married to him—in name only, of course—the law said he had to provide for her. And if there was one thing Jenny had found immutable and constant in her life, it was the law. This marriage was her chance to ensure financial security for the rest of her life. What did she care if it was a marriage of convenience to a man who did not love her? She didn't love him either, but they were friends and she trusted Roland, and that was enough.

"I didn't think it was fair to you," Oscar said.

"Why not?" Jenny asked.

"Because you'll be shackling yourself to a man you don't love for the rest of your life."

"It's not like I want to marry some other cove," she said. "I'm thirty, well past the age to marry, not that anyone is asking."

"Men might ask if you ever went out in public. You're very beautiful for someone so ancient."

Jenny rolled her eyes. Oscar was three and twenty and liked to tease Roland and Jenny about their advanced ages.

"Now that you're attending balls and the theater and taking your nose out of every musty book in the library, you might find more than one man you'd like to know better."

"Roland said once we're married, I can take any lovers I choose and pass the bastards off as 'is." Indeed, he thought the idea of a bastard inheriting the Chamberlayne name and title vastly amusing. *Perfect revenge on my arse of a father*, he'd said.

"I know what he said. What *we* said." Oscar stood. "But I honestly thought you were quizzing us when you asked. And then when Rollie said yes, I worried that you only went along because you feel obligated."

Jenny stilled. Her obligation to Roland was one subject she did not like to discuss. It made her emotional, and she didn't like emotions. She waved her hand. "That 'as nothing to do with it."

"But of course, it does. He saved your life, so to speak. He pulled you out of the gutter."

She pointed a finger at him. "I'd pulled myself out of the gutter long before I met 'im."

"You know what I mean."

She did, and she had felt she owed Roland in those first few years. But since then, she'd learned everything he had to teach and more. Her skills at appraisal had earned Roland pots of money. He hadn't cared about the money so much as the antiquities, but her skills had made his name respected by some of the best in the field. Now he was routinely called in to museums and by private collectors to examine new finds, especially Roman pieces. Jenny hadn't suggested the arrangement because she felt she owed Roland anything. She'd proposed because she wanted security and…well, the rest wasn't Oscar's business.

"Ye can rest easy then if that's wot's troubling ye. I didn't agree out of obligation. I didn't ask 'im to marry me out of obligation either."

Oscar tilted his head, looking very much like a puppy trying to understand a new command. "Then why did you ask?"

She laughed and bent to lift one of the pigeons at her feet. "The blunt, of course."

Oscar smiled. "He does have plenty." He was obviously letting the matter go, but Jenny got the feeling he didn't really believe her.

She released the pigeon. "I should go down. Want me to close the aviary or will ye?"

"I'll do it. You go down and start on your work. The pigeons pay more attention to me than either of you do once you have an old coin in front of you."

He was right, she thought as she started down the steps. Both of them could lose track of time once they began studying an artifact. And that sort of focus and attention was exactly what she needed today.

Two

"Well?" Aidan asked as soon as the Duke of Mayne entered the dining room at the Draven Club on King Street in St. James.

Phineas scowled at him. "Might I at least have a drink before you bombard me with questions."

"Here." Aidan offered his glass of port, but Phin gave him a strained look and waved his hand. He insisted on taking his time sitting at the table then removing his gloves. Porter, the Master of the House, who had escorted the duke to the paneled wood room, signaled a footman to bring the duke a glass of wine. The duke accepted it and then asked one hundred and one questions about the menu. In the meantime, Aidan paced back and forth between the tables covered with white linen. Neil Wraxall and Colonel Draven were also dining tonight, but they were on the far side of the room and seemed engrossed in conversation. Draven threw Aidan an annoyed look, and Aidan pulled out his chair and sat opposite

Phineas, who seemed to have finally decided to eat the same meal he always ate at the club.

"You've come from Westminster, yes?" Aidan asked.

"I'm fine, Aidan, how are you?" Phineas said. "Why, my wife is doing very well, thank you for asking."

Aidan rose. "Never mind. I'll go to the offices of the *Times*. They'll have the news from Parliament."

"Come back," Phineas said, laughing. "I'll tell you."

Aidan didn't even pretend to think it over. He sat back down and raised his brows. "The tariff bill?" he asked.

"Failed," Phin said, and Aidan sat back in relief. There would be no new tariffs to cut into his profits. Now he needed to find someone to introduce a bill to repeal existing tariffs. He eyed Phineas with interest.

"You must have called in favors," the duke said, sipping his wine. "I thought it would pass."

"You have no idea," Aidan admitted. He'd waged an all-out campaign against the bill these past few days. He was exhausted but also exhilarated by his victory. Actually, he was elated at the thought of making more money. Money always invigorated him. "How did you vote?" Aidan asked, still thinking about introducing more bills.

Phin raised his brows. "Don't look at me like that. I don't owe you any favors."

"True, but surely a repeal of some of the existing tariffs would suit your interests as well." Aidan withdrew the notebook and pencil he always kept in his pocket. "Here, let me show you—"

Phin waved the notebook away. "I don't want to discuss tariffs and I don't want to discuss the Lords. I want to drink my wine and eat my dinner and talk of trivialities. That's all my brain box can handle after all the speeches I was forced to listen to tonight."

Aidan tried to think of trivialities to discuss. And tried.

Phin must have seen the futility of waiting for Aidan to suggest a topic because he began, but not before glancing longingly at Draven and Neil's table. "Have you been to any mills lately? Seen Chibale Okoro's new fighter?"

"No, you?"

"No. I thought you were one of the Fancy, traveling to watch the boxing exhibitions and such."

"Not as interesting now that Rowden retired," Aidan said.

"I've noticed"—he gestured to Draven and Wraxall— "we've all noticed that now that Rowden is no longer fighting, you've become rather...obsessive about your work."

Aidan had no idea what he was talking about. He'd always been obsessed with making money. "I thought I'd miss the mills more, but this new crop of fighters doesn't interest me. Besides, the stakes are usually too low."

"It always comes back to money for you, doesn't it?" Phin said. "Even your pastimes need be profitable."

Aidan bristled. "There's nothing wrong with making a profit. We weren't all born a wealthy duke." Aidan immediately regretted the words. Phineas Duncombe had been the youngest of five sons born to the Duke of Mayne. His four older brothers had died or been killed before he could inherit, causing terrible pain to the family. Aidan saw the shadow cross Phin's face. "I'm sorry. I didn't think before I spoke."

He'd been distracted and feeling off all day, thanks to his encounter with Jenny. He had to keep pushing her from his mind and reminding himself that she did not want to see him and that she wanted him out of her life. That was the least he could do for her.

Phin waved a hand. "I was born privileged. That's true. But even the lowliest night soil collector has a pint with friends once in a while." Night soil collectors had the unenviable job of emptying the cesspools and privies of the upper classes and carting the excrement away.

"You and I are having a drink," Aidan argued as a footman delivered Phin's soup, supervised by the watchful eye of Porter. Aidan raised his glass to Draven and Wraxall. "A toast, gentlemen," he said.

"Did you buy another factory?" the colonel asked as he raised his glass.

Aidan scowled. "No." He turned back to Phin who had his napkin to his lips and appeared to be clearing his throat. It was a poor disguise for the laughter shaking his shoulders.

Aidan sipped his port, a drink which he hated but ordered because it was expensive. "You've made your point," he said.

"Actually," the duke said, "my point was that you need a life outside of making investments and counting profits. You only go to a ball if there's someone you want to speak to about business. You only dance with a woman if her father is a man with whom you want to partner. You only come to your club"—he gestured to the room—"when you want news about a bill on tariffs."

"Now that Rowden is leg-shackled, I hardly have reason to come," Aidan said. "I'm the only bachelor of the lot, save Nicholas, and he's hiding in the country. I hardly want to sit here for hours and listen to all of you wax poetic about your wedded bliss. And if all the weddings weren't bad enough, now there are the babies. I saw Lady Lorraine the other day, and she's as big as a house. Ewan had to pull her out of her chair."

"Then I suppose you won't enjoy hearing the news that Jasper will be a father before the end of the year."

Aidan put his head in his hands. "First the weddings, now the christenings."

Phin ate more soup. "Have you ever considered marrying?"

"Gad, no. I don't have time for a wife."

"You would if you allowed the army of clerks and assistants you employ to do their jobs instead of checking every notation they make for accuracy."

Aidan scowled. Even if he'd wanted to do such a thing, it would have been impossible. He had far too many employees to go over everything they did.

"Aidan, I didn't marry because I had time to fill. I married because—well, I fell in love—"

"No." Aidan held up a hand. "No love stories."

Phineas grinned, and Aidan could have sworn he was enjoying himself at Aidan's expense. "Companionship is part of what makes life worth living. It's human nature to want to share our experiences and hopes and dreams with another person. Not to mention, Annabel makes me laugh. She adds to my experiences of life. Her way of viewing the world is interesting and novel—"

"Duke, if I want a woman in my bed, I can have a woman."

Phineas rolled his eyes. "You aren't even listening. I am speaking of more than mere carnal relations. Marriage is more than having a woman in your bed every night, and even that act is different when the woman is your wife."

"I don't need a wife. I don't want a wife." He wanted lower tariffs and it didn't appear as though that could be accomplished tonight. He rose. "I need to go back to my office and look in."

"It's past ten o'clock," Phin pointed out.

"Still early. Give my best to Her Grace and to Lord Jasper, if you see him." He stopped by Draven's table and asked after Mrs. Draven and her sister, who had recently married, and he sent his greetings to Lady Juliana, Neil's wife, but made sure to leave before Neil could regale him with any anecdotes about the orphanage he ran. An orphanage—the idea was appalling. Where was the profit in that?

Somehow Porter, who had been in the dining room but a moment before, was in the vestibule with Aidan's coat and hat at the ready. He allowed Porter to help him don his greatcoat as his gaze paused on the large shield opposite the door. A medieval sword bisected the shield that was embellished with eighteen fleur-de-lis. Those were for the eighteen men of the troop they had lost during the war. Aidan remembered each and every one of them—Guy, Bryce, Peter, George, Harold...

But he had come home. Against all the odds, Aidan had made it back to England, and he would not squander his second chance at life now. He stepped out of the club into the brisk April evening. It was cool and sometimes he found the night air cleared his thoughts. He told the footman waiting for him to send the coach home as he would walk to his offices and could take a hackney home if he did not wish to walk. The truth was, he often slept, when he slept, in his office. There was little to go home to. He had a large house in Grosvenor Square, but only the rooms he used for entertaining had been furnished or decorated. The rest of the house was quite empty, except for his bedchamber. And really that was cold and empty as well.

He stuck his hands in his pockets and started for the building he used for his offices on Piccadilly. It was a short walk, and he was far from the only man out in St. James's this evening. He stayed well clear of the drunk young lords stumbling about or tossing up their accounts. He wondered how many of them would go home to a pretty young wife this evening. Was he the only man in London sleeping alone?

He didn't have to sleep alone. There were plenty of widows and even married women who had made their interest plain. But he'd been so focused on building his empire for so long that he had begun to think he didn't have the same physical needs other men had. Aidan counted himself lucky in that regard because he remembered all too well the way he had burned for Jenny Tate when he'd been younger. Back then a touch of her hand or a glimpse of her ankle could arouse him for hours. And when she wore trousers—well, he'd needed a plunge in the cold Thames to cool off then.

But he'd been a youth, undisciplined and unruly. Now he was a man, ordered and efficient, and even seeing Jenny the other night had not brought back those lustful urges— well, not many of them. Seeing her had reminded him of the time they'd spent together, some of it nearly naked. But she was engaged to marry Viscount Chamberlayne, and Aidan didn't feel quite right about lying in bed imagining her on her knees with his cock in her mouth when she was soon to be another man's wife.

Of course, now that he did have that memory in his mind, it was hard to dislodge it. She hadn't known what to do, and he hadn't any experience either, but they'd made it up as they went along, and he thought they'd done a fair job of it.

He'd just turned onto Piccadilly when a coach slowed, and a man leaned out of the window and called to him. Aidan, mind still on fellatio, turned distractedly then started as he realized the man calling to him was Viscount Chamberlayne himself. Aidan felt the color rise to his cheeks. But the viscount was saying something—repeating it now—and Aidan made himself focus. He tried not to look into the coach windows, tried not to squint to see if Jenny was inside, but he couldn't quite help himself.

"—we'd be happy to take you there," Chamberlayne was saying. He rapped on the roof of the coach, and it slowed, causing the coachmen in the conveyances behind it to protest quite loudly. Chamberlayne swung the door open, and Aidan couldn't fail to see Jenny in the light from the carriage lamps. She wore a red dress and leaned forward to peer at him. Her dark hair had been pulled up and away from her face except for a long curl that snaked over one breast, much of which was exposed in the low-cut gown.

A thousand thoughts went through Aidan's mind in that moment, not the least of which was that he had no idea what Chamberlayne had been saying or where he was headed. But

Aidan, who a moment before had been congratulating himself on overcoming the physical needs other men succumbed to, couldn't quite stop staring at the tendril of hair caressing Jenny's breast, and the next thing he knew he was in the coach.

He found, once he entered, that Chamberlayne and Jenny were not alone. Another man was also present, and he was seated beside Chamberlayne. This meant Aidan had to sit beside Jenny. He did so, and the coach started away. The coachmen behind them cheered and whistled.

Jenny looked over at him. "Good evening, Mr. Sterling," she said in her cultured voice. Chamberlayne made introductions.

"Might I present my good friend, Oscar Lexum," he said, introducing the man beside him. Aidan nodded at the man with the overly tousled brown hair and sleepy eyes.

"Miss Tate said you were tall, dark, and handsome," Lexum said. "She was not exaggerating."

"I said no such thing," she retorted, and Aidan was inclined to believe it. Jenny didn't give compliments.

"Should we drive you home?" Chamberlayne asked. "Or were you off to one of the other events of the evening? We've just left the theater. The play wasn't over, but Miss Tate found it rather dull."

"I was actually—" He paused, remembering Phin's words from earlier that evening. *Even the lowliest night soil collector has a pint with friends once in a while.* How pathetic would he seem if he admitted he was returning to his offices to work while the rest of London danced and laughed and drank?

"Which play was it?" Aidan asked, turning to Jenny. He didn't know why he'd asked. He never went to the theater. He had a box, of course. He had the best box at every theater, but he never used them.

She named the play, still playing her part as a lady of the upper classes, but it meant nothing to him since he hadn't seen it. But instead of expecting him to comment on the production, she changed the subject. "Lord Chamberlayne will not say it, but he would be endlessly grateful if we could have a peek at your recent find. If you have other plans for this evening, perhaps we could call on you another day, but if you are amenable to allowing us a glimpse this evening…"

"Oh, do say yes," Chamberlayne said.

"Please," Lexum added. "I beg you. If you don't agree, he shall go on about it for days."

Aidan had quite forgotten about the trunks the workmen had found when doing repairs on the ground floor of the old house. If he had remembered, he would have ordered a footman to have them sent to Montagu House for the British Museum to appraise and hopefully buy. But he saw no harm in allowing Chamberlayne to take a look. He had mentioned Chamberlayne's offer to appraise the items to his private secretary, and Pryce had said the viscount was widely respected in that area.

"Of course," Aidan said. "Have the coach drive to my house in Grosvenor Square." It wasn't until the viscount had relayed the directions and the coachman had turned the conveyance in that direction that Aidan had time to regret. He was aware, again, of Jenny at his side and of their shared history in the rookeries of London. To have Jenny in his house—his very large, very ostentatious house—seemed somehow vulgar. They'd practically starved to death together, and now he would be showing off one of the largest, most expensive properties in Town.

She moved slightly, and the silk she wore rustled, reminding him that she had come out on top as well. It might have easily gone the other way. She might be dead in a pauper's grave right now. But somehow, for some reason, Fate had put her in his path again.

Jenny and her betrothed.

"Would you mind telling me how you came to find the trunks, Mr. Sterling?" the viscount asked, producing a notepad and a pencil from the pocket of his coat, much like a Bow Street Runner might do. Much like he himself did when talking business.

"Not the notebook," Mr. Lexum said under his breath.

"It sometimes helps in our work to know a bit about the discovery," Jenny said. Aidan would never get used to hearing her speak in that upper class accent. It was practically flawless, but that didn't mean he liked it. Of course, when they'd lived on the streets together, he'd perfected a lower-class accent. He'd had to else he would be beaten by anyone who heard him open his mouth. He wondered if he could still affect it. He'd tried so hard to forget those years.

"Let's see," Aidan said, bringing his mind back to the antiquities. "I bought the house about two years ago and took possession almost immediately. I did some refurbishment of the bedchambers and servants' quarters, but I hadn't thought much of the areas belowstairs until my housekeeper mentioned that she would like to move the coal cellar to the other end of the house and might I allow her to authorize workmen to open up a wall."

"Which wall was it?" the viscount asked, scribbling furiously.

"One of the walls of the larder," Aidan answered. "I don't know if it was always the larder, but that was how we used it, as had the previous occupants."

"And you had no idea there was a room behind the wall?"

"I suspected there was something. I'd walked about the exterior and noted that the structure went on past the section we were using. I saw no reason for Mrs. Woodson not to have the wall opened." He was distracted by the rustling of Jenny's skirts again. She seemed restless or perhaps bored. He made an effort not to glance at her again, as his eyes were continually drawn to that lock of hair over her breast.

"And when did the workmen tell you they had found something? Was it the first day of work?" Chamberlayne looked up from his notes, pencil at the ready.

"I don't know which day it was. I'm not home all that often, but at some point, they let me know they had found several old trunks stacked in that walled-off antechamber."

"I assume you went to investigate right away," the viscount said.

Jenny laughed, and Aidan did look at her then. "I'm certain he was far too busy making money to do anything of the sort," she said.

Chamberlayne gave her a quelling look. "We can't all be gentlemen of leisure, my dear," he said. Aidan found he did not like it when the man used terms of endearment toward her. He'd never done that himself. If he had, Jenny would have laughed in his face. But she seemed unperturbed.

"No, we can't," she agreed. She looked at Aidan, and though he couldn't see the pale gray of her eyes, he could imagine them fixed on him. "At some point you found a moment to examine the find," she suggested.

"Yes. I found papers and clothing items. A few books. It all looked rather old. No jewelry or plate, nothing terribly valuable."

"As though you would know."

He opened his mouth to retort that he wouldn't know because she had always been a better thief than he, but he remembered her betrothed sitting across from them and his promise to keep his potato hole shut and said nothing.

The viscount either hadn't heard Jenny or was pretending he had not. He closed the notebook and smiled at Aidan. "I expect that within the hour I will be able to tell you if there's a possibility you have anything of any real value. Regardless of the monetary worth, it sounds like an exciting find."

"Yes." Aidan drew out his pocket watch. "An hour, you say?" he asked, glancing at the time. It might be after midnight before he was able to return to the office.

"Do you have another engagement?" Jenny asked sweetly. "A paramour from whom we are keeping you?"

From whom? This was thick even for a born charlatan like Jenny Tate.

"Dear girl," Chamberlayne chided, reaching over to squeeze her knee. Aidan followed the movement with his eyes before forcing himself to look away. "I'm sure that's none of our concern."

"It's nothing pressing," Aidan said, though of course it was. His time was money, and money was always pressing. But he did need to attend to the trunks on his ground floor before the workmen could continue, and if Chamberlayne could give him some direction that would at least tick one thing off his list. "This is it," he said, as his town house came into view.

The viscount rapped on the roof of the coach while Lexum let out a low whistle. "Now *that* is a house," he breathed. But for some reason Aidan found himself looking at Jenny. She shook her head, looking disappointed.

Aidan glanced past her, trying to imagine how the house must seem to her. He couldn't see anything wrong with it. It looked as well-maintained as always. The outdoor lamps were lit, so the house could be seen in the dark. The flickering light showed fresh white paint, new black shutters, flower boxes bursting with blooms, and hedges trimmed within an inch of their lives. The gravel at the drive was smooth and almost soundless as the wheels rolled over it then stopped.

Almost immediately, the door opened, and his butler came out with two footmen.

Everything was perfect. And yet Jenny turned to him with a pitying look on her face. He knew that look because she'd given it to him often enough when she'd first found him sleeping on the streets. "Well," she said quietly, her tone full of scorn. "Ye finally got wot ye always wanted."

***

The house was ridiculous, Jenny thought as she was led inside an enormous vestibule lit as brightly as the day with a crystal chandelier that must have boasted a hundred candles. Why it should be lit, when they had not been expected, was beyond her. But then judging by the amount of gilt and marble around them, Aidan spared no expense.

She didn't know why she expected him to live in one of the terraced town houses. She should have known when he mentioned Grosvenor Square the house would be free standing. She just hadn't expected it to be so large. When the coach had driven through the gates and onto the circular drive, it appeared the house went on and on before them. She'd actually peered out the window to look up and up at the massive stone façade. Aidan had always talked about one day living in style. He'd said one day he would have the biggest house in all of London. She'd laughed, thinking it was the idle talk of any youth starving on the streets. She'd say how one day she'd own a hundred silk dresses and buy a whole sweet shop so she could eat as much as she liked of the confections. She'd been fantasizing, but Aidan had been planning.

A servant took her wrapper and Roland and Oscar's greatcoats, and Aidan offered to give them a tour. He did not want to give them a tour. She could see his reluctance in the way his eyes did not crinkle when he smiled and made the offer. He was doing what he considered polite, not what he wanted. He probably had a woman waiting in a flat across town and would rather be rogering her than poking about in musty old trunks.

"If you don't mind, I'd like to see the trunks," Roland said predictably. Oscar rolled his eyes, and the four of them followed the butler down the stairs and into the servants' domain. This area of the house was not blazing with light. Most of the servants would be up with the sun and had already retired. The butler's lamp was all the light they had to see by. And yet, Jenny noted that the quarters were clean and comfortable. At least Aidan took care of his servants.

Finally, they reached the larder, and though the debris of the excavation had been mostly swept away, there were still large chunks of plaster and rock that dug into the sole of Jenny's flimsy shoes. Ladies didn't wear shoes that were actually good for anything because ladies didn't ever have to walk anywhere or do anything. Jenny rather hated that part of being a lady. Sometimes she longed for her boots and trousers.

She winced as she maneuvered around the worst of the rubble and stopped before three large trunks. Not only had they been walled in, they had also been set inside a wooden cupboard. The workmen had torn the cupboard down, if the stacks of wood pieces around her were any indication. That was too bad. The workmanship of the cupboard might have told them something about the period when the trunks were put away.

One of the trunks had been pulled off the top of the stack, and Aidan went to it, opening it with his gloved hands. Strange seeing him in gloves, but they suited him. In fact, everything about this house and the wealth oozing from his every pore suited him. He'd always been too good for her, and they'd both known it.

"May I?" Roland asked, gesturing to the latch on the trunk. He'd inspected the outside and made murmuring noises, but Lexum was making motions with his hands, obviously eager to see inside. If she had done that, Roland would have scolded her and told her there was as much to learn from the outside as the contents, but Oscar really didn't care about antiquities. He just wanted to open the trunk and see the surprise.

"Go ahead," Aidan said. "Pierpont." He gestured to the butler to raise the lamp higher so they might see. Roland reached for the latch, and Jenny held her breath. It was exciting, almost as exciting as thieving had once been. In some ways the work she did now was not dissimilar. She went into people's homes—invited, of course, which was different—and studied their treasures. She never knew when she arrived if she would find anything of value. Sometimes Grandmama's old vase was just a cheap trinket. And sometimes Grandpapa's sword was priceless.

Roland raised the lid of the trunk with a flourish, and too late Aidan said, "Slowly now."

Dust rose up, and they all coughed for a good thirty seconds before it settled and Pierpont could hold the lamp steady again. The first item they saw was an old piece of burlap. Jenny would have tossed it aside, but Roland took out his notebook and made a note. He squinted at the cloth and then looked at Aidan. "Is there any way we might have more light?"

"I can fetch another lamp, sir," the butler said.

"Very good," Aidan said. Because no one else moved forward to take it, Aidan finally took the lamp from the servant and raised it up. Jenny saw his hand stray to his pocket, where his watch resided. He did not appear the sort to have the patience for the tedious work she and Roland did on a daily basis. Roland looked down at the trunk and withdrew a sheaf of papers, squinting at the writing on them. "Hmm. Perhaps sixteenth century," he murmured. "Much older than I expected." Then he looked up. "Do you know when the house was built, Mr. Sterling?"

"I…" Aidan opened and closed his mouth. "I don't remember at the moment. I am sure that information is in the records I received when I purchased the house. It has quite a history, I'm told."

Apparently, he hadn't cared enough about the history to read the records, but then she had always been the one drawn to the old coins and pieces of jewelry the mudlarks they knew pulled from the Thames. Aidan had just wanted to know how much they were worth. Jenny had been interested in the value too, of course, but she was also interested in their history. The mudlarks learned very young how to identify older finds and separate them from something only lost in the river recently. She liked to talk to them and learn how they could distinguish.

Roland was at war with himself. Jenny saw the way his mouth tightened and his eyes flicked back to the open trunk. He wanted to know what was in those records, but he couldn't very well order a man like Aidan Sterling to fetch them or report back about their contents.

"I'm afraid I'm not dressed for this tonight," she said, indicating her flimsy slippers and the hem of her gown, now gray with dust.

Roland's eyes widened in horror. "I should not have dragged you down here. I'll take you home, my dear."

"Nonsense." Her gaze met and held his. They'd known each other long enough that he could see she was warning him to let her take the lead. "We just arrived. Perhaps Mr. Sterling would be so kind as to allow me to sit in his study and peruse the house's records. I'm sure he has more important tasks to attend to than holding a lamp in the larder while you poke around, my lord."

"I don't mind at all," Aidan said. She gave him a look that said, *liar.* He looked away and cleared his throat. "Of course, if the lady is uncomfortable, I would be happy to show you to a more restful room." He glanced at the lamp, and Oscar stepped forward and took it.

"I'll hold the lamp."

"This way, Miss Tate," Aidan said, gesturing back through the larder. She stepped into the kitchen, but the farther she moved away from the work area, the darker the quarters became. She hesitated, allowing her eyes to adjust. "Where is Pierpont?" Aidan asked, moving past her. His arm brushed against her back before he realized how close he was and adjusted his path.

He stood in front of her. "Should we wait?"

"I can see well enough now," she said. He led the way, and as they moved out of the kitchen the sound of Roland and Oscar's voices faded. Funny how more than a decade had passed but now that she was creeping about in a dark house with him again, it felt like they'd never been apart.

"The stairs are this way," he said, the shape of him moving off to the right. At the base of the stairs, he waited for her to reach him. She gathered her skirts in one hand and started up behind him. But she hadn't quite caught all the material of the gown because she stepped on the hem and started to fall forward. He pivoted and caught her under the arms, steadying her and pulling her upright.

"Feck," she breathed, forgetting she was supposed to be a lady. "I almost cracked my 'ead open."

"I have you," he said, his voice low and reassuring. He lowered his hand to her arm, brushing—quite inadvertently, she thought—against her breast. "Let me help you."

"A moment. My slipper is caught on the material. Bloody worthless shoes," she said, dislodging the hem of the dress.

"I see your language hasn't improved." There was a hint of amusement in his voice. The comment rankled. She might never be a true lady, but she'd worked hard to get where she was now, and unlike him, she hadn't had a rich, titled uncle to help her.

"I beg your pardon," she said sweetly. "I know your ears are innocent."

He snorted and started up the stairs again, still holding her arm.

She tried to tug free. "I can walk on my own."

"I'd prefer to hold on just to make certain you don't fall and break your neck. The last thing I need is the magistrate here tonight."

If she had needed more confirmation that their presence here was an interruption to him, his words were it. Still, she allowed him to hold onto her, if only because she didn't quite trust herself in the shoes and the gown, until they reached the door at the top. They had to pause then. He fumbled for the latch in the dark and she, waiting on the step below him, tried not to notice how close she was to his broad back or how his coat smelled of tobacco and clean wool.

He finally opened the door, and just as he stepped through a light appeared as the butler holding a second lamp neared. "Sir!" he said, looking surprised. Well, as surprised as a servant of his training ever managed to look. "Madam. I would have escorted you up the stairs."

"We managed, Pierpont," he said. "Hold a moment." He took a candlestick with a taper from a counter in the anteroom and gestured to Pierpont to assist him so he might light the candle with the lamp. That accomplished, he led Jenny through the house and back the way they'd come. The candle was unnecessary as they passed through the foyer again, but the chamber behind the wooden door he opened toward the rear of the house was dark, and he lifted the candle to shed light on the room as she entered.

This was obviously his library. Shelves and shelves of books lined the walls and went up and up as far as she could see. This was no ordinary library. It extended past the first floor and into the second. Tall windows would allow light in during the day, and though it was too dark to see through them now, she imagined the view they showcased was a manicured garden.

While she stared at the books and the winding staircase, the painted ceiling and the various ladders on this floor and the one above, he lit a lamp on the desk, two wall sconces, and stoked the fire. When she looked back, he was standing behind the chair at his desk, watching her. Her gaze flicked to the desk, and she knew instantly this was his private space. This was where he lived. The piles of books on the desk, the open ledger, the inkwell and numerous quills spread about indicated he worked here. She had never known him to be particularly fastidious. He tended to spread out and leave things where they fell. She'd lectured him about it time and again because if they had to make a hasty exit from a roof or an abandoned building where they'd found a place away from the elements, it would take too long to gather up items strewn about. He'd learned to keep his few possessions close and tidy. But she saw now he'd reverted to his old ways.

"Would you like to sit?" He indicated a grouping of chairs and couches upholstered in a red that matched her gown. "I could ring for tea."

"No need," she said. "I'll have whatever that is." She pointed to a table behind the desk with crystal decanters filled with amber, pale gold, and ruby liquids. She could have fetched the drink herself, but she liked the idea of him waiting on her, so she took a seat on the couch and watched as he selected what appeared to be brandy, poured her two fingers, and replaced the stopper. She would have told him to go back and add two more fingers, but he started toward her then and she forgot about the drink altogether. He'd been sixteen when she last saw him, not quite a man and no longer a youth. He'd been tall and thin, sinewy from the hard work of survival and the thin rations. He was still tall, but he was no longer thin and rangy. His chest stretched the front of his shirt, his shoulders needing no padding to fill out the coat, which tapered nicely into a V at his slim hips. His breeches, fawn-colored and snug, showed off muscled thighs and well-shaped calves.

Her gaze traveled back to his face. Before he'd sprouted a patchwork of facial hair that he needed to shave every few days. They'd stolen a razor and shaving soap for him. Now he had a dark shadow along his jaw. She imagined he had to shave every day to keep his face smooth. The dark eyes were the same. The hollows around them were gone as were the dark shadows underneath, but they were the same murky eyes that told her nothing of what he was feeling.

He stopped in front of her. "That was rather obvious," he said, handing her the drink. "I doubt your betrothed would appreciate the way you just undressed me in your mind."

She almost said he wouldn't care a whit but remembered herself in time. "I was just noting the changes in you."

"I could note some in you," he said, "but I'm more circumspect." His gaze lowered to her breasts pointedly before returning to her face. The glance had been brief, but it didn't matter. Her nipples hardened inside her stays, and she felt an old heat she'd almost forgotten begin to pool in her belly. He turned away. "I imagine you'd like to see the house plans." He crossed to a cabinet and opened a drawer. "I have them here." He rummaged through papers and produced a folder. She had no doubt that what appeared to be chaos to others was perfectly arranged in his mind. He flipped the folder open and perused its contents under one of the sconces. His dark hair gleamed under the light, and she wondered if it was as soft as it looked. He'd worn it short when she'd known him before, but the longer length now—just long enough to fall over his forehead—suited him. She sipped her brandy, glancing at the glass after a taste. The brandy was very good, probably the best she'd ever had. She was no connoisseur, but this was smooth and didn't burn as she swallowed.

"Ah, here we are," he said, still looking at the papers. "Built in 1728. One of the first houses in Grosvenor Square. There have been changes and additions, of course," he said, carrying the folder to her. "It's all here."

"Interesting." She took the folder. "Roland said the cloth looked to be from the sixteenth century."

"I thought it rather old myself, but perhaps we are both mistaken."

She shook her head. "He's rarely mistaken."

She looked up at Aidan, surprised at how close he was. He had leaned down to hand her the folder and not yet straightened. Their eyes locked. "Is that so?" he asked.

She nodded.

"That's another thing the two of us have in common."

Three

He should have known Jenny wouldn't take the bait. Her level gaze remained cool and direct. Finally, he was the one who straightened and looked away. Ridiculous to be jealous of another man after all this time. Would he rather Jenny be alone? Or worse, stuck in the rookeries, shackled to a drunkard who foisted a new baby on her every year? He should be glad she had caught the eye of a viscount. Even more importantly, she had found meaningful work. She'd always had a good eye. She could distinguish the valuable from the paste far better than he, and she'd been interested in the history of items. She'd spend hours with the mudlarks, learning how they knew what century a find might come from. Aidan just wanted to find something else and pawn it so they would have coin in their pockets.

They never seemed to have enough coin.

"Take your time looking through that," he said, moving to his desk and lifting a document. He pushed the jealousy down with practiced efficiency. He was used to the feeling of wanting what others had. It was why he was so successful in business. It wasn't that he wanted Jenny or begrudged Chamberlayne for what he had. It was second nature to Aidan to want a horse or house or piece of land someone else owned. That's all this was.

He lifted another document just as Jenny whistled. He looked up, and she waved the bill of sale at him. "Ye paid a fortune for this 'ouse. *This much*." She snapped the parchment. "For a 'ouse!"

"I think I liked it better when you couldn't read."

"Ye shouldn't 'ave taught me then." She set the folder on the cushion beside her and sipped the brandy he'd poured for her. "Just 'ow much blunt 'ave ye got?"

Unlike many men in his position, Aidan knew exactly how much money he had. He knew his profits, losses, and the value of his investments down to the pound, if not the penny. "Enough," he answered because it was none of her business how much money he had, and if he told her, she'd balk.

"I doubt that." She lifted the folder again and rifled through the papers. "Even when our bellies were full and our pockets bulging, it were never enough for the likes of ye." Her voice was bitter.

She knew him well, but she didn't know everything. "I daresay that was true once upon a time," he said, pulling out the chair behind his desk. "But I'm quite content now." Aidan managed to say it all with a straight face. He didn't even gag on the word *content*.

She gave a disbelieving snort then went back to the folder and this time several minutes of silence stretched between them as she quietly turned pages and he shuffled papers from one side of his desk to the other. Finally, he surreptitiously glanced at his pocket watch.

"Are we keeping ye from something?" she asked, her gaze still fixed on the papers. How the devil had she known?

"No." He slipped the watch back into his pocket.

"A midnight rendezvous?" she asked, finally glancing at him with a teasing look in her eyes.

That teasing look had always been his undoing. She'd been such a serious girl. But when she gave him or anyone that teasing look, it made his heart clench painfully. It did so now, and he spoke without thinking. "I wanted to go back to my office and look over a contract."

Her smile faded. "To yer office? Is that wot ye do in the wee hours? Work?" She shook her head. "Ye never were one for any fun."

"If you mean did I want to spend our last shillings to sit in Astley's Amphitheater for an hour instead of eating for the next week, then I'm not any fun. But as I recall a bunch of prancing horses hardly make up for days of being cold and hungry."

"This again?" She dropped the folder and stood, hands on hips. "Are ye really still 'eated about that?"

"We gave up eating for a week to watch horses prance in a circle."

"They did more than that," she argued, "and not all of us were born the bastard of a nob and 'ad seen it before." She'd raised her voice. Now he stood and raised his.

"I could have sneaked us in."

"I wanted to sit in a seat and not watch my back for once. And ye didn't starve for a week. It were one night. Two at most." She'd moved across the room, anger making her skirts swish as she walked. He met her at the side of the desk, looking down at her. For a moment, it was almost as though those thirteen years melted away. She was clean and smelled of flowers, but her eyes were the same and the argument familiar.

"That's not the point, and you know it. That was *our* blunt, not yours. You should have asked me."

"Why? Ye would 'ave said no. Ye can't fault a girl for wanting some fun."

"I could have shown you fun," he said. It was what he'd said all those years ago, and he said it now without thinking. Her eyes darkened to blue, her pupils dilating.

"Ye might have been 'ungry that night, but ye weren't cold." Her voice was low and seductive.

"No, that was the night after. We were too angry that night to…" His gaze dropped to her lips.

"To do this?" Her hand slid up the side of his coat and fisted on the lapel. With the slightest tug, she brought his mouth down to hers, his lips a fraction from her own. His hands circled her waist out of habit. She was still slim, but when he stretched out his fingers, he could feel the swell of hips that hadn't been there before. His heart beat so hard that his chest hurt. The blood pounded in his head as he brushed his lips over hers.

Her lips were soft, softer than he remembered, and her breath smelled of brandy. Her hand slid up to his neck, grabbed his hair and tugged him down into a real kiss. His mouth touched hers, and he was struck by the heat of her, but then she'd always been fire to his ice. Why had he ever let her go?

Aidan pulled back so abruptly that Jenny had to grasp the edge of his desk to keep from stumbling. He had let her go, and now she was betrothed to another man. He was kissing another man's intended. Thank God the kiss had not gone far. They'd barely tasted each other.

"Wot are ye doing?" she asked.

"I'm sorry. I shouldn't have done that."

"I kissed ye, nodcock."

"Then you shouldn't have done that. Your betrothed is downstairs."

She opened her mouth to say something then closed it again and nodded. "You're quite right," she said, and he could almost see her step into the persona of the viscount's betrothed. "I don't know what came over me. Nostalgia, I imagine."

"You'll tell him, of course," Aidan said. Jenny was a lot of things, but she was not a liar. Well, until she began pretending to speak like one of the nobs she hated so much.

"I'll tell him." Her brow creased as though she were considering how to do this.

"Should I call my second?"

"For?" Her brow smoothed. "A duel? No," she said on a laugh. "He won't challenge you to a duel. I'll tell him it was the good-bye kiss we never had. I told him a bit of our history together."

Aidan might have preferred pistols at dawn to having his sordid past discussed over tea. He could hardly fault Jenny, though. It was her past as well.

He took a step back. "It won't happen again. I can assure him of that myself."

"Don't," she said. "I won't be kissing you again. Ever." She straightened her shoulders and seemed to make a decision. "I haven't a watch like you, but I think it is time we were away. If I don't drag Roland from the larder, he's likely to stay all night."

Aidan lifted a lamp. "I'll show you downstairs."

Jenny followed him out of the library, and as they walked, her head looked this way and that. "He will want to know if he can come again," she said, head tilted back to look at the foyer's high ceiling.

Aidan stopped and she almost slammed into him. "Even after you tell him…"

She gave him a wry smile. "There's little that will keep him away from an archaeological find."

"My secretary did say he was one of the best."

"He is," she said. "He's very good, very thorough, and honest. If you have something of value down there, he will tell you." Her tone implied that there were plenty who would say he had nothing and buy it off him for pennies then sell it for an enormous profit. Men like that didn't last long as appraisers because it was a profession that demanded trust and honesty, but Aidan had seen greed corrupt the best of men. "But you won't want us to come back," she said. "We would be here all day for hours. Surely, we would be in your way. Perhaps you should send the trunks to Chamberlayne's town house—"

"No," he said. He didn't know why he said it. She was right. He didn't want people in his home at any hour of the day. He especially didn't want Jenny Tate in his home. She'd already proved herself a temptation.

"No? Wot the 'ell, Aidan?"

Aidan saw a nearby footman's head snap back. Jenny must have seen it too because she said, "I mean, pardon me, Mr. Sterling. I don't think I heard you correctly."

He jerked his head toward the servant's door and when they were alone again, standing at the landing of the stairs to the kitchens, he said, "The trunks are mine. They stay here."

"No one disputes those trunks are yours, but if we take them—"

"They stay," he said again.

She glared at him.

"And if the issue is having to see me, I assure you I am rarely here. I doubt we'll see each other again." He opened the door and led her down the stairs, toward the light in the larder. He found Mr. Lexum leaning against the ragged door frame, looking tired and bored. His arm was raised to shed lamplight over the figure bent above the trunk. Lord Chamberlayne didn't even look up when Lexum greeted them.

"Deep in concentration, I see," Jenny said, taking the lamp from Lexum who looked happy to lower his arm for a moment.

"There are quite a number of letters and journals here," Chamberlayne said, indicating he had heard them after all. "Fascinating. I haven't had time to read them yet…" He looked up. "Did you discover when the house was built?"

"Yes, 1728," she said. "One of the first houses in Grosvenor Square." She glanced at Aidan when she said it.

"Hmm." Chamberlayne lifted a paper and squinted at it. "That's interesting. Mr. Sterling, I've only had a cursory glance at these items, but I think we have something quite interesting. There may be nothing of value, except historically speaking, but I'd like to have a closer look."

Aidan waved an arm. "My larder is at your convenience."

"Shouldn't have said that," Mr. Lexum murmured under his breath.

"Brilliant!" The viscount held out his hand and Aidan shook it. As he looked into the smiling face of Jenny's betrothed, he wondered if the man could tell Aidan had kissed his bride-to-be just moments before. "I promise to keep you abreast of anything and everything we find. I'm happy to give daily reports."

To the side and slightly behind the viscount, Jenny shook her head vehemently. Aidan pressed his lips together. "I am afraid I am rarely home, but you may report any progress to my private secretary, Pryce. I will have Pierpont give you his card."

"Very good, sir." He looked longingly over his shoulder at the trunks.

"We should leave Mr. Sterling to enjoy the rest of his evening," Jenny said. "And I do believe my bed is calling to me."

"Of course, my dear," the viscount took her hand. "I will take you home."

Aidan had a sudden image of the viscount in bed with Jenny, but he pushed it away. She was not his. He had made the decision to let her go, and he did not regret it. He had everything he could want now. He'd done the right thing— for both of them. After all, she would soon be a viscountess.

The small group departed, and Aidan stood in his foyer and debated going to bed himself. And if he did that, he'd lie there, alone, remembering the kiss and the past. He didn't want to think of the past. He wanted to think about the money he would be making in the future. "Pierpont," he called. "Have my coach brought around."

***

The next morning, Jenny sat at a desk in Chamberlayne's sunny parlor. His artifacts were kept in the library, away from heat and light, but this adjacent room was used to store notebooks, brushes, shovels, and even pickaxes. She had moved several pieces of pottery into the sunny room to catalogue them. The pieces were from an excavation in the countryside a few weeks ago. Though Roland preferred that the pieces be kept in the dark, she preferred to work in the light, and this morning he was happy enough not to object. He had a large sack open in the center of the room and he was going from drawer to drawer and shelf to shelf, picking items he might need to study Aidan's find. They'd travel to Grosvenor Square after noon. She and Roland might wake early to work, but no one expected a man like Aidan Sterling to receive them before midday.

"I am certain he is already up and at work," she said, choosing her words carefully while noting the item number of the shard in front of her. The upper-class accent was becoming more second-nature to her. "He never was one to lie abed."

Chamberlayne paused, and she looked up a moment later to see him watching her draw the pattern of the pottery in the notebook. He lifted his teacup from the edge of the desk and sipped. Then he sat across from her. "I believe I have only had glimpses of your past with Mr. Sterling. Perhaps you should elaborate."

She replaced the quill in the stand. "I think you're right, especially after what happened last night."

Roland raised a brow but didn't interrupt.

"I kissed him," she said.

"Was that wise?" he asked. "I'd rather you kiss men after we wed."

"No, it weren't wise," she said, scowling as she heard herself slip into her old dialect. "I wasn't thinking, I just did it. Afterward, he asked if I would tell you, and I said yes. Now I suppose he expects you to throw down your glove or whatever men do before dueling."

Roland looked horrified, and Jenny bit back a laugh. "I told him I would explain everything. It was just a good-bye kiss. No need to call your seconds."

"I could play the role of the jealous fiancé, but I don't know how convincing I might be. Surely I can affect a cool demeanor when I next see him, though."

"Just blame it on the woman," Jenny said. "That's what men always do." She lifted her quill again and held it above the inkwell. "In this case, I am at fault. I did kiss him."

"Why?" Roland asked, taking the quill from her and replacing it before she could wet the nib with ink. "I mean, he's an attractive man, yes, but you manage to refrain from kissing other attractive men. Why him?"

She shrugged. "It won't happen again. He's the last man I ever want to kiss." She made a motion to end the conversation.

"Oh, no, Miss Tate. I think it long past time we had a discussion about Mr. Sterling and his role in your past."

"You always said you would never pry into matters that didn't concern you." She lowered her voice to sound like him.

"But now you've kissed him, and we're to spend the next several weeks in his house. This matter does concern me."

She couldn't argue. Well, she could, but Roland would win. He was right. She did owe him an explanation. The problem was Aidan's history wasn't really hers to tell. She supposed she could keep to the parts that pertained to her or were common knowledge. "Fine, I'll tell you how we met."

The door to the parlor opened and Oscar poked his head in. "Good morning. Why the serious looks?" he asked.

Jenny rolled her eyes. Oscar Lexum was like a bloodhound. He could scent gossip two miles away.

"Jenny was about to tell us how she and Mr. Sterling first met," Roland said. "Sit down."

Like a child with a new book, Lexum rushed to a chair and sat, hands folded in front of him.

Jenny leaned back and closed her eyes, not because it was difficult to remember, but because it was all too easy. She always felt that the rookeries lingered at the edges of her existence, waiting with long fingers to drag her back down.

"I thought he was dead," she said, and painted a picture of the filthy street in Spitalfields where she had seen him lying in a mud puddle, barefoot and motionless. "But then he woke up, and as much as I wanted to leave him there, I couldn't."

"You always had a soft heart," Oscar said.

"No, I didn't. I'd stepped over plenty of half-dead children before. I don't know why I didn't just leave him." She gazed out the window, not seeing the view of the garden but those filthy streets and that little girl who'd been clutching her mother's skirts and watching her. "He was ridiculous. He didn't belong there. He gave me his hand to shake and told me his mother was dead and his father was an earl. I thought he was lying. Everyone in the rookeries has a Banbury tale like that."

"What made him different?" Roland asked.

Jenny thought back. So much had been different about him. "He asked about me—if I was an orphan. No one had ever asked about me before, or cared." She laughed at the next memory. "And then he asked if we could be friends. I didn't even know what a friend was."

"Your first friend," Oscar said, smiling.

"It wasn't like that at first. We were partners in crime. He would distract the costermonger, and I would swipe an apple or a plum." She held a piece of pottery, rubbing it as she spoke, and she set it down now.

"How did he distract them?" Oscar asked, leaning forward.

"He'd stand up and give speeches. I didn't know what they were then, but he had whole sections of Shakespearean plays memorized. He'd stand on a chair or the pedestal of a statue and start yelling, 'To be, or not to be? That is the question.'"

Roland and Oscar exchanged a look.

"He did," she insisted. "I know it's difficult to believe now, but he wasn't always so stuffy and serious." He hadn't been that way at all once she had started to know him. He'd been funny and silly and such a change from the people she knew, who had all been worn down by poverty and want. Of course, over time, he was worn down as well.

"He's the son of an earl?" Oscar asked. "Then shouldn't he be *Lord* something?"

"The bastard son," Roland said. "Cranbourne acknowledged him but apparently didn't think to provide for him in his will. It sounds as if the new earl was not aware of him. But he found Sterling a few years later and took him in, yes?" He looked at Jenny.

That was exactly what had happened. Aidan couldn't wait to be rid of her. She clenched her hands at the rush of rage. "You asked how we met," she said coolly. "That's how we met."

"I asked about your history," Roland corrected. "I asked why you kissed him."

Oscar gasped. Jenny rolled her eyes.

"And now I need to know what, exactly, we should do about your obvious attraction to Mr. Aidan Sterling."

Four

"I hate to ask this of you," Colin said that afternoon at the Draven Club. Aidan had a rare free hour between appointments and had come into the club for a drink and to read the paper. Now the paper sat folded in his lap and his drink sat untouched on the table. He'd thought no one would find him in the Billiard's Room.

He'd been wrong.

"This is far out of my area of expertise," Aidan said. "You should ask Neil. He knows all about orphans."

Colin scowled at him. "I just told you Neil agreed to take her in. I want you to find her. I'd find her myself, but she knows me, and I have the feeling every time I get close, she goes into hiding."

"Then wear a disguise. Isn't that what you're known for?"

Colin's green eyes narrowed. "I wish I'd thought of that."

The sarcasm in his tone was unmistakable. "She saw through your disguise?" Colin made a gesture that indicated this was obvious. "Then why not send—"

"Were you listening at all?" Colin demanded. "Lord Jasper has another job. He can't do it. And when he's not working, he wants to be home. His wife is—"

"Yes, I know."

"Good. Then you'll do it? I wouldn't ask you, but Lady Daphne is worried about the child. We haven't seen her for weeks now. I've written down a description." He handed a piece of paper to Aidan, and for some reason Aidan couldn't fathom, he took it.

"This describes practically every urchin in London."

"Her name is Harley."

"That's not her name."

"Well, it's a start, and with your resources, you can hire men to flush her out. Once you have her, bring her to me, and I'll take care of the rest."

Aidan folded the paper again. "If this is about resources, ask Mayne. He's in Town and has plenty of resources."

"But he doesn't have your background," Colin said. "You know your way in and out of that world. If anyone can find her, you can. Well, Jasper could find her, but you're the next best choice."

"I think that's supposed to be a compliment." Aidan rose and Colin followed. "Listen, FitzRoy, I would like to help, but I have business to attend to. I can't waste time and money on finding one urchin out of the fifty thousand living in London." He dropped the paper on the chair and started away.

"And that's your answer?" Colin said. "A friend comes to you for help, and your answer is, I'm too busy making money?"

Aidan paused. He considered telling FitzRoy his real thoughts, but he wasn't even sure he understood them himself. When Rowden had married, leaving Aidan as the last man standing, so to speak, he felt he'd lost his last friend. He was the lone bachelor, save Nicholas who enjoyed being alone. He hadn't been jealous of Rowden really, but he'd realized that unlike during the war, his former comrades-in-arms now had people in their lives who meant more to them than he did. Even if Colin's request hadn't come on the heels of seeing Jenny again, Aidan would have resented it. FitzRoy wanted help because his wife was unhappy. Well, who cared if Aidan was unhappy? Did Colin understand that if Aidan went back to the rookeries, he wouldn't be able to stop thinking of Jenny? Everything would come rushing back, everything he had had with her and lost.

Worst of all, the memories of that fruitless search years ago when he'd returned from the army. He'd been so hopeful that he'd find Jenny and sweep her into his arms and carry her out of that hell. Instead, he'd found dead ends and had to finally walk away without any answers. He'd mourned Jenny as though she had been dead because he'd thought she was dead.

And now she'd come back into his life and was unreachable as she'd been during those frantic weeks of searching years ago. He rejoiced that she was alive and well, but the joy was tinged with the pain of knowing she'd never again be his.

Aidan turned to face Colin. "If you needed help, FitzRoy, I would be the first in line, but just because you're tired of hearing your wife whine, doesn't mean I need to rearrange my life to step in. Get her a different urchin or tell her to whine in private."

For a moment, Aidan thought Colin would strike him. Colin wasn't the violent sort—not like Ewan or Duncan—but the look in his eyes was murderous. "You really don't care about anything but yourself, do you? You ever wonder why you're alone? Take a look in the mirror and think about what you just said."

And with that verbal slap, he strode past the billiard's table and out of the room. Aidan almost went after him, but he couldn't think of a rejoinder. Instead, he caught the reflection of himself in the mirror on the far wall. He strode to it and studied his features. He didn't have green eyes like Colin or a halo of blond hair like Mayne. He had brown hair and brown eyes and a crooked nose. He wasn't an unattractive man—at least he didn't think he was. But he did look stuffy as hell. In fact, he looked like the sort of humorless person that he used to feel sorry for.

Aidan walked away from the mirror, lifted a cue stick and aimed at a ball on the table. It appeared someone had abandoned a game in the middle, and he knocked a ball into the pocket easily. "I'm not selfish," he said, walking around the table, looking for another shot. "There's nothing wrong with wanting to earn money. What does FitzRoy know about it? He never slept under a bridge or ate grass just to fill his empty belly."

But they'd all been plenty hungry during the war, and they'd slept in worse places than under a bridge. And during those difficult years, Colin had been there for him. Of course, Aidan had been there for FitzRoy as well. He didn't owe him anything. Aidan bent over and took another shot. "I care about more than myself," he grumbled. "I give money to every charity in the city."

He caught sight of his reflection in the mirror again. A man, playing billiards by himself. And that was the argument Aidan couldn't counter. He was alone. And he was pushing his only friends further and further away.

With a curse, Aidan strode to the chair he'd vacated and lifted the paper. "Harley," he muttered. "Not her real name." But it was a start. She was likely to be found near the river and the docks. That's where Colin had first met her. Aidan wasn't as familiar with that area of London. But he knew who was.

***

Aidan arrived home several hours later, his head full of numbers and legal terms from contracts. He held a stack of ledgers in one hand, the accounts from a business he had considered purchasing, and had come home to review them in his library. In the office, the lawyers were yelling about this clause and that, and he couldn't think. But when his front door opened, it wasn't Pierpont who greeted him. It was Jenny, and she was holding a bird.

"What the hell?" he said as she released the bird, and it flew over his head, narrowly missing gouging his eyes out. He almost dropped his folders.

"Oops. Didn't see you there." That was a lie. She was smiling and trying to hold back a laugh. She hadn't even made an effort to lie convincingly, which she could do very well. He would have still known it was a lie, but he would have appreciated the effort.

"Sir, I told Miss Tate to release the bird on the walk," Pierpont said, opening the door wide.

Aidan looked at Jenny. He'd tried all day to put her out of his mind and had finally succeeded. And now here she was, and the sight of her made his breath catch. And he had no right to react that way when he saw her. She wasn't his any longer. "Why are there birds in my house?" he demanded, angrier at himself than at her.

"Not birds, a homing pigeon. We send them when we want to communicate quickly. We only brought three."

"There are two more somewhere in the house?" He walked into the foyer, hunching slightly in case they decided to fly at his head.

"Yes, but we have them in a cage."

Aidan gaped at her. "Oh, yes, the cage makes everything just fine."

"They're very friendly birds. You shouldn't worry."

He was not worried. He'd caught sight of her now and had forgotten all about the birds. "What are you wearing?"

She looked down at the pink and cream confection as though just noticing it. This was impossible as the dress had ribbons and buttons that must have taken a maid an hour to do up. As it was a day dress, the material was a fine white muslin striped with bright pink. The sleeves were full at the shoulder and upper arm then tapered to fit snugly about her forearm and wrist. Tiny pearl buttons extended from each wrist to each elbow as well as from her waist—or what passed as a waist these days—to the base of her throat. A long, thick pink ribbon had been secured about that high waist and trailed down the skirts like a pink tail.

She wore no hat, and her black hair had been gathered simply at the base of her neck and secured with a pink ribbon. Her hair was much longer than it had been when he'd known her. Then she'd hacked at it with blunt knives to keep it above her shoulders. Anything longer might have been used to catch hold of her if she was running away. She'd hacked at his hair too, so it didn't grow so long that he looked like a girl. Now her hair trailed down her back all the way to her waist, the curls and waves of it a river of chocolate against the white of the dress.

"Do you like it?" she asked, turning from side to side like a young girl showing off her first party dress.

"No," he said and stalked away. He had known she would be at his house and had congratulated himself on lingering at the offices as long as he had. He'd told himself when he arrived home, he wouldn't even see her. She would stay downstairs and out of sight. But regardless of where she might choose to venture, he could close himself in his library with the ledgers and forget about her. He'd forget about Chamberlayne too. Her betrothed was probably in the larder studying burlap and not even noticing the dollop of cream that was his bride-to-be. Aidan briefly wondered if she had confessed to the viscount about their kiss. Since he hadn't been greeted with a glove to the face, Aidan assumed she either hadn't told him yet or he wasn't angry.

Though that was ridiculous. If Jenny had been his and she'd kissed another man, Aidan would have killed him.

He gritted his teeth and shoved the unwanted thoughts from his mind. He paused a moment at his library door, noting the door was already ajar when he typically kept it closed. He stepped inside and realized why the door had been open. The curtains had been pulled wide and near the window sat a large cage, where two pigeons cooed and preened. He turned to his desk and found two dusty bound books in the center with a sheet of paper beside them and a quill at the ready. He spun around to find Jenny walking into the room behind him, behaving as though she owned the place. Apparently, she had been behaving thus all day in his absence.

"What is this?" He pointed to the cage and the desk.

She raised a brow. "Those are birds," she said as she crossed to *his* desk and sat in *his* chair. "And these are journals Roland found in the trunk. He's asked me to read them and determine when they were written." She indicated the paper and quill. "I haven't read much yet—the handwriting is awful and the language very old-fashioned—but I've made a few notes, as you see."

Aidan didn't know what annoyed him more. The fact that she sat in *his* chair and was using *his* paper and pen or the fact that she insisted on using that accent that made her voice sound nothing at all like the Jenny Tate he knew.

"And you thought to undertake this work in my library?"

She sat back. "No, I *thought* to undertake the work in the parlor in Roland's house, where I usually do such work," she said. "But you...what is the word? *Decreed* that we couldn't remove anything, so I am forced to work here."

He set the ledgers he'd been carrying on the edge of his desk. "And where am I supposed to work?"

"You don't think I've considered that?"

He waited.

"I sent the pigeon to request that Roland's staff send a small desk here. I thought I would have them place it by the windows and Peggy and Percy, and I will work there."

"Peggy and Percy?"

"All the pigeons have names beginning with P."

Of course, they did. Aidan pulled a hand down over his eyes.

"Oh, not that look," she said. "Not the *poor me* look."

"I don't have a *poor me* look. This is my *God give me strength not to toss you out on your arse* look."

She raised her brows. "I'd like to see you try."

He laughed in spite of himself. He'd won his share of tousles with her, but he didn't want to remind her—those tousles, when they'd gotten older at any rate, had usually led to his hands up her skirts and their mouths locked in heated kisses.

Aidan looked away.

"If you want, I can take my journals to the couch over there." She pointed to the couch where she'd sat the night before.

He was supposed to be a gentleman, and he had better act like it. "No. I'll sit there. Until the desk arrives," he qualified. He would have rather gone to his bed chamber and worked at the desk there, but he wasn't about to cede the library to Jenny. He'd never get it back. At least, that was the reason he'd acknowledge.

He sat on the couch. "How long does it take for a bird to fly from here to—" He waved a hand as he didn't know where Chamberlayne lived.

"Only a few minutes," she said, pulling on a pair of white gloves. "Birds needn't contend with carriages or pedestrians." She looked down at the journal and carefully opened the cover. "But the footmen who bring the desk will have to deal with both, so I imagine it will be several hours before the desk arrives."

"I see."

She made a sound of acknowledgement and appeared to study the journal. Aidan opened one of the ledgers and tried to make sense of the numbers. But he was acutely aware of Jenny sitting just a few feet away. He tried to concentrate, but he couldn't seem to stop looking at her from the corner of his eye and seeing her reading then lifting his quill and scratching something on the paper. What was she writing? Moreover, what was she reading? What journals had meant so much to someone that they had held on to them for—well, that was the question, he supposed—then secreted them in this house in Grosvenor Square and kept them safe for all this time?

"Stop," she said, still looking at the journal.

"What did you say?" But he'd been caught staring at her. He knew it.

"I said stop. You're staring at me." A lock of hair had fallen over her shoulder, and his eyes kept tracing it down over one plump breast. "I know it's strange to be together again, but we'll make the best of it. It's temporary."

"I was wondering if you told Chamberlayne."

She dipped the quill in ink and made a note without looking at him. "Told him wot?" Her concentration on the journal had caused her accent to slip. He didn't point it out, preferring it.

"Told him you kissed me."

The scratching of the quill ceased. She didn't look up, but she took a deep breath. "I told 'im."

"And?"

Now she looked up, her gray eyes steely. "And 'e said 'e understood. It was good-bye."

She was lying again. She was more convincing this time, but he knew her face. He might not know this clean scrubbed version of it, but he knew it all the same. When she lied, she looked directly at someone. Her gaze was fixed and intense. She did this because most people wouldn't look others in the

162 | Shana Galen

eye when they lied. But it was such a direct gaze, that it gave her away—to him, at least.

"Does he know you are upstairs, alone in this chamber with me right now?"

"No," she said, looking back at her paper. "But if 'e comes upstairs, there's nothing to see. Yer over there, and I'm 'ere. I mean, *h*ere," she corrected herself.

"I like it better when you drop the H," he said. "It sounds more like you."

She gave him an annoyed look. "This is me now. The girl you knew is gone."

"Where did she go?"

"Wherever the boy you were went, I suppose."

Well, she had him there. "Direct hit," he said. She inclined her head, taking the point with characteristic smugness. He rose and wandered toward the birds, who watched him with small reddish eyes. "Something does not make sense," he said.

"Then you'll need to add the columns again," she said, sounding distracted by the journals.

"Not with my math." He turned to look at her. She quickly looked down at her paper, pretending she hadn't been watching him. "With your engagement."

Her head snapped back up. "Wot's that mean?"

He must have hit close to the mark to make her forget her accent again. "It means, that if I were your intended and you kissed another man, I would not be so forgiving."

Her eyes darkened to blue with interest, but her voice was droll. "Roland is an even-tempered cove—er, man. And he trusts me. If I say it's a good-bye kiss, then 'e—*he*—believes me."

"Then he's a fool."

Her eyes turned icy. "Wot was that?"

"He's a fool. That was no good-bye kiss."

She rolled her eyes. "Men. Always thinking they're irresistible."

Aidan shrugged. "I'm plenty resistible to any number of women. I'm just saying, that wasn't a good-bye kiss."

"Care to wager on it?"

He'd forgotten her penchant for wagers. When they'd lived in Spitalfields, they'd wagered on everything from whether a bird would land on a roof or an awning to how much they'd make from pawning a pair of stolen candlesticks. At first, they'd wagered food—whoever won got the apple. And then when they'd gotten older, they'd wagered...other things.

"Jenny and her famous wagers," he said.

"Aidan and *his* famous wagers," she countered.

This was dangerous. He shouldn't talk to her so much or play games with her. It would only make him want her more, and that road led to more heartbreak. But one look at her, *his* Jenny, finally here and gloriously alive, and he couldn't resist. "I'm game." He started for the desk, startling the birds who nervously fluttered in the cage. "What's the wager and what are the stakes?"

He stopped on the opposite side of the desk—*his* desk— and pulled out one of the chairs. He plopped into it and put his feet on the desk.

"Isn't the wager obvious?" she asked.

"Indulge me," he said.

She leaned forward, pressing the pearl buttons of her bodice against the wood of his desk. How was he ever to sit there again and not think of her breasts pushed against the wood? "I say it was a good-bye kiss. You say it was not. If I don't kiss you again, then it *was* a good-bye kiss. If I do, then it wasn't."

His heart was beating fast now at just the *idea* of kissing her. "You have to kiss me," he clarified. "What if I kiss you?"

He saw her swallow before speaking again. "Neither of us can kiss the other, but if you kiss me, I win. I also win if I don't kiss you."

"If you do kiss me, I win."

"Yes, but I won't, so you might as well pay me now."

"Pay you what? The stakes are…?"

"I set the wager, you set the stakes."

That was only fair, and it was the way they'd done things in the past. "I set the stakes," he said, buying time as he considered what he wanted.

"Must be difficult to decide what to ask for," she said. "A man like you who has everything." She folded her hands on the desk before her, looking like one of his clerks—except much prettier.

"I know what you want," he said.

She gave him a look that said she very much doubted that.

"You want to take the trunks out of here."

Her brows went up. "Very well. If I win, we take the trunks to Lord Chamberlayne's house to finish the appraisal."

"Agreed. And if I win—"

"—you won't."

"—you help me find a girl." He realized how that sounded as soon as the words were out and before she stiffened. "It's not like that," he said.

"So you don't want a girl," she said carefully.

"I don't want her, but I need to find her. For a friend."

She shook her head even as he protested. "I want no part of that."

"That's not what I mean. You know me well enough to know I'd never be part of that. His wife wants to help her."

"Then why—"

He held up a hand. "When I win, I'll give you the details."

She sat back. "I suppose I'll never know then because I wouldn't kiss you if you were the only man left in London."

A challenge. Oh, but he loved a challenge even more than a wager. He couldn't resist one, in fact. "You're so sure of that." He rose and stalked around the desk. She watched him with her eyes, not deigning to turn her head.

"Wot are ye doing?" she asked, her accent slipping slightly. Good, he had her on edge. Even better, he had an excuse to be close to her.

"Getting a drink," he said, starting in the direction of the drinks table. Instead, he paused behind the desk chair—*his* chair—and pretended to remember his manners. "Would you like one?" he asked, putting his hands on the back of the chair, close to her shoulders. She sat ramrod straight now, that river of black waves cascading down her back. He wanted to touch it.

"No, thank you. I am working." She lifted the quill again.

"I see your penmanship has improved," he said, bending over her shoulder to peer at her notes. "I can almost read your scratches." His cheek was beside her ear, but he kept his gaze on the paper laid on the desk. She held the quill in one slim hand, her fingers very steady. He'd always thought she'd make an excellent pickpocket. But in a crowd, she was unable to avoid detection. There was something about her that drew the eye. She might approach a man silently from behind, but just as she reached for his pocket, he'd turn round and say, "Oh, hello there."

It was a definite liability in the rookeries. She'd had to work very hard to avoid the notice of the gangs and the arch rogues.

"It's shorthand," she said. "Perfectly legible." Her voice was clipped and sounded annoyed, but he wasn't fooled. She was as affected by their closeness as he was. It was her scent, he decided, that made him lightheaded. He remembered her always smelling of dirt and grime and sweat, but he'd smelled the same and over time, he didn't notice those smells any more. What he'd noticed was the scent of *her*. There was always something musky and earthy about the way her skin smelled. Now it was masked by a light floral scent, not dirt, but he could sense it all the same.

"Shorthand," he said, his voice low. "How clever." He shouldn't be doing this. She was betrothed. But even as he chided himself, one hand slid off the back of the chair and grazed her shoulder. She flinched as he lifted the strand of hair that had fallen over one shoulder and slowly drew it back. For a man who spent very little of his time flirting with women, he was pretty good at this.

She caught his hand in a tight grip—tighter than he would have thought her capable of—and pushed it back. Then, she gave him a steely stare. "You're wasting your time. I'm immune to your charms."

"That's not how I remember it," he quipped.

"Oh, really? Because as I recall, you wanted me as much as I you."

He couldn't argue. "I recall a great deal," he said, drawing his arm back and causing her to move closer to him as she still held onto his hand. He wasn't the scrawny boy of twelve or even sixteen any longer. He was bigger and stronger than she, and he held her close. "I recall that you always liked it when I kissed you right behind your earlobe. Do you still like that, Jenny?"

Her eyes were no longer gray. They were bluer than blue. He couldn't tell if her breathing had sped up because he was all but panting. In that moment, he didn't care if he won or lost. He just wanted to kiss her.

The sound of someone clearing his throat broke the tension, and Aidan looked up. Pierpont stood in the doorway, his gaze on a point close to the ceiling. Of course, he couldn't have missed the fact that Aidan and Jenny's lips were mere inches apart, but he knew better than to see anything that happened in this house. Jenny released Aidan's hand, and he straightened. "What is it, Pierpont?" Aidan was vaguely aware of Jenny dipping the nib of the quill in the inkpot and going on about taking her notes as though nothing had happened.

"Two men are here with a desk, sir. They say they were instructed to bring it in here."

"Ah," Jenny said, still writing. "My desk. Yes, have them put it by the window."

Pierpont looked at Aidan, and Aidan made a reluctant sign of agreement. And then he did go to the drinks table and poured himself a glass of sherry because he was suddenly hot and thirsty. The footmen worked efficiently, but Jenny seemed more particular than he remembered, and had them move the desk this way and that and then wasn't certain about the placement of the chair. The process took so long that he went back to the ledgers, which was probably her plan to begin with. But far from being annoyed, Aidan considered her attempts to keep the footmen present as long as possible a victory. If she'd trusted herself alone with him, she wouldn't have gone to those lengths.

Finally, the desk and chair were where she wanted and her papers were arranged just so, and Aidan was able to take his rightful place behind his own desk. They worked in silence for some time. He'd always found profits and losses absorbing. He could lose himself for hours, but he couldn't quite lose himself today because Jenny was just on the other side of the room, and his mind kept drifting to her, despite his attempts to keep it occupied. Even as he scribbled numbers and made notes as to where the ledgers indicated a shortfall he could exploit, another part of his mind worked on a different sort of problem—how he could entice her to kiss him so he might have her help in finding Lady Daphne's Harley.

Of course, he'd called two Bow Street Runners to his offices after he'd left the Draven Club and hired them to find her, but he doubted they'd have any success. He'd never had any trouble evading Charleys or Runners when he'd lived in the rookeries. And Colin said this girl was particularly elusive.

A tap on the open library door drew his attention, and Lord Chamberlayne smiled at him. "Hard at work, I see," he said cheerfully.

Jenny, who had situated the desk so her back was to Aidan and she faced the garden, turned. Her face lit up when she saw the viscount, and Aidan immediately wanted to hit something. "I thought I would have to drag you out," she said.

"My belly did that." He patted his midsection. "I'm starving." He nodded at Aidan. "Sterling, I hope we're not disturbing you."

Aidan looked for an underlying strain, something to indicate the viscount was annoyed that Aidan had kissed his betrothed, but he didn't see it. "Not at all," Aidan said. "I hardly knew she was there."

Jenny gave him an aggrieved look at that statement. She probably didn't believe him, but she clearly didn't like the idea that she could be so easily forgotten either.

"Care for a drink?" he offered, looking first at Chamberlayne then Jenny. He really had quite a lot of work to do, but he meant the offer sincerely. He was interested to see Jenny and the viscount together. The man seemed so unlike the kind of man Aidan would picture Jenny with. Of course, he wasn't sure why that should be. The only man he could picture with her was himself.

"No, no," the viscount said. "Not for me. You, darling?" He looked at Jenny. She shook her head.

"I should go home and change. We're attending that lecture tonight."

"Ah, yes. We should be on our way then if we're to eat anything beforehand." He looked at Aidan. "We'll be back tomorrow, Sterling. Really just getting started and organized, but I should have a better idea of what it is we're looking at in a few days. I'll give you a report then, shall I?"

"Very good. Have a pleasant evening," he said as Jenny joined the viscount at the door and took his arm.

"You too," the viscount said.

"Good night," Jenny said, not even looking at him. Instead, she smiled up at Chamberlayne as he led her away. Aidan barely restrained himself from throwing the glass of sherry across the room. He would have done it if he hadn't known Jenny would hear it and know she was winning.

Lecture. What lecture were they attending? He'd lost her once. He didn't want to lose her again. "Pierpont!" Aidan bellowed when he was certain the viscount and his betrothed were out of the house.

"Yes, sir."

"I want Pryce."

"Yes, sir."

"Tell him to bring me a list of all the public and private lectures being given tonight, especially any having to do with antiquities."

Pierpont showed no surprise at this odd request.

"And, Pierpont, tell him to hurry."

Pierpont nodded and strode away, seeming to take his time. Aidan considered he might have told Pierpont to hurry. He brought the sherry to his lips and then paused at the sound of a coo. He glanced at the window and realized Jenny and her viscount had left the two pigeons in his library. What the hell was he supposed to do with two pigeons? He supposed one of the maids could clean the cage and perhaps a groom knew what they ate, but—

He stood and started for the cage, slowing when he saw the birds fluttering their wings nervously. The cage was raised on a sturdy gold stand. It looked adjustable, perhaps so the birds could be raised or lowered depending on the height of a nearby window. Three-fourths of the way to the top of the cage what looked like a handle bisected the stand. Hanging on either end of the handle were small rucksacks.

Aidan looked at the birds, then at the sacks, judging the size and fit. Then he lifted one of the little sacks and smiled.

Five

"I need you to go to Suffolk," Roland said in the coach later that evening as they traveled to Montagu House for the lecture.

He watched Jenny's gaze dart from the window to his face and then to Oscar's. Oscar wasn't looking at her because he and Roland had discussed it earlier, and he knew Jenny wouldn't like the suggestion.

"I beg your pardon," she said carefully. She always spoke carefully when maintaining her upper class accent. "What is in Suffolk?"

"The Duke of Suffolk, of course," he said. "He recently bought several items of dubious Greek origin and wants a second opinion on their value and age."

Jenny narrowed her eyes. "You received that request a fortnight ago and said it was a waste of time. You said the items were almost certainly a forgery and at any rate—"

"I'm not an expert of Greek artifacts. I know what I said. I've changed my mind. I think you should go."

175

She gave him a long look, and he didn't look away, though her gray eyes were piercing. People said his blue eyes were intense, but he had nothing on Jenny and her gray.

"If you want," he added. Jenny did not speak, and Roland blew out a breath. Her dark hair looked red-tinged in the carriage lamps. "It's only that you and Sterling—it's not working."

She blinked. "I know we didn't expect him to come home this afternoon, but once my desk arrived, he did his work and I did mine."

"Did you? What can you tell me about the journals?"

She opened her mouth then pressed her lips together as though thinking. "I've only just begun. I made some notes on the quality of the binding and the style of handwriting."

She knew as well as he that answer was vague.

"He's distracting you, Jenny."

"I didn't even know he was there," she said. She was a good liar, but he'd seen them together.

"I could practically feel the heat between you two when I stepped into the room."

"Ooh!" Oscar sat forward, his eyes wide. "Go on."

"There's nothing—"

"Jenny." He used his paternal voice because he wanted her to listen. For once. "I've known you for over a decade.

Don't tell me there's nothing between you and Aidan Sterling."

She met Roland's gaze. He hoped it held no judgement or condemnation. He just wanted honesty. That's all they'd ever asked of each other. "I can 'andle it," she said. "I *am* 'andling it."

"You don't have to handle it. If you want him—"

"I don't!"

Roland exchanged a look with Oscar.

"The lady doth protest too much, methinks," Oscar said, quoting Shakespeare.

"I don't want 'im," Jenny said again, her voice even. "Not after wot 'e did."

"Which is?" Roland asked.

She waved a hand, indicating she didn't wish to speak of it now. "I don't want to go to Suffolk."

"I'd never make you, but you understand that if you and Aidan Sterling are caught, er—"

"Making the beast with two backs?" Oscar suggested. Jenny smiled.

"Yes, if you are caught together, then what might that say about me? I'll have to call off the engagement and not only will that make our professional relationship difficult— at least to outsiders—but it might cause speculation."

178 | Shana Galen

He knew he didn't need to tell her what sort of speculation. The entire reason she'd suggested this engagement was to avert speculation that he was a molly, or a man who preferred to engage in sexual congress with other men.

"I'd never put ye in danger, Roland," she said. "Aidan and I might flirt, but there's nothing between us and won't be anything between us." She reached across the carriage and grasped his hand and then Oscar's as well. "The engagement was my idea, wasn't it? I won't back out now."

"I think what Roland is saying is you don't owe us— him—anything."

Roland hoped she believed that, but he worried she felt as though she owed him her life and that marrying him was the least she could do. He didn't want her to make that sacrifice.

She squeezed their hands. "Yer my friends. I'd do anything to keep ye safe."

"The right word in the wrong ear, and we end up like the men from the White Swan," Roland said. "James Cook had a wife and they still pilloried him."

The White Swan was a molly house that had been raided by the Bow Street Runners some seven or eight years before. Twenty-seven men had been arrested in the raid. Most were released for lack of evidence, which meant they bribed the Runners. But those men had not been members of the peerage. No amount of bribery would keep Roland's name out of the papers were he caught in a similar situation. The penalty for buggery was death, and though it was unlikely a nobleman would be put to death, an example might very well be made of Oscar. He could be hanged while Roland was stripped of his land and titles.

They'd come dangerously close a few months ago. Oscar and Roland had been drinking and found themselves in a room alone at a ball. At least they'd thought they were alone until a man sleeping unseen on a couch woke up to find them in an embrace. Fortunately, Oscar had acted quickly. The man had stormed out to find the host, and Oscar had fetched Jenny then fled the ball. Jenny had thrown herself into Roland's arms just as the host stormed into the room, and the man who'd made the accusation looked like a fool.

Roland had apologized for their improper behavior, and Jenny had intimated that they'd both been overflowing with joy at the viscount's marriage proposal and had momentarily forgotten themselves.

But other men and women at the ball had seen Roland and Oscar talking and laughing together that night, and the seed of doubt had been planted. It was only very recently that

Oscar had taken to being seen in public with Roland again, and always with Jenny between them.

"No one will be pilloried," she said. "I can resist Aidan Sterling."

"But you shouldn't have to," Roland said.

"Oh, it's no 'ardship, I promise ye that," she said.

"He's a handsome man," Oscar said. "I don't know if I could resist him."

"Excuse me?" Roland's tone was indignant.

"Not as handsome as you, of course."

Jenny released their hands and sat back.

"And what makes him so handsome?" Roland asked

"I think it's those dark eyes."

"I thought you liked blue eyes."

Roland continued to spar with Oscar, but he kept an eye on Jenny. She had a sad smile on her lips. Clearly, Aidan Sterling had churned up long-buried feelings. No matter the risk to himself, Roland couldn't marry her until he knew those were sorted and safely put away.

***

Jenny sat with Roland at the lecture. Oscar had spotted friends when they'd arrived and sat in the back with them. Roland was annoyed at this. Jenny could tell because he'd crossed his legs and clasped his hands over his knee. His knuckles were white with the stiffness of his grip. She didn't think he objected to Oscar sitting with his friends, rather it was that Oscar and those friends had left in the middle of the lecture.

She leaned over to Roland and murmured, "I'm sure he will be home when you arrive."

He kept his gaze on the speaker. "Who?"

She rolled her eyes. As though she was fooled. The lecture, which had been on Greek architecture and nothing she didn't already know after ten years of enduring Roland's own lectures, ended and Roland wanted a word with the speaker. Jenny did not want a word with the old man. He had white, bushy eyebrows that reminded her of caterpillars, and she feared she would not be able to stop herself from staring at them if she got too close. Instead, she moved out of the chamber and into the great hall. The grand staircase beckoned her to the first floor, and she need only look up to spot the three taxidermy giraffes at the landing. Not that there weren't plenty of dead animals on the ground floor. Some sort of horned horse stood on a pedestal nearby. She shivered and looked up at the high ceiling, painted with all sorts of pagan gods. Roland would know if they were Greek or Roman, but it didn't really matter to her since she wasn't studying them, only admiring the artwork. She chuckled. Who would have ever thought one day she would be standing in a place like this, admiring artwork?

"A few too many cherubs for my taste," said a voice, "but rather more vulgar than amusing."

With a sigh, Jenny watched Aidan Sterling stroll down the grand staircase, hands in his pockets, black hair swept back from his forehead. She wasn't certain if she was sighing because she was annoyed to see him there or because when he walked like that, he robbed her of breath.

But she was nothing if not quick on her feet. "I didn't think you were interested in Greek architecture," she said, still feeling a bit short of breath as he descended the last few steps.

"I'm not. I listened for five minutes then went to explore the museum."

Thank God he hadn't lingered or Roland would be pushing her out the door to Suffolk.

"I haven't been to the museum in years," Aidan confessed.

Jenny had business at the museum weekly, it seemed, and saw the place as a second home. "Which room did you like best?"

"I didn't see them all, but I was rather struck by the Egyptian sculptures. They're far bigger than I expected." He stopped in front of her. "But you stayed for the entire lecture."

"It's my job to take an interest in that sort of thing." She had to make him leave before Roland saw him. "Don't you have work to do? Ledgers to study? Contracts to sign?"

He smiled. "It occurred to me, after you left, that we never shook on our wager."

"I'm a man of my word," she said.

"So am I. Still"—he held out a hand—"we should shake on it. Make it official."

Fine." She stuck out her hand, eager to finish with him and return to Roland. In the carriage, she might have seemed confident that she could handle Aidan Sterling, but she was far from confident when the man himself stood before her. Oscar was right. There was something about those dark eyes. And it didn't help that it was dark in the hall. The museum relied on natural light, and candles and lamps were only used when strictly supervised. This was to protect the valuable artifacts from any chance of fire. Two lamps did burn in the great hall now, but they gave scant light. Jenny didn't know how Aidan could have seen very much at all on the first floor. But then she'd always thought the Egyptian artifacts best when viewed by moonlight.

His hand closed around hers, large and warm, and she looked down and realized he wasn't wearing gloves. "We never gave our wager an endpoint," she said, realizing too late she should have negotiated this last part before shaking. She should draw her hand away now, while they finished negotiations, but she didn't. She liked the feel of her hand enveloped in his.

"I assumed it would go on in perpetuity."

She wrinkled her nose. "You really have become quite the businessman. But after a week or so—"

"A week or so," he said, sounding choked.

"—Roland will be quite ensconced in your larder and moving the trunks will be more trouble than it's worth."

"Fine. A week. Seven days."

She nodded and shook his hand, but he didn't release her. Instead, he pulled her closer. "If I win, and you kiss me, you help me find the little urchin."

"When I win," she said with a smile, "you will allow us to move the trunks to Chamberlayne's residence." She leaned close, tempting fate. "I might even make you carry them yourself."

He laughed softly, and for a moment she felt dizzy with memories. She remembered so many nights when they lay in an old, creaking warehouse or under a bridge or beneath the stars and that soft laugh of his warmed her in the cold night. He'd pulled her close—or she'd pulled him close—and they'd warmed each other.

"Go ahead," he murmured. "You know you want to."

She did want to kiss him. The remembered desire was making her head muddy and the attraction she felt seeing him now, as a fully grown man, stirred even more in her. But Roland was counting on her, and even if he hadn't been, she always hated to lose a wager.

She pulled her hand out of his. "I will win this wager."

He frowned at her. "I didn't become richer than the King by losing."

"I remember you losing quite a few wagers to me." She stepped back. "In fact, you are already losing."

"Explain," he said.

"I will if you escort me back to the lecture room." And then she'd shoo him out the door.

He offered his arm without protest, and they walked slowly through the shadows and back toward the rumble of voices.

"Go on then."

"Very well. You admitted yourself you have no interest in Greek architecture."

"And?"

"And you obviously have little interest in the museum. You hadn't seen the newer Egyptian pieces."

"I'd argue I have little time for museums, not that I have little interest."

"But you're here now," she said.

"And?"

They paused outside the door to the lecture room. Jenny caught Roland's eye, and he gave her a beleaguered look when he saw who was at her side.

"And I can't think why you would be here unless it's to see me." She gave him a bright smile. "You see, I am already winning."

He took her hand and held it between them. "Keep telling yourself that." He kissed her hand, released her, then walked away.

Jenny watched him walk away, just as she'd watched him all those years ago. She hadn't cried then and she wouldn't cry now at the memory, but she'd rather sleep in a stable dung pile than let him win this time.

An hour later, she was undressed and sitting at a table brushing her hair, when her maid tapped on her door. Jenny called for her to open it. "Norris, I said you could retire."

"Yes, miss, but this came for you from Lord Chamberlayne."

Jenny took the small slip of paper. Why was Roland sending notes to her flat at half past one in the morning? "Thank you. Now go to bed," she said with a smile.

She looked down at the folded note and her breath whooshed out. This was not Roland's handwriting. Her name was written on the outside. She opened the paper and stared at the three scrawled words.

Six days left.

Aidan. The note had to be from him. But Norris had said it came from…

The pigeons, of course. She'd left them in the library. An oversight on her part and Roland's as well. Aidan had obviously found the little satchels that fit over the wings and onto the birds' backs as well as the small slips of paper and sent one of the pigeons home with the letter. But home for the pigeon was Chamberlayne's house, which was why the note appeared to come from Roland.

Had he read it before he'd sent it to her by one of the pigeons who had been trained to see her flat as home? Even if he had, the meaning wouldn't be clear to him. And since when had she started hiding things from Roland?

Jenny rose and tossed the paper into the fire. She simply needed to make it through this wedding. When Roland was safe—or saf*er* at any rate—she needn't worry so much about everything she did. And after all she and Roland had been through, why did Aidan have to come back into her life now, when everything had been going so well?

Her gaze went to the note, slowly curling brown and then black in the fire.

Six days left.

But it didn't have to be six days. She just needed Aidan to kiss her and then she wouldn't have to see him again. She and Roland could move everything to Roland's town house, and she could bury herself in work and forget all about Aidan Sterling. Again.

This time for good.

***

Aidan realized almost immediately he shouldn't have come alone. He could practically feel the eyes watching him from windows above the street and shadowy corners he passed. It was broad daylight, but somehow the light never seemed to reach the cracks and crevices of the poorer areas of London.

Aidan had reread Colin's notes again, and he'd mentioned first meeting Harley near a tavern called The Clipper. To his surprise, his coachman knew the place and had remarked on its excellent fare. Aidan had stopped there first, but when he'd gone inside, he'd sent John Coachman back to Mayfair. The last thing Aidan wanted was his horses stolen and his coach looted.

He'd made sure to take his walking stick, though. A walking stick in the right hands could be a formidable weapon. Aidan had made use with far less.

Not surprisingly, no one in the tavern knew "nothing about nobody." But what did surprise Aidan was that no one knew anything even when he put coins on the bar…and kept putting them there. Finally, he swept them off the bar and put them back into his pocket. He left his card in case anyone remembered something. He walked out of The Clipper knowing he had a target on his back, and kept his head cocked for the sound of trouble. Though he knew he wouldn't hear them. He'd most likely feel them. That was what Jenny had taught him. She'd showed him how to use his instincts, how to notice the hair rising on the back of his neck and the sudden tensing of his body. Once he'd learned to pay attention to those instincts, he'd started anticipating and avoiding attacks by older boys and street bullies. Eventually, as he'd gotten older and taller, he'd been able to fend them off.

Now he paused to chat with two men sitting on a stoop, but a few words with them convinced Aidan that they didn't know about Harley. Perhaps she didn't frequent this area any longer. Perhaps she'd moved on to a different rookery.

Perhaps she was dead.

But he wasn't about to deliver that news to Colin without some proof.

He stopped to ask a woman what she knew, and she just pulled her child close and hurried away. Other people on the street gave Aidan less than friendly looks, so when he heard a loud *Psst* he was a bit surprised.

Without being too obvious, he looked about for the source of the hissed call. He spotted a child—sex indistinguishable—in a doorway. The child cocked its head and stepped inside the door, letting it close behind him or her.

Aidan looked about him. This was obviously a trap. He'd be an idiot if he went through that door. Who knew what might be waiting inside? He'd probably end up beaten bloody, and that was if he were fortunate. Aidan casually strode across the street and to the door. Using the handle of his walking stick, he pulled it open. Darkness lay inside, though he could just make out a wooden staircase to higher floors in the building. Aidan stood there for a long moment before he heard the *Psst* again. It came from the back of the small chamber, behind the staircase. Aidan rolled his eyes. It was so obviously a trap.

And like an idiot, he walked into it. He stepped into the darkness and let the door close behind him. He waited for a minute until his eyes adjusted. "Guv, over 'ere," said a high voice. It was the child.

"We can talk while I stand here if you don't mind."

"I do mind, see. I don't want no one to 'ear me talking to a nob like ye."

"They've likely heard you by now anyway. Tell me what you know about the girl Harley, and I'll give you a copper." He would have offered a farthing, but he didn't carry denominations that small. As it was, he'd had to ask Pierpont for the pennies.

"Two coppers," the child said. Aidan shook his head. The men in Bond Street could learn something from these little negotiators. They seemed born with the ability to bargain.

"Two coppers then. Talk or I walk. I don't plan to stand here while your friends get in position to ambush me."

"Guv! I'd never do that."

Aidan almost believed the child was truly indignant. He turned to leave.

"Oy! 'Old up." The child darted out of the shadows and in front of Aidan's exit. He or she was a tiny thing, all skin and bones. Aidan could have lifted it with one hand. Instead, he raised his brows expectantly. "I know something about this 'Arley."

"Is that her real name?"

"That's what we call 'er, but she don't stay 'ere anymore."

"Where does she stay?"

The child held its hand out, and Aidan put one penny in it. The copper disappeared before Aidan could blink.

"Where?"

"She moved closer to the river and them mudlarks."

Aidan made sure the child saw the second copper. "Does she dive with them?"

The child shrugged. "Don't know. Don't care. I'm just passing on wot I know." The hand came out again. Aidan flipped a copper toward the child, but when the child caught it, he grabbed the grubby, little hand.

"Now tell me how many are waiting for me outside."

The kid tried to pull its hand away, but Aidan held tight.

"Two, maybe three," the child said, voice strained.

"And is there another way out?" Aidan didn't mind a fight, but he didn't relish beating hungry children.

"No."

Aidan bent close, trying not to breathe too deeply. "You're telling me you were about to walk through that door after they were through with me? I'd have thought you wanted to hold on to those coppers."

The child's eyes narrowed. "They said I could keep 'alf."

"And you know they're lying. Show me the back exit, and I'll give you a bob."

The child's eyes widened. "Give it over now."

Aidan reached into his pocket and withdrew the shilling, flashed it so the child could see it, then made it disappear again. He still remembered some tricks from his youth.

The child seemed to consider then said, "This way."

Aidan decided he must be mad to follow the child up the stairs, but follow he did. They reached the first floor, and the child entered an empty flat, opened a window facing the opposite way from which they'd come in, and pointed to a clothesline strung across to the next building. "I'll go across that."

Aidan frowned. "I'm too heavy."

"That's not my fault." He or she held out its hand, and Aidan gave it the bob. Why not?

While Aidan watched, the child climbed out the window, grasped the clothesline with both hands and climbed, hand over fist to the other building. There it ducked inside, paused to wave to Aidan, and was gone.

Aidan sighed and went back to the rickety stairs. Instead of going down, he climbed to the top, using what was more of a ladder than a staircase to access the roof. If chimney sweeps ever cleaned the chimneys in this part of London— which was highly unlikely—they would have used that ladder. Aidan emerged on the roof and carefully made his way to one side. He looked down, spotted five lads waiting to bash his brains in, and cursed under his breath. He shouldn't have given that little shit the bob. He'd give them a half hour to give up and then he'd go back down again. If he was fifteen again, he'd jump to the next roof, but age had given him a sense of his own mortality. Aidan moved away from the edge of the roof and sat. For a moment, all the demands of the day seemed to weigh him down so heavily that he could have sunk back to the ground floor. He would miss his lunch meeting now, and he'd have to reschedule that tour of the warehouse he'd just bought.

But he lifted his head and his gaze roved over what he could see of London. This roof was higher than some others, and he could make out St. Paul's in the distance as well as the trestles of London Bridge. It was almost the exact same view he'd used to share with Jenny.

Damn it. He'd known coming here would dredge up those old memories, and now here he was thinking about all the times they'd played at being emperors of all they'd surveyed. How odd to actually own some of what he surveyed. He'd thought that would make him happy. All those years ago, he'd thought a full belly and a full purse was all he needed in life.

But he had both of those things now, and he wasn't happy. He hadn't been happy—not in the army, not in his new home, not in his offices. Was it possible that he'd been happier when he was penniless and hungry but with Jenny at his side? Ironic to run away from happiness only to look for it elsewhere and then to come back and realize he'd had it all along.

And now Jenny was betrothed to another, and he'd never have it again.

Six

Jenny didn't see Aidan the next day. She worked in his library all day, her ears listening for the door opening or the sound of his footsteps, but he never came. She was surprised. After he'd sent the homing pigeon with the reminder that they only had six days left in the wager, she thought he would go straight to work trying to persuade her to kiss him so he could win. But perhaps he'd forgotten about the wager.

Or perhaps he stayed away because he knew it would make her think and wonder and drive her completely mad. The pigeons were all home at the end of the day, so when she and Roland left Aidan's house that afternoon, she knew she wouldn't receive any missives from Aidan. She and Roland attended a dinner party that evening, and she went home and to bed without any mention of Aidan.

The next day was similar. She worked alone in the library until afternoon then went home early to rest before the ball Roland wanted to attend. It was to be a lavish affair hosted by the Duke and Duchess of Warcliffe, and Roland

197

had instructed Jenny to wear her best dress and jewels. Though she preferred her red dress, she'd worn that at the last ball—the one where she'd seen Aidan again—so she chose her sapphire blue gown and her diamond parure. She was aware the gown made her eyes look more blue than gray, and Norris had ornamented her coiffure with tiny sapphire pins that sparkled in the lamplight. She chose a new pair of pretty blue slippers and then rushed downstairs as she'd kept Roland waiting a half hour.

In the coach she realized she'd made a mistake with the slippers. She should have tried them on before wearing them. They were tight and probably too small. She would be miserable dancing in them for any length of time. Oscar wasn't with them. Roland thought it wise for the two of them to be seen without him sometimes. "And I must warn you, dear girl," he said as the carriage approached the bright lights of the Warcliffe residence, "I intend to show everyone how much I adore you. You'll give me the first dance, of course. And I'll be entitled to one other. After that, feel free to dance with whomever you like."

"If my bloody feet 'urt as much as I expect, I won't be doing much dancing."

"Accent, darling," he said.

Jenny blew out a breath and pasted on a smile as a footman opened the carriage door, and Roland took her hand and escorted her into the massive house. She would have been impressed regardless, but after seeing Aidan's house, her jaw didn't drop at the crystal chandeliers and the ornate gold wall sconces. She went through the receiving line, accepting the compliments and best wishes gracefully, then had only a few minutes to rest her feet before the first dance began and Roland swept her up.

Jenny usually enjoyed dancing with Roland. He'd taught her all the dances, and after she'd danced with a few other gentlemen, she realized he was quite a good dancer. He was light on his feet and always seemed to know when she didn't know the next step and skillfully guided her into it. They danced a quadrille and then a country dance she didn't know the name of, and then he left her to fetch champagne, and she was immediately surrounded by half a dozen young men who wanted the next dance.

Jenny flirted and put them off, wishing she could sit down and slip off her shoes. Most of the men seemed happy to just converse with her, but one man—the son of a baron— continued to insist she dance with him.

"My lord," she said sweetly, "you must allow me to catch my breath."

"The next dance is a waltz, Miss Tate," the baron's son said with a smile, showing his uneven teeth. They looked sharp and carnivorous to Jenny. She cast her eyes about for Roland, but after delivering her champagne, he had been pulled aside by one of her admirers. The two men chatted amiably now, and Roland obviously didn't see Jenny's distress. It wasn't that she couldn't take care of herself. She could handle any one of these nobs. It was that she didn't know how to handle them politely.

"She can't dance the waltz with you, Mr. Harmon," said a voice Jenny recognized.

Mr. Harmon, the baron's son, frowned until the men around them cleared and the tall figured of Aidan Sterling came into focus. The men parted further to allow him to approach.

"Why is that, Mr. Sterling?" Harmon asked.

Aidan took Jenny's hand, bent, and kissed it. "Because she's promised it to me."

Jenny would have dearly loved to contradict him in front of all those men. She would have loved to take him down a notch. He deserved it, the way he swaggered and moved as though this was his ball and he was the most coveted man in attendance. That last part was probably true. Still, she would have liked to knock him down a peg, but if she did that she would have had to dance with tiger teeth Mr. Harmon, and that seemed a decision that would belie her own interests.

Instead, she allowed Aidan to lead her away from the other men, drawing her closer to the dance floor. He paused at the edge and gave her a long look. "I forgot to ask if you know how to waltz."

"Of course, I do," she answered. And then another thought occurred to her. "Don't you?"

He gave a slight shrug. "No, but I'll make it up as we go along."

Jenny stared at him, stumbling when he led her to the center of the ballroom floor. "Why are we in the center?" she hissed. "Everyone will see us!"

He put his hand on her waist and pulled her closer. "It's not as though you can hide in that gown."

"It's perfectly appropriate," she argued.

"You look stunning," he answered, and that comment left her speechless. The strains of a waltz began, and Jenny held her breath as Aidan began to lead her in the first steps. But to her surprise, he didn't stumble or count woodenly. He danced as though he were born to it, which being the son of an earl, he rather was.

After a moment, she forgot her fears and almost forgot her aching feet. He was such a skilled leader, such a consummate dancer, she needn't think of anything but holding on. "Why did you say you couldn't dance?" she asked. "You're wonderful."

He smiled at her. "I like to scare you a little. Keeps things interesting."

"I said that when I was seventeen," she chided. "I don't feel that way now."

"Now you like everything to be boring and predictable. Is that how Chamberlayne won you over?"

She didn't want to talk about Roland. And she didn't want to acknowledge that she wasn't as angry at Aidan as she had been even a few days ago. She needed to remember that he'd left her, and she could never forgive him for that. But this was not the place to air that grievance. "I had plenty of excitement in my youth, and life with Roland is quite exciting. We've traveled the world."

"You always did want to escape London."

"You weren't the only one who wanted to escape poverty and hunger. And I wanted to avoid ending up making a living on my back like my mother." Of course, she had always thought they'd escape together. Aidan had obviously only thought of himself.

"And look at you now," he said and twirled her around. "No one who knew you then would believe it."

"Everyone who knew you would believe it. You never belonged in Spitalfields. Even dressed in rags, you were too good for the place."

His gaze locked on hers, his dark eyes startled.

"You're surprised I said that?" she asked. "Didn't you think you were too good for it?"

"No," he said, and his voice had a familiar timbre. It was the voice she remembered from all those years ago—his real voice—not the voice of the wealthy businessman. "You accused me more than once of thinking I was too good for the rookeries, but the truth is I never thought I was good enough. I would have died if not for you."

She shook her head. "You would have found a way to survive. You were, and still are, a fighter."

He swallowed and looked away. "So are you," he murmured. "You're the only one of us to knock out Meg Hardy."

She smiled faintly at the memory. "One thing I can't fight is these bloody shoes," she said under her breath. "My feet are bloody killing me."

Aidan threw back his head and laughed. If the other guests hadn't been watching him before, he'd garnered their attention now. "You know what I like about you? You always say what's on your mind."

Not always, she thought as she looked up at his handsome face. She couldn't say what was on her mind at that moment because it would most certainly shock him— and he might just take her up on it, which would be disaster for everyone. He skillfully guided her off the dance floor and escorted her toward the refreshment table. He took two glasses of champagne and whispered in her ear, "I know someplace you can sit and take your shoes off. Take my arm."

She accepted it, and he took her for what would appear to others to be a stroll around the room. Instead, they slipped out of the ballroom, through the supper room, and into a dark chamber. A pianoforte stood in the center of the room, a harp beside it, as well as music stands and other dark shapes that might have been other instruments. A plush couch in a color she couldn't make out in the darkness had been placed opposite the instruments, and Aidan led her there.

"I took a wrong turn when I was in the supper room earlier," he said. "I assume this is the music room. The duke has several children and grandchildren, and I imagine this is where they play or take lessons."

Jenny collapsed gratefully on the couch and reached for her slippers, but before she could grasp one, Aidan knelt before her, lifted a foot, and tugged the slipper off. Then he did the same with her other foot. He placed the slippers on the carpet, and Jenny stretched her toes.

"Better?" he asked.

"Much." It was dangerous being here with him. She shouldn't have left the ball. She should have asked Aidan to take her to Roland and had Roland find her a place to sit down. But it was too late to go back and do it again. Now she was alone with Aidan. She jumped when he took her foot. "Wot are ye doing?"

"You said your feet hurt."

"Ye don't need to do that."

"The night is young. You have many dances ahead of you."

"Maybe I'll 'ide in 'ere all night." She laid her head back, giving in to his ministrations. How could she argue with him? His fingers were magic as they rubbed and pressed and eased all the aches from her foot.

"I should fetch your betrothed," he said.

"Yes."

But neither of them moved. He took her other foot and began to massage it. She turned her head to study the pianoforte. "Do ye play?" she asked, lifting her head to sip her champagne.

"No. You?"

She blew out a breath.

"You know how to waltz," he argued. "Maybe you learned how to play the pianoforte or the harp."

"If I sat down and played the 'arp, my mother would turn over in 'er grave."

His hands stilled. "I didn't realize—I knew about your father."

She nodded. " 'E died right before ye left. Me ma, she didn't make it through the winter that year ye left."

He squeezed her foot. "I'm so sorry."

She shrugged and pulled her foot away. "Better off dead, if ye ask me. Couldn't 'ave weighed more than six stone when she passed. All she cared about was the drink in the end."

"Jenny." He tried to put his arms around her, but she pushed him away.

"Don't *Jenny* me. Ye lost the right to 'old me when ye left me. I don't need yer pity."

"It's not pity." He stood. "Your mother died. I know how that feels."

She looked up at him. "Course ye do, but yer mother was a good mum. Mine…" She shook her head. "She'd just as soon beat me as 'ug me. Ye met 'er."

"She loved you. In her way," he added. "Even I could see that."

Her eyes stung, and she swiped at them angrily. "She's gone now. Joined that miserable cove she married in 'ell. Better off without 'er."

"You always were," he said. "You were stronger than her, braver than her. I always knew you were special." He sank into the space beside her on the couch. "I tried to take you with me when I left."

"Not this old argument," she said. "Yer uncle came for ye, not all the 'angers on from the streets."

"You were hardly a hanger on. You saved my life. I wanted to repay the favor."

"By making me a maid in yer uncle's 'ousehold?"

"It was a start," he protested.

"I didn't know a thing about being a maid, and I'd rather be free than work from dawn to dusk for a few coppers."

"In the end, you found your own way." He laid back, his head on the cushions beside her. It felt so much like the past that she could almost imagine they were back in Spitalfields. She closed her eyes.

"I'm still sore at ye for leaving me. Ye said ye never would."

"I've regretted it so many times over the years," he admitted. "I thought about you, worried about you. But tell me honestly, given the same opportunity, would you have stayed?"

She opened her eyes and turned her head to look at him. He'd turned his head too, and their gazes met. Their faces were just inches apart now. She tried to think what to say, but it was difficult to think of anything at all when he looked at her like that. And she couldn't tell him the truth because the truth was that she *would* have stayed. She wouldn't have left him for a thousand pounds. She loved him. She would have stayed with him no matter what.

And the pain she'd felt all those years before hadn't been so much that he'd left, but that he didn't love her enough to stay.

"I would have walked away so fast, ye would have choked on the dust of me shoes," she lied.

He smiled. "That's what I thought. I've never met anyone else like you, Jenny. You're like another piece of me. We understand each other. No one will ever know me like you do," he murmured.

Jenny nodded. No one would ever know her as he did. No one else could ever understand how she could loathe her mother and still mourn her passing. No one else had been there when her father had beat her or when her mother had chased after her. It was Aidan who had bandaged her wounds. Aidan who had told her it was alright to cry (not that Jenny would). It was Aidan who had held her, kissed her, loved her. He was the first person to ever love her.

She lifted a hand and touched his cheek, wishing she could remove her glove so she could feel his skin. She stroked down to his chin, that sharp chin she always teased him was the mark of stubbornness. He gazed at her fondly, his mouth curving in a smile. In the dark like this, she could almost imagine they were back in her hidden cellar, just the two of them, alone in the dark. She leaned forward and brushed her lips over his. They felt the same and yet different. He smelled better and the stubble she remembered had been shaved, making his skin smooth.

She drew back, and his hand cupped the back of her neck, pulling her close again. "I thought kissing you felt like it did because you were the first," he whispered. "But that's not it at all."

She kissed him again, this time more than a mere brush of her lips. This time she let her lips rove over his, let her mouth take his as she'd been wanting to do. He groaned quietly. "God, Jenny."

She knew what he meant. There was something between them, something she could almost touch, that drew them together. And when they touched everything became…*more.* She'd kissed other men after him, men with more skill than a boy of sixteen, but no kiss, no man, had ever made her feel like Aidan. Kissing Aidan was—

Kissing Aidan.

She jumped back, and he sat straight. "What is it?" he sounded alarmed.

"Ye tricked me."

"What?"

"Ye tricked me so ye'd win. I knew I shouldn't trust ye."

"What are you…the wager," he said, sounding defeated. "Jenny, I swear the wager was the last thing on my mind."

"I know ye too well to fall for that. Ye'll do anything to win."

"Fine." He stood. "You think I'm not playing fair? Then let's exclude this ball from the wager. Nothing that happens here counts."

She stared at him, trying to determine why he would say something like that. She didn't see how it could benefit him, except it would put her in his debt. "We'd 'ad to decide that when we made the wager. Or at least before I kissed ye," she said.

"The rules are whatever we make them," he argued. "We can decide it now."

"I see wot yer doing," she said, standing and pointing a finger at him.

"And what is that? I have no idea, so if you can explain it, I'm all ears." He held his hands out, his eyes wide and seemingly innocent and confused.

"Ye just want to kiss me again."

He shrugged. "I should think that would be obvious. I want to kiss you all the time, and the only reason I don't is that you're bloody well betrothed."

Oh, yes. She'd forgotten that for a moment.

"It's probably best if you and Lord Chamberlayne do take the trunks and remove to his town house. I'm obviously not to be trusted."

She shook her head. "And now yer pretending it was ye who did the kissing. *I* kissed *ye*, which means I lost the wager."

"Then I forgive your debt."

"Then I'll be in *yer* debt," she said. "No thank ye. I 'onor my debts, and I'll 'elp ye find that girl like we agreed."

"I don't think that's a good idea."

"Too bad." She started away, ready to return to the ball and Roland.

"Jenny," he said.

"Wot?" She whirled on him. "There's nothing else to discuss. Ye can't send me any messages because all the pigeons are 'ome. So we can talk more tomorrow. In the light of day," she added and started away again.

"Jenny."

"Wot!" She was thoroughly exasperated now. She hated to lose, and she hated that it had been to him. And she really hated that she'd promised Roland she could handle her attraction to Aidan when it was obvious to everyone but her that she couldn't. "Let me be."

"I just thought you might want your slippers." He bent and held up her dancing slippers, which were still sitting at the base of the couch.

With a huff she stomped back, took them, and sat down to shove them back on. They hurt just as much as earlier. "I really 'ate ye sometimes," she said.

"I know." And he strode out of the chamber, ruining her grand exit.

***

"Leaving already?" Colin asked when Aidan stepped outside the ducal residence and called for his coach.

"Yes. Did you just arrive?"

Colin shook his head. "Been here for hours and will have to stay to the end."

Aidan frowned.

"Warcliffe is my father-in-law."

"Ah, that's right. I always forget you're married to a duke's daughter. Must be ten years now."

"Almost. Lady Daphne spied you earlier and was surprised since you weren't on the guest list."

"An oversight, I'm sure," Aidan said. "I'll have to speak to her another time."

"Listen, I want to apologize."

Aidan waved a hand. "No need."

"There is a need. What I said the other day, about you only caring about money—"

"Was true. It is all I care about. I'm going back to my offices now to look over some investments and determine how I might make them more profitable." At least that's what he'd planned to do—before Jenny had kissed him. Now he wondered if he'd be able to concentrate or if he'd spend the whole night imagining her mouth on his. But he also couldn't stand here and let Colin apologize. They'd been through too much together during the war and Aidan had too much respect for Colin. "In any case, I started searching for your Harley."

Colin stared at him, genuine shock on his features. It was rare to see Colin react so honestly. Aidan was most used to seeing the other soldier in disguise. Colin was quite skilled at hiding his emotions or feelings behind a mask or concealing them behind the façade of the character he was playing. Aidan had seen him practically become the character he was playing dozens of times. While Aidan broke into a house or locked room, Colin distracted anyone passing or keeping watch by playing a part. Aidan had stolen important papers from the offices of French generals while Colin coolly played cards with the guards on duty on the other side of the door.

"But you said—"

"I was wrong. You were right," Aidan said in a rush, not liking to admit when he was wrong but having to do it so little that he could tolerate the uncomfortable sensation once in a while. "I may not be able to locate her. It's been years since I lived on the streets, but I made a start, and I have information that might prove useful."

"Aidan." Colin put a hand on Aidan's shoulder. "You don't know how much this will mean to Daphne."

Aidan tried not to grit his teeth. "I didn't do it for her."

Colin nodded. "You don't owe me anything. I never saved your life."

Aidan laughed. "You saved it a hundred times by keeping me from being caught pilfering troop assignments and ammunitions shipments. But I didn't do it out of obligation. I did it out of friendship."

This was wholeheartedly true. Except it wasn't exactly Colin's friendship Aidan had been thinking about when he sat on top of the roof waiting for the lads who wanted to bash his brains in to give up. He suspected if Jenny hadn't suddenly walked back into his life, he would have told Colin to piss off and not given the matter another thought. But he and Colin were friends and after the years they'd spent working together and the times Colin had risked everything to keep Aidan safe—and vice versa, it should be noted—Aidan owed him a few hours in the rookeries.

"Thank you."

"I haven't found her yet," Aidan said as his coach came into view. "And I probably won't. By now she's probably heard someone is looking for her and gone underground. It was already like finding the proverbial needle in a haystack. Now it will be like finding a needle in ten haystacks." Except now he would have help. His carriage arrived, and one of his servants rushed to open the door. Aidan tipped his hat to Colin and climbed inside, settling against the opulent squabs. He had every comfort he could want in this carriage. The seats pulled out to the size of a bed. The cabinets were stocked with an assortment of food and beverages. The upholstery was the finest materials, and even the ceiling had been painted by a renowned artist.

But Aidan couldn't help but notice he was alone. He had everything he could ever have wanted in life—two of everything in some cases—and no one to share it with. It was no surprise why he felt so melancholy. Before seeing Jenny again, he didn't care that he was alone—well, not much. Watching so many of the other Survivors marry had, on occasion, caused a pang in the area of the center of his chest. But Aidan always told himself he didn't have time for a wife. He'd get a wife when he'd made his fortune. When he had financial security.

But he had that. And he'd had it for a long time.

And now he would have to stand by and watch the only person still alive that he had ever loved marry another man. Chamberlayne seemed a decent fellow. He probably cared more about dusty antiques than he did about most people, but then Aidan was living in a glass house and wasn't about to cast stones. He'd spent the years after he'd returned from the war with the single-minded determination to amass the sort of fortune that he could only have dreamed about all of those years when he'd been unable to sleep because he'd been so hungry. He'd wanted to make sure that not only was he never hungry again, but he would never want again. It had been years since he'd gone to bed hungry or with a want other than making more money. And still he wasn't satisfied.

And Aidan had a sinking feeling he knew why. Because for years now he hadn't had Jenny. She'd come back into his life, and he couldn't seem to stop himself from wanting her. If there was one thing about Jenny he understood, it was her loyalty. He'd always loved her for it, and it was a quality he prized highly. She'd given the viscount her hand, and she would be loyal to him. Aidan doubted she would make the mistake of kissing him again. She'd agreed to help him find the child, and she would do that.

But then she would marry Lord Chamberlayne, and Aidan, who was used to getting whatever he wanted, would have to watch her walk away.

Seven

"Where is Lord Chamberlayne this afternoon?" Aidan asked when Jenny climbed into his coach at half past four the next day. She'd sent a note to his secretary that she would be available at that time to aid him in his work. Aidan hadn't needed to wonder what the work was. They would go to see the mudlarks.

"Have you even been home?" she asked, running her critical gray eyes over him. "He's still in your larder. There's a tablecloth in the bottom of one of the trunks, and he's spent the last day studying it. I know next to nothing about needlework, so I focused on the journals." She looked up and then from side to side. "Wot the 'ell?" she said, forgetting herself. "Is this a coach or a moving palace?"

"A little of both. Care for tea? The servants always keep hot water available."

She gave him a look that said he was ridiculous. He shrugged. "Found anything interesting in the journals?"

"Plenty. We aren't taking this bauble into the rookeries, are we? I don't fancy a beating as soon as we step out."

"My coachman will drive us closer and then we'll go on foot." She wore a long cloak, which he'd thought a bit dramatic for early afternoon, but looking down, he saw she also wore serviceable boots. Or at least that's what he thought from the toes he saw peeking out. "Your foot attire looks more comfortable today. We should probably be prepared to run. You're so pretty you're bound to attract notice."

She scowled at him. "That's why I have this." She waved a large hat that looked like something his coachman had given her. As he watched, she pulled her hair into a plait, tossed it back, and stuck the hat on her head, shielding her face from view.

"That might work except the cloak is good quality. Someone will want to steal it." His own clothing was probably too fine as well, even though he'd changed into his oldest coat and the boots he'd scuffed the last time he'd searched for this Harley. Thank God he didn't have a fussy valet who would have thrown these garments out immediately.

"I'll leave it in the coach," she said. "Along with this nob accent." She tossed the cloak off her shoulders to reveal a white shirt, black coat, and black breeches. Aidan's throat went dry. The boots were not ladies' half-boots as he'd assumed. They were men's riding boots and went to just below her knee, which was quite plain to see in the tight breeches. If she hadn't been sitting down, he would have seen more than that, he knew. He supposed the garments were worn and chosen to attract little notice, but Aidan had forgotten what Jenny looked like in breeches and a shirt that strained across her breasts. Come to think of it, she'd been so thin when he'd known her before, she'd never looked quite like this, though by the time she was sixteen and he fifteen, the sight of her bending over in trousers had begun to affect him.

"Wot?" she asked, finally noticing his stare. He looked away.

"You look perfect."

"Where are we 'eaded?"

"The river," he said, opening one of the cabinets and pulling out a bottle of brandy. He just needed a small drink to wet his throat. It felt as though he'd swallowed sand.

"Why the river?"

"The information I was able to gather seemed to indicate she was friendly with the mudlarks."

"Really?" Jenny's smile was wistful. "I like this girl already." She watched him down the brandy. "Where'd ye come by this information? Did ye toss a few coppers at some little cub who then sold ye out?"

"Something like that."

She nodded then looked about again. "Ye don't think this seems a bit...much?" she asked.

"The coach?"

"The coach. The velvet and silks and the gilt on the cabinets. The"—she pointed to the ceiling—"painting."

"I like to have the best. This is the best. Feel how smoothly it rides?"

" 'Ow much did this cost ye?" she asked. He must have made some expression because she waved a hand. "I don't care if I'm not supposed to ask. 'Ow much? A thousand quid?"

He didn't answer.

"More? Three thousand quid? Never mind. I don't want to know. Don't ye remember 'ating men like ye? Men who spent blunt like water when we would 'ave killed for a farthing."

"I give to charities."

She made a face. "Charities never 'elped us. They wanted to lock us away in an orphanage."

"You should probably stop talking like that. This Harley is bound for an orphanage, but from what I've heard it's more like a home and less like a prison."

Jenny gave him a dubious look. She ran her hand over the velvet of her seat. "I always felt sorry for those rich men," she said. "I know ye 'ated them, and I did too, but I felt sorry for them too."

Aidan stared at her and wondered if the brandy was stronger than he'd thought. She wasn't making sense.

"Why is that?"

"Because they didn't realize that all the blunt in the world couldn't make them 'appy. Me and ye, we didn't have two tuppence to rub together, but we were 'appy." Her gray-blue eyes met his. "At least I was."

Aidan started at her words. It was almost as though she'd seen directly into his deepest thoughts. The coach stopped then, and Aidan was relieved for the interruption. Once on the street, Aidan sent the coachman back home and told him he wouldn't be needed again this afternoon. They were close enough to the river that he could smell it, and he wrinkled his nose at the stench. Jenny didn't laugh at him, but her eyes looked merry. "The tide is down, I suppose," she said. "So we will find them 'ard at work. Not the best time to strike up a conversation."

"Actually, there's another hour before it's at its lowest." He tried not to allow his eyes to drift down to those breeches. Did anyone really think she was a man in those? "At least that's what the ship's captain I had my secretary consult said. So now is as good a time as any."

"We'd better go then." They started to walk, she falling into step beside him, and his head was dizzy with the feeling of *déjà vu*. But it wasn't *déjà vu* because he had done this before. It seemed he'd lived a lifetime since walking the streets at her side.

"Ye said ye'd tell me more about this girl. So go on then."

He summarized the information FitzRoy had given him. The girl went by the name Harley and had provided them information that had saved Lady Daphne's life.

"And so they repay 'er by locking 'er in an orphanage?"

"I told you—"

"Right. It's a 'ome. Sure it is."

They made it through the jostling crowds of men and women trudging home after a day's work. Closer to the river the number of people they saw thinned, and by the time they were on the banks, there were only the usual scavengers.

Aidan tried not to look too hard at the haggard women with children clinging to their skirts who bent over, searching for a piece of coal to burn that night or an ounce of iron to sell. One in particular looked so thin and desperate that Aidan had to look away.

"Lend me a crown," she said. Of course, Jenny had not looked away.

"Jenny?" Aidan said with a warning tone but already reaching in his pocket to hand it to her. "If you give her money, we'll have a crowd of beggars around us in no time."

"Give me some credit," she said. He watched as she pretended to search the beach for something she might scavenge. She moved close to the woman, who gave her a warning look. Jenny pretended to take note of the look and moved further down the beach. Aidan followed her, keeping his gaze on the woman. She'd obviously learned not to react when she found something of value—that was the quickest way to have it stolen—but he didn't miss the way her body stiffened as she reached for the crown Jenny had dropped in her path. She pocketed it quick as a flash, and in another minute she and the child were gone.

Aidan wasn't surprised at what Jenny had done. After all, she'd saved him all those years before.

"There. Now she's out of the way," Jenny said as if that had been the reason she'd dropped the coin.

A bit further down the beach a small group of young mudlarks crowded together, combing the beach. They were dressed similarly in clothes that hung off their bodies, loose trousers rolled up to the knee and feet bare. In another half hour they'd venture onto the mud in the river and see what they could unearth there. It was also a good time to dive into the deeper areas of the river, though Aidan didn't know how they could stand it. Sewage flowed freely into the river, and just the smell of the river burned his nose. He couldn't imagine submerging himself in it.

As they approached, one of the boys said something to the others, and they all gave Aidan and Jenny watchful looks. The tallest one, who was also probably the oldest, stepped forward. He pointed a finger at them, and Aidan noticed his hands were red and raw. "This is our spot. Ye go treasure 'unt somewhere else."

"It's a good spot," Aidan commented, studying the section of the river. It bent slightly here, slowing the currents. Anything being carried in the river might have time to sink or be caught on a branch or piece of rubbish.

"Ye one of them inspectors?" the leader asked. "We don't know nothing about that body. They wash up 'ere all the time. We let them be."

"After you empty their pockets, you mean," Aidan said.

Before the boy could lie and say they didn't, Jenny stepped forward. " 'E ain't interested in any bodies or taking wot ye've found."

The boys exchanged looks when they heard her speak. It was obvious that though she was dressed far better than they, she was one of them.

"Then why are ye 'ere?" the leader asked. "If I found a way to get out, I wouldn't come back."

The boys behind him nodded. Aidan noticed there were a few girls as well. They were dressed in ragged skirts, tied up to show knobby knees. One had stringy dark hair and but for the fact that her eyes were dark, she might have been Jenny when he first met her.

"We're looking for someone," she said. "Ye don't know 'er. She's probably moved on from these parts by now." She took Aidan's arm, seemingly ready to move on. Damn, but she was clever. She'd stirred their curiosity, turning the tables so they were wanting information, not she.

"Who is she?" one of the children asked, falling right into her trap.

The leader shushed him, but he was ignored. Another mudlark said, "Who is this girl?"

"Ye won't know 'er," Jenny said dismissively. "If she doesn't want to be found, she won't be. She can 'ide in the shadows like."

"We might know 'er," one of the children said. "Wot's 'er name?"

"I 'ave a name, but it's not 'er real name. She's not so dim she'd ever give 'er real name."

The children nodded, clearly in agreement that anyone who gave his or her real name was quite dim.

"Wot's 'er street name then?" the leader asked, giving up his effort to seem uninterested.

"She goes by 'Arley. I said ye wouldn't know 'er."

But Aidan was watching their faces when Jenny said the name, and some of the children, the younger ones who were not yet so good at hiding their emotions, clearly did know Harley. One piped up, "I know 'Arley!"

"Stubble it," the leader said.

Jenny shrugged. "Probably a different 'Arley."

"There's only one 'Arley," another child said. "We calls 'er that because no one *'arley* ever sees 'er."

"That might be 'er. Might not. Wot's yer 'Arley look like then?"

Aidan held his breath. She'd pushed her luck a bit, and this was where they might call her on it. But she had the children truly invested in proving their knowledge now. One little girl stepped forward. "She's about yea 'igh." She held her hand just above her own head.

"And she 'as brown 'air she keeps tucked up under 'er cap. She always wears a cap."

Jenny pretended to be shocked. "That might be 'er, but then lots of girls wear their 'air tucked up."

"She dresses like a lad," the leader said, unable to keep from joining in. "Like ye. And she sleeps over by the bridge. Don't like being closed in."

"Might just be 'er," Jenny shrugged. She looked at Aidan. "Let's go."

He knew better than to argue, though he could almost smell victory. But he was enough of a negotiator himself to know that was the best time to walk away, even if it physically hurt.

"Why do ye want to find 'er?" the leader asked.

"Wot does it matter?" Jenny said. "Ye won't tell 'er that nob she 'elped last year wants to repay 'er."

The leader shook his head. " 'E wanted to lock 'er up."

"Lock 'er up." Jenny laughed. "These nobs don't know wot to do with all the blunt in their pockets. The lady 'Arley 'elped wants to repay 'er."

The leader crossed his arms over his skinny chest. " 'Ow?"

"Oy, that's none of yer business. If we find 'er, we'll tell 'er. Mr. Sterling, are you ready to go?"

"Absolutely."

They walked on as though they had intended to go this way all along. "Wot bridge ye think 'e means?" she asked as they moved out of earshot. " 'As to be London Bridge."

"That's my guess. It's growing dark. We should come back another time."

She gave him a derisive look. "Plenty of daylight left. And I didn't come without protection." She indicated one of her boots.

"Don't tell me you have a dagger hiding in there."

"Fine. I won't tell ye then." She gave him a look of challenge. "But if yer afraid—"

"I simply wasn't looking forward to having to defend your honor when some of the men see you walk by. You look a lot less like a boy in those breeches than you used to."

She winked at him. "It was the best I could do on short notice. Poor Roland wasn't sure wot to make of me."

Aidan stopped and Jenny had to turn to look back at him. "You told him what you were doing?"

"Where do ye think I got the clothes?"

"And he didn't mind?"

She scrunched up her face. "Well, I wouldn't say that exactly, but 'e didn't try to stop me."

They walked on for a few minutes in silence, Aidan watching his steps as the riverbank could be uneven. He hadn't thought much about her relationship with Viscount Chamberlayne. He hadn't wanted to. But now that he did all signs seemed to point to an open and honest relationship. A real relationship. The viscount obviously knew Jenny very well and if he'd allowed her to borrow his clothing for this little jaunt, he must know her well enough to understand he couldn't stop her if she set her mind to something.

"Did you tell him you lost the wager?" he asked. In the distance, London Bridge was coming into focus.

She seemed to bristle at his words. "Not likely. And 'e weren't 'appy I was slumming with ye, but I told 'im ye'd probably turn up floating in the river if I didn't."

"Your confidence in me is inspiring."

"Ye want my 'elp or not?"

"I want your help. You've already gleaned more information in a quarter hour than I acquired in three. There's the bridge there. Looks empty at the moment."

Although Aidan had crossed the bridge hundreds, if not thousands. of times in the years since his uncle had found him and pulled him out of poverty, this was the first time he had approached it from the river and on foot in thirteen or more years. The landscape was the same and yet different. The same discarded clothing items, rotten vegetables, and broken pieces of wood and crockery had washed up underneath. Small areas had been cleared of rubbish, and this was obviously where people slept when the weather wasn't too cold—and probably even when it was.

This was one of the places he and Jenny had slept on warmer summer nights. This night wasn't particularly warm as it wasn't quite summer yet, but it was mild enough to bring the memories back to him. He glanced at Jenny, but her expression was unreadable.

"I know wot yer thinking about," she said.

"I doubt that."

"Yer thinking about that night when we were 'ere alone."

He had been thinking about that night. It wasn't the first time they'd been together. There had been a few times before that, but those had been awkward stumbling attempts that left them both laughing and only him satisfied and even that was questionable. But that warm summer night under the bridge—how could he ever forget it?

"It's difficult not to think about it," he said. "I haven't been back since then. I'm sure you were back many times and have forgotten all about it." He gave her a sidelong glance. He saw the way her lips tightened and then she glanced at him.

"I didn't forget it. I didn't forget any of it." She walked on ahead, looking about as though searching for some evidence of Harley's occupation here. Aidan understood her implication perfectly well. He was the one who had left her. He was the one who had forgotten.

But watching her now, it was almost as though the decade had been wiped away. She was Jenny and he was Aidan, and though he was warm and well-fed now, all the other feelings—the emotions he'd had for her—were coming back. In the past, loving her had been like breathing. He didn't think about it. He just did it. He didn't know when he had fallen in love with her—it seemed something that had come about so gradually that he couldn't remember when he hadn't loved her.

He'd never told her he loved her before that night under the bridge. She knew he loved her, just as he knew she loved him. But that was the night he'd said the words.

He didn't want to remember those words now, any more than he wanted to remember how she'd cried hearing them. And it was pure torture to remember the feel of her body under his, the way her breath hitched when he touched her and she trembled when he pleasured her.

Or how she'd asked him to promise never to leave her.

And he'd promised.

But he hadn't meant it. Not even then. He rubbed a hand over his eyes. He wished he could go back and mean it. He wished he hadn't ever left her.

***

Jenny could almost see his mind remembering the time they'd lain here together. Jenny tried to remember how she'd felt that night, only a few weeks before he broke his promise and left her, but it was too tainted by the hurt that came afterward. She only remembered there had been something beautiful between them, and then he'd smashed it and left her to clean up the pieces.

She'd thought she'd swept them all away, thought she'd put her heart back together. But it was easy to believe that when the destroyer wasn't standing in front of her. "I'll have a look around," she said and moved under the bridge. The girl they sought wasn't here, and even if they did find something of hers, it wasn't as though it would be marked *Harley*.

She crossed her arms, rubbing her hands up and down to warm herself. Aidan came up behind her, and she expected him to suggest they leave. He probably had bags of money to count.

"I know I have no right to ask this," he said, his voice low as he spoke. She closed her eyes and could almost imagine he was the boy she'd fallen in love with. She turned her head slightly to let him know she was listening. "Are you happy?" he asked. "With him?"

Roland. He was concerned about her engagement. She might have pointed out that it was a little late to worry about her, but neither of them could change the past. "I am," she said.

"Do you…" His voice faded and she knew he was trying to think how to phrase it. But he was Aidan and she Jenny, and she knew what he was thinking without him saying a word. Decades might pass, centuries even, and she'd know.

"No," she said. "It's not like that between us."

"Then how is it?"

"We're friends." She had to tread carefully here. " 'E needs me, and I need 'im."

He was so close to her now. She could feel the heat of his body. *Touch me,* she thought, and as though she had willed it, he put his arms about her waist and leaned down to whisper in her ear, "I need you, Jenny."

The sharp ache of need between her legs almost made her groan. There had been other men after Aidan, and she would have been a simpleton to think there hadn't been other women after her. But she'd never felt with any other man the way she felt with him.

"I want ye," she said, turning in his arms. His forehead rested on hers, his expression pained. She understood his turmoil. She belonged to another man, and he respected that. Hers was different. Roland didn't care if she lay with Aidan. He only cared if she was caught. Taking Aidan to bed wasn't a betrayal of Roland, but would she be able to go through with the marriage, to walk away from Aidan if she allowed this to happen?

Oh, yes, she would. And she might just give him a taste of the pain he'd given her all those years ago. Not that pain was her main impetus for action. She wanted him badly.

"One night," she said, looking into his eyes.

"You're betrothed."

"I'd never do anything to 'urt Roland, and ye'll 'ave to trust me if I say this won't 'urt 'im."

"What about you?"

"Do you bite now?" she teased.

"I might."

She couldn't stop herself from taking his mouth. The image of his teeth grazing her skin made her legs weak. He stumbled back at the force of her kiss, then caught himself, lifted her and pressed her against one of the bridge supports. She wrapped her legs around him, happy for the freedom of the breeches. He was hard where his body pressed against her, and she moved against him. He groaned, his hands digging into her buttocks as he held her.

"If we don't stop now," he said, his voice breathless, "I'll take you here."

"Don't tease me," she said. She kissed his neck then lightly bit his earlobe. "Take me 'ome."

She didn't remember how they'd made their way back to his house. His hand was in hers and everything she saw seemed dim and murky through her haze of desire. She'd thought about taking him in the coach, but he'd given her a look that said *wait.* And when he pulled her into his bed chamber, past the servants who pretended not to notice them rushing through the door and up the stairs, she was glad she had waited. She could see him in the light of the lamp, and all that dark hair and those dark eyes just whet her appetite.

She was aware of a large chamber and an even larger bed, but mostly she was aware of Aidan. He tugged off his coat, and she shook off hers. He inhaled sharply and she glanced down to see how her white shirt stretched across her breasts and how the hips of the breeches looked unusually rounded as they fit snugly over hers.

She unbuttoned the collar of the shirt until it was open in a V that exposed her cleavage. She hadn't worn stays under the shirt. She hadn't worn anything as her breasts weren't so large as to require binding if she had a coat. Now she could feel her nipples hard and rubbing against the soft linen. She imagined that was why Aidan's hand had frozen at his own collar and his mouth had dropped open. "Take it off," he'd said, his voice rough.

She bit her lip and pretended to fumble with the cuffs at her wrist. But eventually, when she'd tortured him long enough, she tugged the shirt tail out of the breeches and up over her belly, over her breasts, and over her head. She dropped it on the floor, standing bare chested before him.

"Christ," he said. "I didn't imagine them."

She gave him a curious look, and he crossed to her, his gaze so hot on her that her sex had begun to throb with need. "Ye forgot I 'ad tits?"

"Never," he said, his voice filled with awe. "But when I remembered them, I always imagined these tips"—one finger brushed over a distended nipple and she let out a breath—"thrust upward. I imagined that dusky rose color. I wasn't sure I'd remembered them correctly. But I remembered perfectly." His gaze met hers. "Can I touch you?"

"I'm not 'ere for ye to just look."

He cupped one of her tits then and ran his thumb along the upward slope until it circled the darker center and made the point so hard it almost hurt. While one thumb played with that point, he did the same with her other breast, until she was breathing hard. With a wicked look in his eyes, he bent and took one nipple in his mouth, rolling it over on his tongue then sucking harder and biting lightly.

She was wet now and clenching her thighs together to stop the insistent throb. "Take yer clothes off," she demanded. "I want ye inside me."

"If I only have one night," he answered, "I want to make it last." He crowded her back against a papered wall then caught up her hands and held them above her head. She didn't fight him. He would have let her go if she'd said one word, but there was something about letting him take control that made her even hotter. He kissed her then, his mouth skillfully taking hers, opening it so his tongue could explore her with long, lingering strokes. With his free hand, he skimmed over her shoulders, her arms, the side of her breast, her waist. Then his hand dipped into the breeches, and he stilled and pulled back.

"You're bare beneath those as well?"

"Where would I get drawers?" she asked.

He uttered an expletive she didn't realize the upper class knew, then picked her up and carried her to the bed. He dropped her on it, unceremoniously, and she frowned up at him. "Oy. Wot 'appened to the one night and making it last?"

"That was before." He pulled off his own shirt, and her throat went dry. She remembered him very clearly, and at sixteen he hadn't had those broad shoulders, that muscled chest, or that smattering of hair. She followed it down to the bulge in his breeches then sat and reached for the fall.

He caught her hand and gave her a reproving look. "Boots off." He bent and tugged them from her bare feet. She lay back, enjoying the feel of the soft bed beneath her until he bent over her and kissed her belly. Her hands went into his hair as he unfastened the fall of her breeches and slid them off. She was naked now, and she wanted to feel his chest against her skin. He bent over her, kissing her, and she arched up, pressing her tits against him. He groaned and slid up and down, teasing her. Then his mouth made a slow trail over her neck, up to her ear. He breathed against it, whispered something very naughty, and bit her earlobe. It was repayment for what she'd done to him earlier. The nip was sharp and hard, and her sex clenched with desire.

"You like that." His hand slid between her legs. "Yes, I can see you like it a lot."

He hadn't had this confidence when they'd been young and still learning how to please each other. Now his hand moved with assurance as he parted her folds and wet his fingers.

"Yes," she said. She parted her legs and told him what to do with his fingers. He bit her breast lightly, and she groaned when he took her nipple in his mouth again as he complied and slid two fingers inside her.

She knew what she wanted now, and she moved against his fingers. He suckled her as she pressed against him, her quick breaths turning to pants. His mouth moved lazily down her body, his teeth nibbling and his tongue licking. His thumb had found that little nub that gave her the most pleasure and he circled it slowly, making her moan.

She had always been bold and taken what she wanted, but she'd never come so close to climax so quickly. And then he pulled his hand away, and she cried out in protest. "We have all night," he reminded her. She called him a name that would have made most ladies blush, but he just kissed her navel and moved lower until he nuzzled the hair at the juncture of her legs.

"Are you—" she began and then his mouth dipped between her legs, and she didn't need to ask. He was. He most definitely was. His mouth brushed against that intimate part of her, and she went rigid with surprise and pleasure. He licked her, long and slow, and her hands delved into his hair as she arched her back.

She had heard about this—of course, she had—but experiencing it was...she was completely lost to the sensation, to the pleasure, to the absolute mind-numbing climax that came after only a few flicks of his tongue.

As she lay panting, trying to catch her breath, she was vaguely aware that he undressed. She made a Herculean effort to lift her head and watch him, surprised as her blood began to heat again at the sight of his lean hips, his long, hard shaft, and those muscled legs. He climbed beside her on the bed, opened a drawer, and lifted out a long case. He opened it and withdrew a sheath.

She raised her brows. "A French letter?"

"I bought this a few months ago at a shop owned by a Mrs. Perkins. I haven't had the opportunity to use it. Do you want me to? It's the most effective way to protect you."

It protected him as well, she knew. Being a bastard himself, she understood he would not want to sire any children.

"Too bad we didn't 'ave these all those years ago," she said.

He stilled and turned his head to look at her. "You didn't—"

"No, but we 'ad a few scares, didn't we?"

He nodded. "Put it on then," she said. She let her gaze travel down to his erection. "Or did you want me to do it?"

"I think I can manage," he said, sounding hoarse. He tugged the sheath on and tied the red ribbon at the base then reached for her, but she squirmed away and threw a leg over his hips. His dark eyes went darker as she slid into position.

Eight

Aidan forgot to breathe as the heat of her body joined with his.

"I've learned a few things too," she said, bending to kiss him. His hands slid down her back and over her bottom. Her skin was so soft. He didn't remember it being this soft, but then he'd never been able to touch her like this, undress her fully, take her in. She was beautiful with her pert breasts, her slim hips, her small waist. She wasn't skinny like she'd been when he knew her before, and the rounding of her hips aroused him. He took those hips in his hands and guided her to his cock. She raised her head, and their eyes met. With a wicked look in her eye, she sank down over him, taking him in very slowly.

Aidan couldn't think of anything but the feel of her hot channel taking him in. She moved so slowly that he would have urged her to hurry if he hadn't seen in her face the act was giving her as much pleasure as it gave him. They'd always coupled in dark chambers, cellars, or under London

Bridge. He'd never seen her face when she'd come. Now, watching the way her gray eyes went violet and her nipples hardened and turned crimson was a revelation. When she had sheathed him fully, her head fell back, and she moaned in undisguised pleasure.

He thrust playfully, encouraging her, and she tightened around him. Christ, even with the sheath on his cock, he could feel her heat, feel the clench of her muscles. Her hips, those nicely rounded hips, moved under his hands as she began to ride him. Her movements were slow at first, but as she found her rhythm they increased until not only was he having to focus on not coming too early, he was having to look away from the way her breasts bounced lest he lose his concentration.

He let her take her pleasure, reveled in the feeling of her muscles clutching him like a vise as she climaxed again. The sound she made was half plea, half cry as she collapsed on his chest.

Aidan didn't give her time to recover. He rolled her over without pulling out and pushed her ankles up onto his shoulders. And then he drove into her. She gasped and cried out a strangled, *"yes."* Aidan saw stars as he thrust deeper into her. She reached for the headboard, grasping it to hold steady as he gave one last plunge and came with a shout and the rasp of her name.

His forehead touched hers for a moment, his lips caressed her mouth, and then he lowered her legs and pulled free, standing to discard the preventative. She must have rolled over because he felt her hand on his buttocks. " 'Ow can a man with that much passion sit at a desk all day staring at numbers and ledgers?" she asked.

He turned to look down at her, rosy-cheeked and dark-eyed from the pleasure he'd given her. "I'm passionate about a great many things."

She moved over and he lay down beside her, turning to look at her, as he used to do. "Ye've learned a few things."

"So have you," he said with a laugh. But the truth was that it had been so long since he'd been with a woman that he hadn't been able to hold back. He'd needed her, needed this release. He threw one arm over her, hoping it wasn't too obvious that he wanted her to stay.

Her gaze roamed about his bed chamber, and after a moment, she moved his hand and sat. *Don't leave*, he silently begged her. "Ye really are rich," she said, climbing off the bed to peer at a painting on the wall. She moved about the room, touching the draperies, the walnut tall boy, and even bending to run a hand over the Aubusson carpet. He didn't mind as he liked watching her body in the lamplight. She'd never been modest, never worried about undressing in his presence, even before they'd been lovers, and she moved with an easy confidence in her nudity.

She wandered into the adjoining chamber, his dressing room, and Aidan had a moment's panic as he hadn't checked to be sure his valet wasn't inside. But as there were no masculine screams at the entrance of a nude woman, Aidan breathed a sigh of relief.

A moment later she came out and put her hands on her hips. Aidan wet his lips.

"Ye have three and fifty shirts," she announced.

"Do I?"

"Yes. And one and thirty coats. Wot does any man need with that many shirts and coats?"

He shrugged, feeling slightly uncomfortable and exposed now. He pulled the coverlet over his nudity. "I didn't realize there was a limit."

"Ye 'ave fourteen pairs of boots and—I forgot 'ow many pairs of pumps. Ye don't think that's a bit excessive?"

"Clearly, you do."

She moved toward the bed. Aidan would have sworn she had no idea how sensual her movements were, how the sway of her hips tempted him. "Ye never liked wearing rags and being dirty," she said. "I suppose yer afraid ye might not 'ave enough."

He kept his face neutral. He hadn't ever considered that, but if he considered recent trips to his tailor, he definitely remembered a feeling of panic that he might not have enough. That he should buy two of everything because what he'd ordered might not be *enough*.

"I was the same when Roland took me in," she said, climbing onto the bed and then sliding under the covers and close to him. She was cold, and he pulled her close to warm her. "I would eat too much or 'oard food, books, pens— anything. When ye live with nothing for so long, it's 'ard to believe it won't all be taken away."

She looked up at him, and Aidan didn't dare speak. She'd spoken so simply and succinctly about fears that often overwhelmed him or felt so large he'd never be able to conquer them. Even when he told himself that he had so much that it was impossible for it all to be taken away, there were nights he'd wake in a cold sweat, afraid he'd be back on the street or sleeping in the cold if one of his ships didn't return or his latest investment failed.

"How did you meet the viscount?" Aidan finally asked. It wasn't a topic he wanted to mention. Why speak about her betrothed when they were naked and in bed together? But he wanted to speak about his fears even less.

"I broke into 'is 'ouse. I cased it and waited until I thought 'e was out, then climbed in a window."

"How long after I'd gone was that?" he asked.

"Some months but not so long as a year," she said. "Ye know I 'ad a weakness for antiquities even then, and I'd 'eard 'e 'ad a collection."

"And he caught you?"

"With my 'and in the jewel box, so to speak. Instead of calling the magistrate, 'e offered me a job."

"Smart man."

She gave him a sharp look then frowned when she realized he wasn't teasing.

"He obviously saw what I saw in you. You're smart and learn fast, and I'm sure he recognized your eye for anything valuable."

" 'E said I 'ad potential," she added. "I proved 'im right. We've worked together for years now, and 'e taught me everything I know. Everything about antiquities," she amended. "I read Latin and Greek now. I know the names and reigns of all the Roman dictators, and I can identify them on coins too."

"Impressive."

She shrugged. "Roland 'as a special interest in Roman 'istory. We've spent months in the countryside digging up ground looking for bobs and bits."

"And that's when you fell in love?"

She elbowed him, and he winced. "I told ye it's not like that."

"Then how is it? Why marry him?"

She didn't speak for a moment, and then she said, "I'm like ye. I want security."

It was a lie. She spoke it convincingly, but he knew her well enough to know that security had never been her main worry. That had always been his concern. She'd rather explore than eat, rather take the chance than play it safe.

"I should go," she said. "It's late."

"Oh, no." He grasped her about the waist and pulled her back against him. "I've hours left yet. You promised me the night."

"Ye've already made me see stars twice," she said. "And I think ye saw a few of yer own. I thought we were done."

"Oh, I'm not done." He pulled her down and wedged himself between her legs.

Her eyes widened. "Already?"

"What can I say? Watching you strut about my bedchamber bare-arsed gave me ideas."

"Wot kind of ideas?"

He kissed her and slid his hand down her belly. "Let me show you."

***

When she woke, the room was streaked with shafts of sunlight that slitted through the drapes. Aidan's arm was heavy and warm around her, and she had to take a breath at the familiarity of his body pressed against hers. He was bigger now—taller and more muscular—but he still felt like Aidan. She pushed at him, and he rolled onto his back, still dead to the world. That didn't surprise her. He'd exerted quite a bit of energy last night. She felt pleasantly sore all over from her attempts to match his efforts. She turned her head and studied him. His eyes were closed, veiled by his dark lashes. His hair was tousled and fell over his forehead in disarray. His jaw was dark with stubble, but his mouth was red from her kisses. She'd spent many mornings watching him sleep, wishing she could sleep so peacefully. Once upon a time, the weight of caring for both of them had fallen on her shoulders. Now he was perfectly capable of caring for himself.

But the scars from the years he'd lived in the rookeries were becoming more visible to her. He surrounded himself with excess—a huge house with more chambers than he could ever use, more clothing than he could ever wear, servants and coaches and material items that gave him the security he'd lacked for so long. Jenny wondered if any of it really eased his fears or if they merely plastered over them like an imperfection in a wall.

And he had walls. She had known the boy he'd been inside and out. But this man was still a stranger to her in some respects. The war had changed him, hardened him. But when she'd asked him about it, he dismissed the question and changed the subject. He didn't like to talk about their past. He seemed an insular man, concerned only with acquiring wealth.

And what was she? It wasn't as though she had dozens of friends and an active social life. She spent most of her time shut up with old artifacts. Not to mention, she was betrothed to a man she didn't love and who would never love her. She'd never really be a wife, which didn't bother her as she didn't see anything to covet in the wives she knew. But she did wonder if she would look back some day and wish she'd been a mother. She might wish to have something or someone in her life besides Roman coins and dusty books.

But those were questions Aidan couldn't help her with. She'd trusted him once but never again. It was best to leave before he woke and tried to convince her to stay a bit longer.

She climbed out of the bed, careful not to wake him, dressed in her male garb, and tiptoed across the floor. In the corridor outside the bed chamber, she found a chair and sat to tug on her boots. She didn't relish the looks the servants would give her when she walked past them this morning, but she also didn't really care. She'd spent most of her life not being respectable. The main thing was to hurry so they did not realize the woman in men's clothing leaving their employer's bedchamber was also Miss Tate. She'd walk quickly and keep her chin tucked so they'd have little opportunity to get a good look at her.

To that end, she rushed down the stairs, turned her face to the side as she passed a maid polishing the banister, pulled her collar up as she passed a footman at the bottom of the stairs, and was so intent on keeping her face hidden she ran right into a person coming toward her in the foyer.

With a start, she glanced up, an apology on her lips. But it died away when she found herself gazing into the disappointed eyes of Roland. And then his gaze shifted away, and he stepped out of her path, pretending not to know her.

She muttered something and hurried out the door, running into the street and hurrying several blocks before she dared hail a hackney. She sat in the conveyance, hands clasped tightly together, all the way to her flat.

Once there she ran inside and locked the door behind her. Then she went to the window. Most of Roland's pigeons were trained to view his town house as home. A few had been trained to fly to her flat. That way they could send messages to each other. Now she opened the window and waited. It wasn't even an hour before the pigeon arrived. Jenny pulled the little note from the backpack.

We should talk. My parlor at three, please.

Jenny brought the bird in and went to change and wash before going to see Roland to try and explain. Again.

***

Aidan woke alone as he always did. The pillow beside him was dented, so he hadn't dreamed Jenny had been with him. But the sheets were cold, which meant she had left some time ago. He rolled over and lifted his pocket watch from the table. And then he shot up.

It was almost noon. What the devil? Why had no one wakened him? He should have been at his offices hours ago.

Of course, he never asked to be wakened because he was always up with the sun. And he had bellowed for no one to disturb him when he'd run in with Jenny last night. Now he yanked the bell pull viciously and rose, pulling on a robe. He ordered his valet to have a bath drawn, then changed his mind because he didn't have time. And then he changed it back again as he sorely needed to wash.

He washed quickly and then had to succumb to a shave, and the entire while his mind tread over and over the night before. Jenny's moans when he'd entered her, the way her eyes darkened to sapphire when he touched her, the way she looked when she straddled him. He cursed, and his valet apologized even though he hadn't so much as nicked Aidan.

Finally, after what seemed an eternity, he was washed and dressed. He walked briskly down the stairs and reached for his hat and walking stick from his waiting butler. From behind him, someone cleared his throat.

Aidan turned and found Viscount Chamberlayne standing with arms crossed on one side of the foyer. "Sir," the viscount said, his voice icy. "Might we have a word?"

Aidan started like a guilty boy. He wanted to tell the viscount no, they could not have a word. He wanted to tell him, *hell no*. He didn't want to speak with him or look at him or even think about him. Not to mention, Aidan was late and eager to be away.

But running was the thief's way, and though Aidan felt very much like a thief this morning, he hoped he was a better man than the little thief he'd been forced to be in the rookeries.

"Of course," he said, waving Pierpont away. "Is my library acceptable?"

The viscount inclined his head, and Aidan led the way. As soon as he entered the library, he couldn't stop his gaze from darting to the desk Jenny used. She was not seated there, and Aidan wondered where she might be. Had she gone to Chamberlayne this morning and told him everything? Was this the meeting where his presence at dawn would be demanded?

The viscount entered, and Aidan closed the door. "Should I ring for tea, my lord? I'd offer you something stronger, but it's a bit early."

"I'll take a brandy," the viscount said, and Aidan raised his brows. But he went to the drinks table, poured it, and handed it to the viscount who had settled himself on the opposite side of Aidan's desk. Aidan took his own chair, but for some reason he felt as though he were the one being called to task.

The viscount was older than Aidan by a few years and had the kind of looks most ladies would swoon over. He had blond hair that seemed to naturally fall into the popular style most men of the *ton* spent hours to attain. His blue eyes were sharp and clear, and his features were unmistakably aristocratic, especially the long nose and pinched lips. "You are a man of business, so I hope you don't mind if I come straight to the point," the viscount said. He sipped the brandy and nodded his head in approval.

"I prefer it, actually," Aidan said.

"Good. I met my assistant coming down your stairs this morning as I was coming in."

"Your assistant?" The words were out before Aidan remembered that Jenny had worked for Chamberlayne before they'd become betrothed. Odd that the man should refer to her as his assistant and not his bride-to-be. Or perhaps not so odd considering the conclusions Chamberlayne must have reached when he saw Jenny.

"Miss Tate," the viscount said. "She was making a great effort to keep from being recognized. I have no idea how successful that was, but I imagine it is only a matter of time before the two of you are seen together."

Aidan opened his mouth then closed it again. It was not what he'd expected. Jenny had said she and Chamberlayne were friends and not in love, but any groom-to-be would be more upset at finding his affianced leaving another man's bed in the morning. Aidan wasn't quite sure what to say in this moment. He waited for a challenge but none came. The viscount did seem to be waiting for him to say *something*.

"My lord," Aidan began. "I want to apologize. I assure you I am not in the habit of poaching other men's brides-to-be—"

Chamberlayne waved a hand. "I know that. And I know the history you and Jenny have together. I understand why you find it hard to keep apart," he said. "What I need to know now is whether you intend for this relationship to continue or if last night was the end of it?"

Aidan frowned. This was the strangest conversation he had ever had. "My lord, I do not want to beleaguer this point, but it appears you don't mind that Jenny spent the night in my bed."

"Of course, I mind," the viscount said, taking another sip of the brandy. "I wouldn't be here if I didn't mind. But I don't mind for the reasons you think." He studied Aidan a moment over the rim of the glass. "You really do not understand, do you?"

Aidan's entire world had been shifted 180-degrees. "I'm afraid I don't."

"Jenny told you she doesn't love me, and I don't love her. Not in a romantic way, at least. I love her as a friend, of course. She is like a younger sister to me, I suppose. And I am protective of her in the way a big brother might be."

"But you are marrying her."

"I'm coming to that. How are you so successful in negotiations if you have no patience?"

Aidan closed his mouth at the chastisement. Was he really being lectured on his patience by his lover's bridegroom? He would have thought himself still asleep if the entire situation wasn't even more ridiculous than any dream.

"Jenny actually proposed to me. I didn't accept at first," Chamberlayne said. "But she eventually talked me into it."

Aidan tried to wrap his thoughts around this notion. That Jenny would propose marriage to a man did not surprise him. She was unconventional enough to do such a thing. And if Chamberlayne declined initially that made sense as well if the two were only friends. But why would Jenny feel the need to talk the viscount into a marriage with her?

"I needed the marriage to her more than she ever needed the security I could offer to her. You see, there have been rumors about me murmured here and there, and I needed to squelch them before they grew into more than a whisper."

"What sort of rumors?" Aidan asked.

"That I have unnatural sexual proclivities," the viscount said. His gaze met Aidan's directly, the challenge in his eyes clear.

Aidan didn't consider this any of his business, but he did consider Jenny his business. "And do you?" he asked.

"No. I don't consider them unnatural at any rate."

Aidan rose and went to the drinks table. He could see why the viscount felt the need for a brandy this early. He poured a splash in a glass and took a large swallow. He was not the sort of man who had any interest in what other men, or women, did in the privacy of their bedchamber. He didn't read the Society pages because he didn't care who was seen with whom. He knew nothing about the rumors surrounding Chamberlayne, but Aidan did know Jenny. She'd saved him and others many times. She'd given that woman at the banks of the Thames a coin last night. If someone needed help, Jenny would give it, whether it was to her advantage or not.

The viscount did not love her, not like a husband would, and he would never feel that way about her. But he needed a wife to protect him from scandal. He looked back at the viscount. "Am I to understand you have no intention of consummating the marriage?"

The viscount inclined his head. "It will be purely in name only. Jenny will live in the town house with Oscar and me. She'll have her own suite of rooms and the freedom to do as she likes as long as she acts with discretion. If she were to get in the family way, I would claim the child as my own."

Oscar and me. The statement confirmed Aidan's deduction. Of course, she had chosen to marry a man who would never want more than friendship from her. Her parents hadn't loved her. She didn't trust love—and why should she? He was the only one who had ever loved her, and he'd left her. No doubt she didn't want to risk her heart again.

And then there was her loyalty. She would do most likely anything to keep her friend, the viscount, safe from accusations of sodomy. As a peer, he would probably not be sent to the stocks, hanged, or jailed. But he could be made a social pariah. And if the viscount's lover was not a peer, he might very well suffer mightily for the relationship.

"I see you are beginning to understand," the viscount said.

"Perfectly."

The viscount seemed to wait. Aidan supposed he expected some expression of disgust or a lecture on depravity or even mild censure. Aidan had none of those to offer. He'd lived four years not knowing if he would survive to the end of the day. And then he had served in a war where his death was pretty much a foregone conclusion. He'd been in a troop of thirty and eighteen men hadn't come back.

Life was short, and why shouldn't a man or woman take what pleasure they could from it?

Aidan had always thought his pleasure came from making money, but now he began to wonder if he wasn't using wealth as a shield the way Jenny and the viscount planned to use their marriage.

"And so I return to my original question," the viscount said, his voice bringing Aidan's thoughts back into focus. "Do you intend to continue this relationship with Miss Tate?"

"I don't know." Aidan sat again and stared at his glass then looked at the viscount. He understood why the man asked this of him now. His future depended on whether or not Jenny would marry him. Aidan could be a hindrance to that. "I don't know how to have this conversation with you about your betrothed."

"Think of me like her brother."

"That doesn't help."

The viscount smiled. "Clearly there is a mutual attraction. Jenny told me that you and she have a history. You were her first lover, and I assume she was yours."

Aidan put his head in his hands. "This is so awkward," he groaned.

"Do you wish to keep…how shall I put it delicately? Fucking her?"

Aidan groaned. He could have sworn the viscount was laughing at his discomfort. He removed his hands from his face, which felt quite warm, and downed the rest of the brandy. He needed more. "I want her in my bed for as long as she'll have me," he said. "Last night was supposed to be our one and only together. I might convince her to reconsider."

"You're that good, are you?"

Aidan leaned back and tried to pretend this was not happening. "I've learned a few things since I was sixteen."

"Will it bother you that she is marrying another man? That she can't marry you? That she won't live with you? That, in the eyes of the law, she is my property and will bear my name?"

"Christ." Aidan tilted his head back to stare at the ceiling. He hadn't thought of any of this. He didn't want a wife. He didn't have time for a wife. This might be the perfect arrangement for him. He could have his life and share his bed when it suited him.

But this wasn't any woman. This was Jenny. And Aidan didn't particularly like the idea of sharing her. He didn't like sharing in general. He wanted it all.

"And if she were to bear you a child, that child would have my name as well," Chamberlayne said. "Not a bad lot as he or she would be the child of a viscount. My heir if she birthed a son. Jenny always says she doesn't want children, but I've seen her with them, and I do wonder."

Aidan sat forward. He didn't have answers and he felt rather backed up against a wall. He usually came out fighting in those cases. "And what about you?" he demanded. "Are you willing to take her chance at a real marriage away from her?"

"She's thirty, Mr. Sterling. Not on death's door certainly, but well past what most consider a marriageable age for a female. If she were four and twenty or even seven and twenty, I would never agree to this plan. As it is, until you arrived at Lady Birtwistle's ball, she had no prospects and only the occasional lover."

"It seems you have an answer for everything," Aidan said.

"And you have none," the viscount shot back. "If you are truly concerned for Jenny's welfare, if you care about her as more than a bed partner, you should come up with some answers of your own."

Aidan would have answered the viscount with a few choice words of his own, but the man stood, gave a bow so slight it was almost insulting, and strode out of the room.

Nine

Jenny found only Oscar in Roland's parlor at the appointed time. He'd been lying on a couch, reading a book, but he dropped it the moment she entered and sat up. "Tell me everything," he demanded, patting the cushion beside him. Jenny laughed and shook her head, but she came to sit beside him.

"Where is Roland?"

"Who cares? Tell me about your wicked night before he arrives and ruins everything. It must have been good. Rollie says he met you leaving this morning."

Jenny gave him a superior look. "A lady doesn't kiss and tell," she said in her best nob accent.

"Good thing you're not a lady. Now tell."

She laughed. "I don't know where to begin."

"Where did he begin?"

"With 'is mouth," she said.

Oscar began to fan his face with his hand. "Where did he put that mouth?"

"Where didn't 'e put it is a better question."

"Oh, my. Is he as delicious without his clothes as he is in them? He looks so hard and muscular."

"Are you quite through?" a voice asked from the doorway. Oscar rolled his eyes at Roland.

"I told you he'd ruin everything," he whispered loud enough for Roland to hear. But Oscar stood. "I'll be off so you can have your tête-à-tête."

As he passed Roland, Jenny heard the viscount murmur, "I'll show you hard and muscular later."

"Ooh, promises, promises." Oscar closed the door and was gone.

Jenny pretended not to hear but seeing them spar made her smile. She was also aware of a tugging in her chest, dangerously close to the area of her heart. She'd never have the sort of relationship they had—their closeness, their love, their spats. Ridiculous to envy them their arguments, but she did. Perhaps if she'd never had a love like that, she might not miss it and would simply find their behavior curious.

But she had loved like that, and it was unfortunate that Aidan Sterling had chosen now to step back into her life.

"Before ye speak," Jenny said, "I want to say that was the end. Aidan and me, we agreed on one night together. It won't 'appen again."

"That's what you said about the kiss." Roland strolled across the parlor, pausing to lift a curious metal object they'd found a few years ago and still hadn't been able to identify.

"This time I mean it. I'll write and ask 'im to 'ave the trunks from his larder sent 'ere, and we won't 'ave to see 'im again."

"He wants to see you again."

Jenny froze. "Ye spoke to 'im?"

"Of course. Someone has to ask about his intentions."

Jenny jumped off the couch. "Roland! Ye 'ad no right."

He waved a hand. "Yes, I realized rather quickly I had probably overstepped. But you hadn't even told him about Oscar and me."

"Ye told 'im?" Jenny practically screamed.

"He doesn't seem to know what he wants," Roland said almost to himself. "Probably discomfiting to a man like him. But I can see quite clearly that he wants you, even if he won't admit it to himself yet."

Jenny folded her arms across her chest. "Well 'e don't always get wot 'e wants."

Roland looked at her. "But why shouldn't you? Why shouldn't you have everything you want, Jenny? You could have a real marriage with him, children, more money than you'd know what to do with—"

"First of all, Aidan 'asn't asked me for any of that, and 'e won't. 'E loves money. It's everything to 'im. Second of all, I want to marry ye. We 'ad it all planned out, and I don't see why anything should change. I've spent the night with other men. This isn't any different."

"You act as though you actually believe that."

"Because it's true. And if ye doubt me, then let's get married now. Take yer carriage over to Doctors' Commons, and we can marry this evening."

Roland gave her a long look. "If your suggestion of marrying in haste with a special license is meant to comfort me, I assure you it has quite the opposite effect." He leaned a hip on the desk. "Sterling certainly has you scared to make you run so."

"Scared?" Her hands landed viciously on her hips. " 'E's the last man to scare me."

"Then there's no rush."

There was a tapping on the door, and Oscar opened it and poked his dark head inside. "I hate to interrupt."

"No, you don't," Roland said. Oscar entered brandishing a paper. "I have the *Morning Chronicle*."

"Rubbish," Roland said.

"Rubbish people read," Oscar added. "See here."

Since Roland didn't seem inclined to take the paper, Jenny held out her hand, and read aloud from the article.

"'And finally, dear reader, a certain Lord C—, who is newly betrothed to a lovely miss, raised eyebrows when he was lately seen not once, not twice, but more than three times this past week in the company of a Mr. L—. The two seemed more than friendly, and as the miss was often seen with them, one must wonder if they are inspired by the example of the infamous late duke, and if we haven't what the French like to call a *ménage à trois* in our midst.'"

"So now I'm sleeping with both of you," Roland said.

"Wot duke do they mean?" Jenny asked.

"Must be Devonshire. He had the duchess and his mistress living under the same roof for years," Roland said. Jenny rolled her eyes. She would never get used to the excesses of some of these nobs.

"I suppose I had better stay hidden away for a few weeks," Oscar said, sounding wistful. "I shall work on a new painting."

"Probably for the best," Roland said, putting a hand on his arm. Everyone knew Oscar loved Society and attending the theater and the Vauxhall Gardens, which was where they had planned to go the next evening.

"I shall call it *Solitude*," Oscar said.

"Or," Jenny suggested, "we can quash the gossip and marry now. People may say whatever they like, but ye'll 'ave a marriage license to wave in front of anyone who challenges ye publicly."

"Fine," Roland said.

Jenny's throat suddenly felt too tight, and it was difficult to swallow, difficult to breathe.

"I'll go to Doctors' Commons and fetch the license. And if I see no reason not to marry, we marry at the end of the week."

Jenny's gaze strayed to the calendar on the desk. Today was Tuesday, which meant she'd be a blushing bride in no more than four days.

***

"Well?" Oscar asked that night when the household had gone to sleep and all was quiet. He entered through a secret door that connected their chambers, and he was careful to close it now. Roland glanced at the other door to the room, noted it was locked, and then patted the bed. His servants were known for discretion and paid well. It was a necessity when one had priceless objects about. Roland knew a few probably suspected the true relationship between Oscar and himself, but he wouldn't give them any proof.

"Well, what?" Roland asked, setting his book aside and turning to face Oscar.

"Did you go to Doctors' Commons and fetch the special license?"

"Of course, I didn't," Roland said, settling back on his pillow as Oscar climbed under the covers beside him. "Jenny will marry me out of loyalty, but I can see now I was wrong to ever entertain the idea."

Oscar propped his elbow on the pillow and then rested his cheek on it, facing Roland. "You couldn't have known Aidan Sterling would walk into her life again. You didn't even know they had a past."

"I knew there was someone who'd hurt her. I knew part of the reason she wanted the marriage was to escape being hurt again. And I almost went through with it. She'd never forgive me if she were leg-shackled to me and couldn't marry the man she loved."

"Considering you've known her more than a decade and never seen her attached to any man or woman, you can hardly blame yourself for assuming there never would be anyone. But Aidan Sterling." Oscar lay back and stared up at the ceiling. "The man is richer than the King."

"I feel quite sorry for him."

"Why?" Oscar looked at Roland. "He's handsome and rich."

"And alone. I walked through his house the other day. The servants were all busy cleaning, and I pretended I was lost. He has entire chambers that are completely empty or with furnishings wrapped in Holland covers. No one but his secretary ever comes to call on him. The earl's family doesn't do more than grudgingly acknowledge him as a by-blow of the last earl. I don't think he knows his mother's family."

"Now you have me feeling sorry for him, except I just remembered he wants to steal Jenny away. Our little Jenny—"

"Can take care of herself. Besides, I don't think the man knows what he wants, and if he wants her, he'd better be decisive."

"Then she may marry you, after all."

"I think we had better make another plan."

"What's that? Oh, Rollie! Could we go to Italy? You know I have always wanted to go to Italy."

Roland blew out the candle and snuggled close to Oscar. "You and your lust for travel. I need to think about this. No rash decisions."

"You'll figure it out. You always do."

***

Lord Jasper was at the Draven Club. Aidan had asked Porter to notify him when the bounty hunter arrived. It was late, and Aidan was alone in his office. He'd finally allowed his clerks to go home. He didn't need the papers writing about how he worked his staff to death. He gave the messenger a coin then gathered up his documents, straightened his desk, and headed out.

On the walk to the Draven Club, he passed several groups of young men laughing and calling to each other from carriages. They stumbled in and out of clubs drunk on wine or flush with their winnings from a night of gambling. Others sat in coffee houses discussing politics or horse racing or women. Aidan watched them almost as though they were another species entirely.

Though the son of an earl, he'd never had a carefree night with friends in his youth. He'd spent the first twelve years worried about his mother's health, wondering why his father never came to see him, and doing his best in school as he knew it cost his mother dearly to send him. Then he spent four years stealing and starving and surviving only by luck and the kindness of Jenny Tate. The next decade was spent on the Continent, fighting for England. He'd made friends with the other Survivors then, but he'd never formed the sort of close friendships some of the men had. He expected every single one of his comrades-in-arms to die. He expected to die every day. The fact that some of his fellow soldiers had come home was a relief but also a quandary. How was he supposed to treat them now that they were no longer under fire?

Added to the uncertainty was the fact that he'd come home before many of them. When Nash Pope, their sharpshooter, had been blinded in a fight, Aidan had also been hit by a pistol ball. It was a minor injury. The ball had gone through his arm, but it was enough that he was sent home with Nash. Nash felt guilty for having to leave the other men. He felt responsible for their protection. Aidan, whose skills tended more toward stealing provisions, horses, and weapons, was less remorseful. Once he was back in London and on his feet again, he set about selling his commission and investing the money. He'd listened to the Duke of Mayne talk about investing. One could invest in shipping companies, imports or exports, mining for coal or iron or other minerals.

Most of the men in Draven's troop were younger sons with no great fortune of their own. They'd be given small stipends and must make their own way in the world. That was why they were in the army, so even though Aidan had listened and not asked questions, some of the other men had, and he'd thought carefully about everything he'd learned. And then he'd put it to use.

Then the men he'd fought beside had come back, and he hadn't known how to be with them. The only soldier he hadn't felt that way about was Rowden. They'd always had an easy friendship as they had common interests in boxing. But the rest of his fellow soldiers often made him remember the war and the nights he'd spent shaking in fear and wondering if he'd survive the coming dawn. He didn't want to be reminded of that time or that man, just as he hadn't wanted to be reminded of the boy he'd been in the London rookeries.

But lately all of it had come flooding back into his life. Jenny was a powerful reminder that he'd once had nothing and been no one. And FitzRoy's request to find this Harley was a subtle nudge back to those long, terror-filled nights when they'd all vowed to give their own lives to save the others. They'd joked about dancing with the devil in the morning, but Aidan had meant those promises. So had the others, especially the eighteen who had died.

He stopped before the Draven Club, climbed the stairs, and opened the door. Porter wasn't there to greet him, which was unusual, but Aidan didn't mind.

He heard Porter on the staircase carpeted in royal blue and waved a hand. "No need to come down, Porter." If he could save the one-legged man from another trip up and down, Aidan would prefer to do so. He started up the stairs so that Porter wouldn't come down. Porter started back up, and Aidan met him on the landing.

"Lord Jasper is in the dining room with Mr. Fortescue."

"Thank you, Porter." Aidan hadn't seen Stratford Fortescue in what seemed like a year. He entered the paneled wood room with its low ceiling and whitewashed walls and spotted the two right away. They sat at one of the round tables covered in white linen. They had a bottle between them and two glasses.

"And he just keeps telling us 'Dinnae fash, dinnae fash. It's a scratch,'" Stratford said in a Scottish accent. "And then he went pale and—" Stratford noticed Aidan and paused. "Oh, hullo, Sterling. I was just telling Jasper about the time Nash shot Duncan."

Aidan smiled. He'd heard the story, but he sat to listen again anyway. The conversation shifted to shared experiences in battle, and though Aidan generally hated remembering the war, tonight, the way Stratford and Jasper told the stories, the battles almost seemed like adventures.

Finally, Stratford rose to go, presumably home to his sleeping wife. Jasper finished his wine and began to rise, but Aidan put a hand on his arm. "Stay a moment, my lord, if you will."

"Of course." He sat back in his chair and gave Aidan a curious look.

"I believe congratulations are in order. I understand your wife is in the family way."

"News travels fast. And people say women are the gossips." He didn't wear his mask as much as he'd used to, and he wasn't wearing it tonight. The ravaged flesh of his face was pink where the fire had burned it. Another war wound, though this one was on the outside whereas most of them wore theirs inside. It was hard to look upon, but Aidan was still glad he felt comfortable enough to go without his shield, so to speak.

"What is this about?" Jasper asked. "I don't have any money to invest, and you'll have to speak to Phineas if you want the Lords to enact some law or other."

Aidan felt as though he'd been slapped. "You think I only want to speak with you when I want something?"

"You don't want something?"

Aidan sighed. "I do want something, but it's advice. Not help making money."

"I doubt you need any help in that area, and if you did, I wouldn't be the man to go to. Is this about the little girl FitzRoy has been looking for?"

"He told me he went to you first."

"He did, but I can't take that on at the moment."

"I've agreed to find her," Aidan said, surprised at the vehemence in his voice. "I'll find her."

Jasper eyed him coolly. "You know that world as well as I. Probably better."

"And yet I've been unsuccessful thus far."

"My advice is to stop looking."

Aidan raked a hand through his hair. "I didn't intend to start looking, but now that I have, I want to find her."

"The harder you look, the deeper underground she'll go. Unless you give her a reason to come out. I imagine Colin wants to put her in an orphanage."

"Neil's orphanage, which isn't exactly a workhouse."

"That's a discussion to have with her later. For now, offer her something she wants."

"What's that?"

"What did you want when you were in her position?"

He'd wanted so many things, chiefly love and security. Instead, he said, "Blunt."

Jasper nodded. "As I recall she helped FitzRoy find Lady Daphne. Offer a reward and see if that convinces her to crawl out of her hidey-hole."

Which was precisely what Jenny had hinted about to the mudlarks last night. She was always a step ahead of him.

"Good advice, my lord," Aidan said standing. "I'm sorry to have kept you."

But Jasper didn't rise. He just looked at Aidan and waited. "What's your real question? What I just told you"— he waved a hand—"you know all of that already."

Aidan grasped the back of the chair and dug his fingers in. He'd always felt a certain kinship with Jasper. Perhaps because Jasper had spent so much of his time in the places and among the people Aidan knew. Perhaps because, despite being a lord, Jasper was the most unpretentious man he knew. Perhaps because Jasper had been injured risking his life to save another of their troop, and a man like that was rare.

"Why did you marry?" he asked.

Jasper's brows went up in surprise. Aidan shook his head. "Never mind. Ridiculous question."

"Sit down," Jasper said.

"I think I'd prefer to stand."

Jasper poured more wine. "It's not a ridiculous question. I doubt you've ever asked a ridiculous question in your life." He sipped the wine and considered Aidan. "There are only two reasons men in our position marry."

"Men in our position?"

"Men who don't need an heir for the title."

"And what are those reasons?" Aidan asked, wishing he had taken a seat and poured himself more wine.

"Love or money." Jasper sipped his wine again. "Olivia has no money, and I can make my own way, at any rate, so the answer is obvious. Which is it for you? I shouldn't think you needed the money, but I'm not sure any amount would ever really satisfy you. Have you found a wealthy heiress?"

"Not even close."

Jasper set the wine glass down. "It can't be love."

"It was a useless question," Aidan said. "It has nothing to do with me. Give your wife and son my best," he said, turning to leave. "I'm sorry to have kept you."

"Let me know when Harley finds you!" Jasper called.

Aidan waved a hand and was finally away. He started home, ignoring the drunk young lords, but he passed one in a passionate embrace with a young woman, most likely a courtesan, and felt his heart lurch. What was waiting for him at home? An expensive bed where he would sleep all alone. Jenny's scent would probably still be on the pillows. How was he supposed to fall asleep like that?

Before he could think what he was doing, he changed directions. He knew where Jenny lived. As soon as he'd seen her at Lady Birtwistle's ball, he'd asked his secretary to find out where she resided. Aidan had told himself it was because he wanted to be certain she had decent lodgings.

Now he headed that way, walking quickly until he reached the door to the building housing her flat. He paused outside then and considered returning home. Putting his head down, he opened the door to the building and walked up the stairs, stopping outside her door before knocking loudly.

No one answered, so he knocked again. She was probably sleeping. He knocked again, and the door opened, leaving his hand to hang in midair.

"Are ye trying to wake the whole of London?" she demanded, looking up at him with tousled hair and cheeks pink from sleep.

"Just you," he said.

"Come in before my neighbors complain to the landlord." She pulled him inside and closed the door. She held a candle with one hand, and the faint light illuminated her white nightdress. Her unbound hair hung down her back, and she tapped one bare foot on the wooden floor. "Wot are ye doing 'ere, Aidan Sterling? Should I even ask 'ow ye knew where I live?"

"Probably not." The nightdress wasn't sheer, but the material was thin, and the neck left one shoulder revealed.

She caught the direction of his gaze. "I told ye last night was the only night."

"You think I came for that?"

She raised a brow.

"Fine. It did cross my mind, but that wasn't the only reason. We made a wager, and you lost."

"Ye seemed quite willing to forgive my debt that night."

"And you said you'd honor it. I want to lay some breadcrumbs for our friend Harley."

"Ye don't need me for that."

"I didn't think you'd want to miss out on the adventure."

"I'm not seventeen anymore. But a debt is a debt. Give me a few moments to dress." He made to follow her, but she held up a hand. "Alone." She left him in near darkness in the small room which looked as though it served as a parlor or drawing room. The flat couldn't have had more than two or three rooms. From what he'd glimpsed, this room was furnished with a few chairs and a couch. They looked as though they'd come with the flat. That made sense as Aidan couldn't imagine Jenny picking out furniture.

In the dark all was quiet, but he heard a faint cooing sound, and looked toward the window. A large cage was positioned there, and he moved toward it, opening the shutter to let in a bit of moonlight. Two pigeons were inside, blinking up at him, looking sleepy.

"Planning to send more messages?" she asked, coming into the room and shining more light on birds with her candle. They were gray and brown with a bit of rust mixed in. Their necks were an unusual iridescent greenish blue.

"Are these also homing pigeons?" he asked.

"Yes, they'll return to Roland's town house and are useful if I need to send a message. I should probably do that now," she said, moving toward a small table with scraps of paper on it and a pen. She scribbled a message, inserted it in a small backpack and opened the cage, allowing one pigeon to move onto her arm. The birds were wide awake now, sensing something interesting about to happen.

"What did you tell him?" Aidan asked.

"That I'll be late coming in tomorrow morning and not to wait for me." She fitted the backpack on the pigeon, opened a window, and waited for the bird to take flight. The pigeon paused, tilted his or her head this way and that, and then, seemingly sure of the path, it took off. The remaining bird cooed, and Jenny said, "Ye'll get yer chance." She gave it what looked like a piece of dried fruit and looked up at him. "Ready?"

286 | *Shana Galen*

But once the pigeon had flown away, Aidan noticed what Jenny was wearing. She wore the trousers again with a white shirt and a man's coat over it. Those trousers defined her legs nicely, and it was hard not to imagine her *out* of the trousers.

"Stop looking at me like that. One night, I said."

"One night," he repeated and forced his gaze away. He offered his arm, and she rolled her eyes at the gesture, instead stomping to the door, opening it, and cocking a hip impatiently. She moved just like a man—a somewhat curvy, delectable man.

He followed her down to the street, where she looked about. "No coach?"

"I walked."

"Didn't think nobs like ye knew 'ow to use yer feet."

He gave her a tight smile and hailed a hackney. When he gave the address, Jenny raised her brows. "That's not the rookeries."

"Not far outside, and she's been seen in the area."

She shrugged, folded her arms, and stared at him. "If this is a ploy to make me change my mind, it won't work."

"Change your mind about the one night?"

She raised a shoulder.

"I'd hardly put you in a hackney and drag you across town for that. Easier to seduce you in your flat."

She snorted. "I won't be seduced. I agreed to one night. We 'ad our fun. I'll be marrying Roland by the end of the week. 'E went to fetch the special license today."

That news rather alarmed Aidan, but he wouldn't allow it to show. "Good," he said.

The silence dragged on just long enough that he wondered if she would take the bait.

Finally, "Good? Wot does that mean? Good?"

"It means exactly what I said. It's good that you are marrying."

"Why?"

"So you'll be taken care of, of course. I shouldn't need to worry about you."

She snorted again. "Oy, go on then. Ye weren't worried. I can take care of myself."

"Of course, you can," he agreed far too readily.

"Ye don't think so?"

"I said I did. It's really a perfect arrangement for both of you. He needs you, and you need him."

She looked as though she wanted to argue, but she made a sound of annoyance instead. Finally, the hackney slowed, and Aidan climbed out. He offered his arm to Jenny, but she hopped down without his assistance. While he paid the jarvey, she looked about.

It was a rather ordinary street lined with closed shops and yellow lights spilling out of taverns. A few men walked along the street, holding lanterns to cut through the dark. But this area of the city was quiet, unlike much of Mayfair. The people who lived here would need to wake early and go to work tomorrow.

The hackney pulled away, and Aidan pointed across the street. "There it is." He gestured to a tavern with a picture of a tall ship on the sign hanging above the door.

"The Clipper," Jenny read. "Why 'ere?"

"She's been seen here before, and more importantly, I'm hungry. I've heard the food here is excellent."

"I should 'ave known. Yer stomach always did lead the way."

She followed him into the dark interior of the tavern, which looked much like any other she'd stepped foot in. There was one woman listlessly wiping a table and a few men sitting at tables, drinking or eating. The publican, a stocky, brown-skinned man with close-cropped wiry black hair, scowled as soon as they walked in. "I don't know anything," he said.

Jenny scowled right back. "Didn't ask ye anything either, did we?"

"We came to eat," Aidan said, smoothly.

"Sure ye did." The publican went back to wiping the bar.

Aidan waited a moment and as no one came forward to show them to a table, Jenny finally stomped across the floor and chose one. She dropped into a chair. Aidan followed, sitting so his back was to the room. He didn't like that position, but he supposed he should have gone first so Jenny couldn't take that prime seat.

The tavern wench came over and leaned a bony hip on the table. Aidan raised a brow at her familiarity. "If yer 'ungry, yer in the right place," she said. "Our cook is the best. Pinched 'im from the palace, we did."

Aidan rolled his eyes. "Two plates of whatever the cook is serving and"—he glanced at Jenny—"ale or something stronger?"

"Ale is fine."

Aidan nodded at the serving woman, who sauntered off.

"Stop acting like a prig," Jenny said.

"I *am* a prig." The words had the desired effect, and she laughed. Aidan liked to see her laughing, and he felt as though his breath was stolen away by how beautiful she looked in that moment.

Jenny's smile faded. "Stop looking at me like that."

"Why? You'd rather spend the rest of your life with a man who won't look at you at all?" He hadn't meant to say that. He didn't even know why he did.

"And yer offering me something else?"

Aidan took a breath. "Maybe I am."

Ten

Jenny felt her heart lurch. "That's a romantic proposal, if I ever 'eard one."

The server returned, thumped the glasses of ale on the table, and walked away. Jenny took hers and swallowed a large gulp. Her throat was unaccountably dry.

"I can certainly offer you a place in my bed," Aidan said, making her heart tighten. This time from desire, not anxiousness. "That's more than Chamberlayne will do."

"Ye think I can't find men to keep my bed warm?"

His dark brows drew together, and she could tell he didn't like that image. Now he took a long drink. "I think it interesting you choose to tie yourself to a man who will never be able to give you what you need."

"And wot is it ye think I need?" Her tone was sarcastic to hide her anger. What did Aidan know about what she needed?

"Love," he said simply.

"Oh, please."

"Everyone needs love," he added. "You've all but ensured you'll never have it. It doesn't surprise me, of course, based on your history."

Jenny had meant to level some criticisms at Aidan, but she forgot them all when he mentioned her past. It wasn't like him to play dirty. "Wot's that mean?"

"Your parents, of course. Ah, thank you," he told the serving wench, who had reappeared with two bowls of thick stew and crusty, warm bread with a bowl of butter. Jenny's stomach lurched, and she realized she too was hungry.

"This 'as nothing to do with my parents," she said, sniffing the stew. It actually smelled rather good. Perhaps she was becoming as much of a prig as Aidan. She took a bite.

"It has everything to do with your parents," Aidan said, breaking the bread and handing her half. The image of his doing so was such a reminder of the hundreds of times he'd done that in the past that she had to blink and remind herself she was no longer that girl and he no longer that boy. For a moment, she held the warm bread, trying to reorient herself.

"That's not to say that my own parents were saints," he said. "My father might have claimed me and provided for me, but he made no lasting provisions for me, and we never had a true relationship. He was just a man I saw perhaps once a year. He meant nothing to me."

Jenny hadn't known Aidan when his father had been alive, but she'd always envied him his relationship with his father, distant as it had been.

"At least yer father didn't beat the snot out of ye," she said. "I learned early to stay out of my dad's way. If 'e'd been drinking, 'e'd cuff me for no reason other than 'e didn't like the fact that I existed."

"I remember your father well," Aidan said, and she knew he was thinking about the time her father had come after her and Aidan had offered to kill him. Aidan had been willing to do anything to protect her. Her father was unpredictable.

Jenny had learned to stay away from home when she'd been seven and her mother had tried to sell her for a few extra coins. Jenny had kicked the man where it hurt and run off. That night she'd waited until her mother was sleeping and returned, taking everything she wanted from the house, which wasn't much. The next time her mother had tried to sell her, she'd been ten and she'd kicked both the man and her mother then found her father in a gin house, reeking of drink and told him. He'd gone home and beaten her mother until she couldn't walk for a week. Jenny had felt badly about that, but her mother had never tried to sell her again. But Jenny had never believed she could rely on her father to protect her. One month he'd be kind and the next he'd try and kill her. Aidan had been the first person she truly relied on.

"If that was your experience of marriage, I see why you wouldn't want it," he said. "But you deserve love."

She curled her lip. "Wot do ye know about love?"

"My mother loved me. Yours never did, and I think you grew up thinking no one would ever love you. Now you're scared to take a chance, so you marry Chamberlayne and never need to risk your heart."

Jenny stared at Aidan, whose expression was one of surprise. She didn't think he'd planned to say any of that. He opened his mouth, perhaps to take it back, but then he said, "I loved you, you know. I told you that night."

"And ye lied."

"I never lied to you."

"Ye left me, Aidan," she hissed, aware that some of the men in the tavern were watching them.

"I tried to help you." He held up a hand. "And before you tell me—again—that you were insulted by the offer to be a maid in my uncle's house, you're right. That was insulting. I didn't know how else to help you, and I knew I couldn't help you by staying. I was a liability to you."

"Never."

"Jenny." He shook his head. "You were a better thief than I was, and without me, you only had to feed yourself and watch your own back."

"Maybe I liked watching yer back. Ever think of that?" she shot back.

"And I liked watching yours. I'm still watching it. Don't marry someone who can never love you in the way a husband loves a wife."

"Roland needs me—"

"And you're his friend and want to help, I know." Aidan paused, then continued, "When I left you all those years ago, it was because I had to save myself. I know you're angry I left you behind, but there are times we have to save ourselves. Maybe if you'd loved me, you would have been happy to see me go."

Her face must have betrayed her thoughts because he reached for her glass of ale, moving it out of her way before she could do as she wanted and toss it in his face.

"Ye 'ave a lot of nerve to question my love back then."

But he was right, of course. She'd wanted him to stay for selfish reasons. She had loved him, but it had been a selfish love. Of course, she'd been seventeen and never known love. She'd lashed out, and in the years that followed, she never reconsidered those feelings. Now that he forced her to, she knew he was right. But she'd be damned if she'd admit that.

"Ye might 'ave watched my back all those years ago, but I don't want ye watching it now. My engagement is my business, and if that's wot ye brought me 'ere to talk about, I'll go." She stood.

"That's not why I brought you here. I told you, I want to lay breadcrumbs for Harley."

"And 'ow do ye plan to do that?"

He glanced at the publican, and she shook her head. "Ye'll get nowhere with 'im."

"But *you* might."

"Yer an arse, ye know that?"

"You've told me enough times." He leaned close, and she tried not to inhale his scent as he spoke quietly about his plan. It was difficult to concentrate with him so close. She could feel the heat of him and the scent he wore now, something expensive, but underneath it was the scent of Aidan—the scent she remembered from all those years ago.

"Can you do that?" he asked, bringing her back to the present. Jenny wasn't sure she'd heard a word he said, but she rose and walked on unsteady legs to the bar, where the publican was still listlessly cleaning. He gave her a wary look. "Another ale?" he asked.

"Please." She took one of the stools and sat, leaning her elbows on the bar.

He went to the cask, opened the spigot and efficiently filled a mug. Then he set it down in front of her. "Put it on 'is tab," she said, jerking her head toward the table where Aidan was probably sitting and watching her.

"Done." He started to move away.

"Ye own this place?" she asked.

He sighed as though he knew what had been coming.

"Wot's it to ye?"

"Just curious." She shrugged.

"Me mother said, curiosity killed the cat."

"My mother said, good thing yer not a cat."

He smiled wanly. "I'm part owner."

"The food is good."

"I know. I don't 'ave all night. Whoever 'e's looking fer"—he gave Aidan's table a pointed look—"I don't know 'im."

"Ye can't know everybody."

"Exactly."

"I don't want to ask ye about anyone. I want to tell ye something."

"Why?"

She shrugged. "I like to talk."

"Sure ye do."

She lowered her voice enough to make the men nearby strain to hear her but not enough so she couldn't be heard. "My friend over there is rich. Ye know the saying, rich as a king."

The publican nodded.

" 'E's richer than the king. 'Is name is Aidan Sterling. Ask around if ye don't believe me."

The publican said nothing.

"There's a girl who goes by the name of 'Arley." She raised a hand. "Don't tell me. Ye don't know 'er."

"That's right."

"She saved the wife of a friend of 'is." Another jerk of her head toward Aidan. "Mr. Sterling wants to thank this 'Arley, so 'e's offering the girl a reward."

"Wot's this to do with me?"

"I'm just talking."

"Sure ye are."

"Ye don't want to know 'ow much the reward is?"

"I'm sure ye'll tell me." His eyes moved past her to the other patrons. "Ye'll tell us."

"Just ye," she said. She leaned over the bar, and the publican hesitated only a moment before leaning close enough so she could whisper in his ear. She wished she could see his face, but she could imagine his eyes opened wide when she whispered the amount. She had no idea if that was the amount Aidan had told her. But it was enough to make people talk. She leaned back. "So if ye ever 'ear of this 'Arley, tell her to find Mr. Sterling and collect 'er reward. 'E's done looking for 'er."

She hopped off the stool, and Aidan was at her side. He tossed the publican a sovereign, and the publican caught it. "This is more than ye owe."

"A round for everyone then," Aidan said. He placed his hand on the small of Jenny's back and led her out the door and into the street. "Three, two," he counted. "One." The sound of conversation exploded behind them. "If news spreads as fast as it used to, she'll hear about it before dawn." He looked down at her. "You were magnificent. Haven't lost your charm."

"Did ye doubt it?"

"No." His gaze met hers and held. Prickly heat climbed up her belly, and she was the one who looked away first. One night. She'd promised herself just one night. "I'm going 'ome now," she said.

"I'll take you."

"I'd rather go alone."

"Fine. Then we'll part ways when I put you in a hackney."

She gave him an indulgent smile. "Ye think I can't take care of myself."

"I think I'd like to make sure nothing happens to you."

His hand touched her back again, and she scooted forward and started walking to avoid his touch. She'd promised herself. She'd promised Roland. She would be married in a few days. She could not go to bed with Aidan again.

He seemed to understand she didn't want to be touched and moved to walk beside her, his hands in his pockets.

"Ye know," she said as they walked quickly, but not so quickly as to draw notice. "Ye seem to think ye know everything about me and my scars from the past."

"I think I know more than most."

"I know more than most about yers too. And maybe the only reason ye want me now is because ye can't 'ave me."

"Ridiculous."

"Why?"

"Because I can have you."

She gave him a look, and he nodded at her. "I saw them too," he said quietly. "Keep walking."

"I can 'andle myself," she repeated. "Just wanted to make sure ye were ready. When they come for us, if ye want to run, I'll take care of them."

"I counted five," he said. "I don't think you can handle five on one, even if I were inclined to run, which I'm not."

The men following them had started moving closer, starting to edge out of the shadows, and Jenny knew the attack would be soon. "Ye seem rather sure of yerself. That ye can 'ave me, I mean. I'm not one of yer 'ouses or 'ats or coats. Ye can't buy me."

"The thought never crossed my mind."

"It will. To ye, blunt is everything. Ye never 'ad enough all those years and now ye 'ave to make sure ye'll never be without. If ye 'ad me, ye'd just put me on a shelf and forget about me or leave me again for the next bright bauble."

Aidan stopped and looked at her. "I'd never treat you like that. And I'd never leave you again."

"Won't ye?" She raised a brow. "Watch yer back. They're coming."

He grinned at her, and she couldn't help but grin back. And then he swung around and faced the five men who'd come up behind them, hands on his hips. "Can I help you, gentlemen?"

"I think maybe ye can," the one in the middle said. He was the shortest and the brawniest. " 'And over yer coin and we'll let ye live."

"I see. I have a counteroffer."

"Wot's that mean?" the tall, lanky one asked.

"Close yer potato 'ole," the leader said. He looked back at Aidan. "Wot's that mean?"

"You walk away now, and I'll let *you* live."

Jenny rolled her eyes. Aidan was buying time, as he always did. Usually right about now he would yell something like, "What's that?" and when they all looked, he took off running. But she could already see two of the men inching around him and toward her. They both wore dirty black caps that had probably been gray at one time.

The leader grinned and slammed a fist into his hand. "Get 'em, boys."

Jenny braced herself as the two who'd flanked Aidan rushed for her.

***

Well, that was annoying, Aidan thought as he took a swing at the tall lad who reached him first. The leader hadn't even considered his counteroffer. He lifted his walking stick and slammed the other man who rushed at him over the head. He went down hard, and the leader cursed and took off his coat.

Aidan glanced back at Jenny. One of the men had grabbed her arms and held them behind her back, but she'd used him as leverage to kick the other man in the jaw. Then she reared her head back, butted the other man in the nose, and tumbled free. Aidan returned to his own two attackers. The tall one was coming for him again, but when Aidan swung the stick, he leaned back and just out of range.

"Be a man and fight with yer 'ands," the brawny leader said. No surprise as a direct hit from him would take Aidan out.

"Two against one," Aidan said. "I hardly think that's sporting." He heard a grunt behind him and wondered if Jenny had already finished with her two. She was probably impatiently waiting for him."

"Swing that stick one more time, and I'll use it to smash yer brains in," the leader said. He'd been watching from the side, not wading into the fray.

Yet.

"That will give the Charleys something to charge you with. Hullo, boys!" He waved at the imaginary men of the Watch and almost laughed when the two attackers believed it. They both looked behind them, and Aidan smacked the tall one in the head, bringing him to his knees. The leader turned back to him, and Aidan was too close to swing the stick now.

He dropped it, kicked it away, and brought up his right fist then his left. The man went down. Aidan turned to find Jenny watching him, her attackers rolling on the ground and moaning in pain.

"Don't say it," he said.

She blinked at him, all innocence. "Say wot? I was only wondering wot took ye so long."

He let out a breath. "I told you not to say it."

She laughed. "Yer boxing 'as improved."

"I've watched a lot of mills." He slid his toe under his walking stick, lifted it into the air, and caught it.

"But ye still like the old *look over there* bit."

"Works every time." He looked down at the men she'd dispatched without a walking stick, studying boxing, or misdirection. "How the hell do you do that?" he asked.

"A lady needs some secrets." She smiled up at him, and he couldn't stop himself. He reached for her waist and pulled her against him. His blood was hot, and he could feel her heart pounding in her chest and hear her breath come fast. Before he could take her mouth, she took his. Her kiss was as rough and savage as her fighting, and the assault made his blood run hotter. He pushed her against the wall behind them, wedged his knee between her trousered legs, and pushed against the heat of her core. She moaned and then someone behind them groaned in pain, and Aidan pulled back.

"We should go," he said, panting. "Before that lot starts thinking about revenge."

She nodded and took his hand, pulling him behind her until they had crossed into an area with lamplight and hackneys. She raised her hand, but two passed her by before he raised his hand and the next stopped.

"How do ye do that?" she asked.

"A gentleman needs some secrets." He handed her into the hackney, his hands lingering just a bit too long on her waist. He forced himself to sit across from her. He'd had his kiss and wouldn't take more unless she offered it. And, oh, but he wanted her to offer it. He needed her like he needed water and food. He craved her. Yes, some of that fervent need was the blood rushing through him, the thrill of the fight, but some of it was just always there when he was in Jenny's presence. She glanced at him, her gray eyes dark, and he couldn't tell what she was thinking. After what seemed years, the hackney stopped, and Jenny reached for the door. "Walk me to my flat," she told him.

Aidan didn't argue. He climbed out after her, paid the driver, and followed her into her building. She took his hand, and the feel of her skin against his made his breath catch in his throat. She pulled him up the stairs, yanked the key from a pocket in her coat at her door, opened it, and stepped inside.

Aidan leaned on the door jamb. "Thank you for—"

"Shut yer potato 'ole," she said.

Aidan closed his mouth.

"Don't say a word, understand?"

He nodded. She grabbed his shirt and yanked him inside.

Eleven

Jenny pushed Aidan against the door, slamming it closed. Then she wrapped her hands around his neck and brought his lips down to hers. She pressed her body against his, the urge to touch and be touched overpowering her better judgment. She knew her reaction was in response to the fight. They might have died—well, *he* might have died; she could handle herself—but the threat and the danger made her blood race. She needed to remember she was alive. That was all this was. It had nothing to do with the fact that the man she couldn't stop touching was Aidan Sterling.

"Jenny," he moaned when they broke apart, and she slid a hand between them to cup his erection.

"I said, don't talk." She stepped back. "Take off yer clothes instead."

He raised a brow, but he didn't argue. He stripped off his coat, and she did the same. She didn't have a waistcoat, so while he fumbled with his buttons, she pulled the linen shirt over her head. She'd bound her breasts lightly with a linen strip this time, and she unknotted it and began to unwind it. When she looked up, Aidan's hands had frozen on the last button of his waistcoat.

"Keep going," she said.

"Do you have a bed chamber or are we to make use of the floor?"

Why did he insist on talking? It made it hard for her to pretend she wasn't yet again betraying Roland with him. "Ye never minded the floor in the past." She dropped the binding on the ground, revealing her tits.

"The floor it is then." He stepped forward to take her in his arms again, but she moved away and gestured for him to follow. She wouldn't admit that he had a point about the floor—they weren't seventeen any longer—so she led him to her bed chamber. Her flat was dark, and he didn't know the way, so there were several thumps and exclamations as they moved, but once they entered her room, the fire burned low in the hearth, giving some light.

She turned to watch him, wondering how he saw the small chamber. His had probably been the size of her entire flat. But her bedchamber only held a dresser, a washstand with a basin, and small bed. The bed was comfortable and the linens clean, but it was by no means luxurious. His gaze skimmed right over the bed and the dresser and went straight to the shelf by the window. She'd forgotten about that. On it were an assortment of trinkets—some extremely valuable, some valuable only to her.

"Still a collector, I see," he said, shedding his waistcoat and moving closer to the shelf. She caught his hand and pulled him back.

"Yer talking far too much."

"And what should I do with my mouth?" His gaze drifted to her tits, and one of his hands came up and palmed one. Now she was the one who couldn't stop a moan. His thumb raked over one hard nipple, and she gasped. He bent to take the hard point into his mouth, licking and suckling with such skill that she couldn't catch her breath. She was writhing against him, and his hands caught her hips, pulling her body against his hard member.

"Yes," she moaned. "Clothes off."

He stepped back and made quick work of his shirt. Jenny exhaled the last of her breath at the sight of his bare chest. If she needed a reminder he was no longer a boy, the muscles and hair on his chest were the perfect prompt. She ran a hand over his chest then sat on the bed next to him while he pulled off his boots. He struggled with the second one, and she helped him remove it then stepped between his legs and pushed him back on the bed. He looked up at her, his dark eyes large in his face. She loosed the fall of his breeches and slid the material down his hips. His erection was hard and lay heavy on his abdomen. She sank between his legs, took his member in her hands, then touched her lips to the tip.

Aidan hissed in a breath. She liked the taste of him and the smooth velvet of his cock against her tongue. Slowly, she took all of him in then slid her lips back to the tip again. His hands fisted in the covers of her bed as his breathing became wildly erratic. She pleasured him with slow, maddening strokes until he put his hand on her head, stroking her hair in a gentle caress. That touch undid her. Even in this moment, when he was close to climax, he was gentle and caring with her. She felt her eyes sting with tears. Damn him. She wanted release, nothing else. No affection. No caring. No…love.

She gripped him with one hand, moving it in time to her lips. He groaned and when she knew he was close, he took her shoulders and pulled her up. "Wot are ye doing?" she asked.

"Your turn," he said and reached for her trousers. "I'll never get used to the oddity of unfastening trousers on a woman," he said.

Christ, but he was talking. *Again*. "Ye don't like it?" she asked.

"Oh, I like it." He wiggled them over her hips then whispered, "Bloody…" He looked up at her. "You're wearing nothing underneath."

"Ye forgot my boots," she said. She stepped away, turned her back to him, and holding onto a wall, bent to remove one boot then the other. A sound like a pained animal came from behind her. She discarded the rest of her clothing, and when she turned, he had undressed and was naked on her bed. Now she was the one who made a strangled sound. Had she ever seen anything like Aidan Sterling naked? He was all muscle and long limbs and dark hair.

She crossed to the bed and made to straddle him, but he took her by the waist and flipped her over, so she was under him. She wouldn't have allowed any other man to take control like that, but this was Aidan. She trusted him with her life.

"I don't have my French letters with me," he said. "It's better if I'm in control."

She wanted to argue, but then he kissed her, and his body was heavy on hers, his skin hot against her own, and she didn't care what he did as long as he didn't stop. His hand slid down her body and between them, finding her hot and wet, she knew. He brushed his fingers over her sex, and she whimpered. She needed him. A few touches and she would come apart. He spread her, one finger sliding between her folds until he found that little nub of pleasure. His thumb flicked over it, and she gasped and writhed. Then his fingers—no, it was his cock—was at her entrance, and he slid partway in, his thumb still working her.

She couldn't breathe, couldn't think as he slowly filled her, all the while bringing her closer and closer to climax. She looked up at him, realizing he'd stopped kissing her and was watching her face. Her gaze locked with his, and she raised her arms and put them over his neck, linking them together. She'd never felt so close with any other man. Never watched a man's every expression as he entered her, pleasured her. She hadn't wanted this to mean anything, but it seemed she couldn't stop it from meaning everything.

His thumb moved again, and the rush of sensation took over. She tipped and fell into the orgasm, bucking her hips and sheathing him fully inside her.

Aidan cursed as she tightened around him. He moved with her, the feel of him increasing her pleasure until she was almost blind with it.

His hands were on her hair, her cheeks, her lips. She opened her eyes and saw Aidan. The love she had felt for him all those years before rushed back over her. She hadn't ever really let it go, and now he'd released it again, and she had to bite her lip to keep from telling him. But she didn't have to say it. He knew.

And she knew.

She could see the love he felt for her in his eyes. She could feel it in the way he touched her. It was in every part of this act.

She felt him swelling and he groaned and quickly pulled away, spilling his seed on the linen she'd tossed on the bed earlier. Then he collapsed beside her, his breath as ragged as hers.

They lay together, catching their breath. Her bed was small, which meant it took barely a movement for him to pull her back against his chest and bury his lips in her neck. Jenny closed her eyes, wishing the outside world would never intrude again. Wanting to stay here, in the safety of his arms forever.

***

She smelled so good. So clean and sweet and yet like his Jenny—though she'd never smelled this good in the rookeries. Her hair tickled his nose, and her skin was soft against his cheek. He thought about saying it—saying the words hanging between both of them—then decided she might hit him if he did. There was a reason she hadn't wanted him to speak. She wanted to pretend this wasn't happening between them again.

She might even want to pretend she didn't love him. But she did. He'd seen it. And he loved her. She was the only person he'd ever known since the age of twelve who could make him forget that he was hungry or tired or hurt. Now she made him forget that he had contracts and meetings and mergers to see to. He didn't care about any of it when he held her in his arms.

Earlier she'd said he'd only leave her again. He'd never walk away from her as he had before, but she might not be wrong about his drive and ambition. If he did have her, would he leave her, figuratively, to seek more wealth and riches? Once he was at work—once he had a contract within sight, negotiations on the table—it was always difficult to think of anything or anyone else. How many nights would Jenny wait for him? Alone? Neglected?

Chamberlayne wouldn't neglect her. They were friends. She'd always have a place with him. But that place would end at the bed chamber door. She'd be alone there, and Aidan knew how long those nights could feel. But would being with him be any different for her? Could he ever believe he had enough? Could he ever be satisfied with what he had and stop needing to acquire more?

He was beginning to think it might be possible. He wanted to believe it was possible with her. But she didn't fully trust that he could put his need for financial security aside. Aidan knew that was because she knew him, and he wasn't sure he could do it either. Just as he knew her and knew the one thing she feared was not being loved. He loved her, but she needed all of his heart, not just a sliver that wasn't devoted to business. She needed all of it if she were going to risk her own heart. She'd sacrificed her chance at love for security, and Aidan wasn't sure he could be that security when he was still seeking it himself.

"Yer thinking too loudly," she murmured.

"My apologies."

"I'd ask wot ye were thinking, but then ye might tell me."

He smiled. He opened his eyes, and his gaze settled on her shelf of treasures. How many times had they lain in abandoned buildings like this, close together to keep warm, his gaze on the twinkling of the metal treasures she'd collected?

"Looks like you've quite the collection," he said, raising a hand to point lazily at her shelf.

"Nothing too valuable," she said. "Or Roland would send it to a museum or insist we keep it locked up." She sniffed. "As though no one can pick a lock."

He rose on his elbow. "I haven't seen much of this flat, but so far nothing reminds me of you except that shelf," he said. He looked down at her. "May I?"

"Ye really want to get up right now?" she said, her voice sultry.

He chuckled. "I'll come right back." He climbed out of bed and reached for his breeches.

"Oy, if yer leaving my bed, at least let me look at ye."

For some reason that made his cheeks heat, but he dropped the breeches and went to the shelf, aware she was probably staring at his bare arse. At first, Aidan looked at the collection as a businessman might—what was it worth? What could he sell it for? There was a coin worth something and part of what looked to be an earring, but then his gaze caught on the small silver cylinder. No, not silver, he remembered. It was pewter. His pinky finger was too big for it to fit over now, but the scrollwork was still lovely, especially as it had been cleaned. He looked over his shoulder.

"You still have this?"

"My prize possession," she said. "I know wot it is now too."

"What's that?"

She rose and came to stand beside him, taking the object. "The top of a needle case. They still make them today. A seamstress can keep her needles inside and protected. It's not worth any more than the price of the pewter melted down."

"But it has sentimental value," he said. His gaze roamed over a few other pieces. "I remember some of these others as well. But these are new."

She followed his outstretched finger. "Roman coin with Domitia, wife of Emperor Domitian. We found about forty of them on a dig."

"And Chamberlayne let you keep one?"

She shrugged. "I didn't exactly ask."

He laughed. "You'll always be a thief at heart."

"Look who's talking," she shot back. "Yer quite the thief yerself. Now ye steal businesses and make schemes, but it's thieving all the same."

"I won't argue." He put the needle case back and sat on her bed. "And I did my share of stealing in the army."

"Oy! Wot's this?" She put her hands on her hips, which might have looked cocky if she hadn't been naked. "And I thought ye liked the army because ye were sure of three meals a day."

"This was later, when I joined Colonel Draven's troop. We had a special mission and no supply lines. We had to sneak behind enemy lines and buy, beg, or steal what we needed."

"Sounds a lot like the rookeries."

"It was. I hated it." He reached out and wrapped a hand around her waist, pulling her between his legs. "And there was no Jenny to keep me warm at night or boost me through a window. Thirty men counting on me to get horses or bread or pistol balls." He felt her hand under his chin and looked up at her.

"Ye got a faraway look," she said. "Was it awful?"

He swallowed. He'd never talked about it before. Never put his experiences into words. "Yes," he said simply. "There were thirty of us and only twelve came back."

"Ye were lucky," she said.

"Exactly. So many people think I came back because I fought harder or outsmarted the French or was some kind of hero. But it was just luck. That's all it was."

She took his face in her hands. "I 'ope I taught ye something in the rookeries. It might not 'ave been *all* luck."

"You taught me everything I know," he said.

She pursed her lips. "Ye learned a few things on yer own."

"Oh? And what might those be?" He slid his hands from her waist up to her breasts and cupped them.

"I can 'ardly think when ye do that." Her voice was breathless, and he liked it that way. He kissed the valley between her breasts and slid a hand between her legs. She was wet for him, and the feel of the moisture there made his cock come to attention. If Jenny really thought this was the last time, she was fooling herself. And he knew she was no fool.

Before she could come to her senses, he rose, reversed positions, and pushed her back on the bed. Then he knelt between her legs and kissed his way from her ankle to that part of her that was warm and aching for him. When he'd teased her to climax, he turned her over, lifted her hips, and drove into her. She cried out with a *yes* so loud he was afraid the other tenants might bang on their door. At the moment, he didn't care. He drove deep into her as her muscles contracted from the last of her orgasm. When he came, he pulled out and spilled his seed outside her. He wanted her, but he wouldn't cheat to have her. If they decided to have a child, they would decide it together, not because he betrayed her trust.

Aidan bent to catch his breath, shaking his head in disbelief. He'd never once thought of being a father before. What the hell was Jenny doing to him?

Jenny rolled over on the bed and looked up at him, then opened her arms. Aidan forgot to worry about the new direction of his thoughts and went to her, sinking into the heat, scent, and sensations that could only be Jenny.

***

She knew she was dreaming, but her feelings in the dream were as raw as the day she'd felt them. She'd sat on the roof—*their* roof—and watched him walk away. His words rang in her ears. "I'll be back for you. When I make a name for myself. I'll come back with fame and fortune, and I'll take you out of here."

The pain at seeing him go had cut her to the bone. She'd rolled into a ball when he was gone and sobbed for hours. She hadn't eaten for days. She'd wanted to die.

And then she'd made herself stand up and do what she needed to do to survive. In the dream, she walked unseeing through the rookeries, alive physically but dead inside. That was how she'd felt for years—dead inside.

Jenny opened her eyes and tried to move. Aidan's familiar and yet not-so-familiar weight was draped over her. One arm was over her waist and a leg thrown over her thigh.

She felt wetness on her cheeks and realized she'd been crying in her dream and then in reality. When Aidan had left her, it had hurt more than anything else she had ever experienced. Her parents had beaten her, ignored her, and cursed the day she was born. But they'd never loved her, and their curses had meant nothing more than those of a shopkeeper who screamed when she stole a trinket and ran away.

But Aidan had loved her. And she'd loved him. If he could leave her, what did that say about her? The truth was something she didn't like to acknowledge, but it was the reason for her tears now.

She was unlovable. No one would ever really love her.

Why was she putting herself in this position again? Hadn't Aidan shown her once that she would never be loved? Did she need him to show her again?

She wriggled out from under him, slid off the bed, and grabbed a shift, pulling it over her head. Aidan burrowed deeper and muttered, "Too early. Come back to bed."

"Get up," she said and lit the lamp.

His eyes opened. "It's not even dawn."

She flung the bedclothes off him. "Get up."

He pushed the hair off his forehead and squinted at her. "Where are we going?"

"Yer going 'ome."

"What's wrong?" He moved toward the edge of the bed and reached for her, but she evaded his touch. "Jenny, what is this?"

"A mistake. I told ye the other night was the last time. This shouldn't 'ave 'appened."

"It did happen, and I suspect it will keep happening when we're together."

She tossed his breeches at him. "I know. That's why this is good-bye."

Aidan stood and shoved his legs into his breeches. "What did I do?"

"The little girl will 'ear about yer offer and come find ye. Ye don't need me for that. If Roland wants to keep rummaging in yer pantry, then that's 'is choice. I'll not be coming to yer 'ouse again. I'm marrying Roland, and that's that." She tossed his shirt and coat at him.

"Can we talk about this?" he asked, easily catching the garments.

"No. Get out." She moved behind him and gave him a push out of her bedchamber.

"Jenny, I want—"

She jabbed him in the back with one of his boots. "Ye want wot? Tell me. Ye want to marry me? Yer married to yer money, Aidan."

"I can change that," he said, pulling his boots on. "If you give me a chance."

"No."

He looked up at her with those beautiful dark eyes. "So this is how it ends."

"Yes." *This time I tell you good-bye*. She raised her chin. "Good-bye, Aidan." She marched to the door of her flat, opened it, and held it while he gathered the rest of his clothing and stepped into the corridor.

"Jenny—"

She closed the door, locked it, and walked away.

Twelve

"She's weeping again," Oscar said, sounding exasperated. Roland looked up from the ledger he'd been using to catalogue the items from Sterling's trunks. Sterling had ordered them sent to Chamberlayne House two days ago.

"You saw her?" he asked.

"I heard her." Oscar leaned against the door. "I heard her sniffling on the other side of the parlor door."

Roland narrowed his eyes. "How does one hear sniffling?"

"One presses his ear to the door." Oscar gave him an unrepentant look.

Roland shook his head. "Oscar, must I give you another lecture on eavesdropping?"

"Rollie, must I give you another lecture on friendship? Go to her. Find out what's wrong."

Roland sat back on his haunches. "I know what's wrong. Sterling did something to upset her."

"Then go challenge the cur to a duel."

The viscount rolled his eyes. "How long have you been waiting to say that?"

Oscar shrugged. "A few days." He shoved off from the door and went to light a lamp. It had been raining most of the day, and the room was dark. "Fine, no duels. I don't want you killed. But go talk to him again."

"And say what? Don't make Jenny cry? Do you think she'll thank me for interfering once more?"

"No." Oscar sat on the couch and stared at the fabric, books, and various other items scattered about. "But you should at least tell her we're leaving. She still thinks you plan to marry by special license any day."

"I keep thinking she and Sterling will work things out, and she'll cry off."

"Clearly that doesn't appear to be in the cards, so to speak."

"Fine. I'll talk to her." Roland rose and started for the door. Oscar was right behind him. "Where are you off to?"

"I'm coming with you."

"No, you'll stay here. It will be better if I talk to her privately."

"Fine," he agreed quickly. Too quickly.

"Oscar, no putting your ear to the door."

Oscar widened his eyes, all innocence. "I would never!"

Roland took his hand and squeezed it. "I'll tell you everything later."

"You'd better," Oscar said, flopping on the couch like a petulant child. Roland left him, walked across the hall to the parlor where Jenny preferred to work, and tapped on the door. "Come in," she called. She didn't sound like she'd been crying.

Roland opened the door, and as soon as he saw her, he knew Oscar hadn't been wrong. Her gray eyes were rimmed with red, and her cheeks were pink. She sat straight and looked composed, but Roland had known her too long. He wasn't fooled.

"How is the inventory progressing?" she asked, sounding like a perfect lady.

"Very well." He took a seat opposite her. "Any idea why Sterling decided to send it all here?"

"None," she said, her eyes not meeting his.

"Jenny, I can tell you've been crying."

She shook her head. "I'm not crying. Something was in my eye."

Roland studied her. "I've known you more than a decade, and I've seen you cry perhaps once. What has Sterling done?"

"Nothing. I'm through with him. I told you, we said good-bye. I'm ready to marry as soon as you are."

"I don't think you are, actually," he said.

"Wot—what do you mean?"

"This marriage was supposed to be a convenience between friends. Oscar and I could be together without suspicion—or at least less suspicion—and you could live here and have easier access to our finds. But I never intended for our marriage to be the way you run from your problems."

"I don't run from my problems." The look she gave him was rather more menacing than he liked.

He steepled his hand in front of him. "You never did before. Before Aidan Sterling."

Jenny jumped up. "This isn't about 'im—him."

"No?"

"No! He doesn't want to marry me."

"He doesn't? Has he asked?"

"He mentioned it, but 'e—*he*—wasn't thinking with his head, if ye know what I mean."

He smiled. "I think I do. But words said in the heat of passion are not necessarily false."

She walked across the floor, looked out the window, and came back. " 'E didn't ask me, and even if 'e 'ad, I would 'ave said no. I don't want to marry 'im."

"Why not? He's handsome, rich, obviously there is some physical attraction between the two of you, not to mention your shared history."

"Exactly. 'E left me once. 'E'll do it again."

"Ah."

She put her hands on her hips. "Wot's that mean?"

When her face was clouded with that stormy look, Roland found it best to withdraw quietly. "Nothing at all."

"Ye don't think 'e'll leave me? 'E will. 'E said 'e loved me before, but I'm smarter now. I know that's all a lie."

"He didn't love you all those years ago?"

"Course not."

"Because he left or because you think it impossible that anyone might love you?"

She pointed an accusing finger at him. "Don't ye start."

"Do you believe I love you?"

She gave him a startled look as though she truly had not considered it before.

"Do you believe Oscar loves you?"

Her hands dropped from her hips as she seemed to consider what he was saying. "That's different. We're friends. Ye don't love me like ye love Oscar."

"I love you like I love a sister, true. But I do love you."

Her cheeks turned pinker, and she picked at a ribbon on her cream-colored dress. "Wot's this to do with anything? I love ye too. That's why we're marrying. To keep ye safe."

"Jenny," Roland said, "we're not marrying."

Her head jerked up and she stared at him.

"I can't marry you when I know you're in love with someone."

"I'm not—"

"You *are*. It was one thing when there was no one and it didn't seem like there would be anyone—"

"There's still no one!"

"—but now it's different. I can't marry you. I won't let you use this marriage to run from Sterling. When you two do work things out, you'll hate me and wish you were free to be with him."

"I won't. Stop talking like this."

"There's more."

She glared at him, almost challenging him to say it. So he took a deep breath and did. "You know Oscar has always wanted to travel more. This seems like an opportune time. Oscar and I are leaving."

"Without me," she said flatly.

"Yes."

"When will ye be back?"

"I don't know. Years, perhaps?"

"Wot?"

"It's not safe for us here."

"It could be if ye'd just listen to me and get the bloody license."

"And if you would just listen to me and go talk to your Aidan, then you'll be that closer to thanking me for doing this."

"Thank ye for leaving me?" she shouted. Roland flinched. Oscar would not need to eavesdrop if she continued at that volume. "And wot am I supposed to do now?"

"Why should you do anything different than you have? You don't need me. Half the requests we receive for appraisal are addressed to you. You've earned your reputation, and you may continue to work out of Chamberlayne House if you like. I'll keep a skeleton staff here to look after things."

The look she gave him cut him to the bone. Roland almost felt sorry for Aidan Sterling because if the look she gave him now was anything like what she'd given Sterling all those years ago, it must have cost him half his heart to walk away from her.

"I'm not leaving because I don't love you, Jenny," he said. "I'm leaving because I do."

"Yer just like 'im. Like all the rest," she said, lifting her skirts and starting for the door.

"Where are you going? Our ship doesn't sail for days yet. Let's talk about this, Jenny. Oscar wants to talk to you."

She ignored him, opened the door, and stepped out of the way as Oscar toppled inside. Roland sighed and directed a look of annoyance in Oscar's direction. Oscar gave a sheepish shrug.

Jenny went around Oscar, and Roland heard her boots clicking on the marble of the foyer. A moment later, a door crashed, making the house shake.

"That seemed like it went well," Oscar said.

"Better than I expected, actually," Roland said. "Probably best to give her a day to soothe her ruffled feathers."

"I hope she doesn't do anything drastic."

"Jenny? She's not the type."

***

"I don't want excuses," Aidan told the manager cowering in front of him.

"But, sir," the manager whined. "The ship sunk in a storm. I can't sell spices at the bottom of the ocean. We're fortunate the crew wasn't lost."

"I hope they don't expect to be paid if they come ashore without their cargo."

"Sir, I will file with the insurance company. The cargo was insured."

"*I'll* file with the insurance company, Mr. Kettering. *You'll* need to find another position. Now out of my office."

"But, sir!"

"Pryce," Aidan said, turning his back to Kettering and staring out the window of the building. It overlooked Bond Street.

"Mr. Kettering, would you come with me, please," Pryce, his private secretary, said.

"How can he blame me for a typhoon? That's why we have insurance."

"Come with me, please," Pryce said, his tone soothing.

The door closed behind the two men and Aidan swore, lifted a model of the lost ship and threw it against the wall, shattering it into tiny pieces. He knew it wasn't Kettering's fault the ship was lost, but he didn't care. He'd been in a foul mood for three days and the last thing he needed was being told he'd lost twenty thousand pounds. What he probably needed was sleep, but that seemed lost to him as well. Every time he went home and laid his head on the pillow, he thought about Jenny. He'd almost gone to her half a dozen times, but he knew better. She'd told him to get out, and she'd meant it. Now he'd probably have to wait another thirteen years before he saw her again. Because that's what these last thirteen years had been—he'd been waiting to see her again. He hadn't realized it until he'd been on his way home from her flat, the sky lightening as the sun came up. But all those years he'd tried to fill the void in his life with the army or making money because without Jenny, he had nothing.

Someone tapped on his door. Aidan stared out the window. "Come."

"Sir?" It was Pryce. "Should I cancel the meeting with the Bainbridge investors?"

Aidan glared at him over his shoulder. "Why?"

"No reason, sir. I'll ready the conference room, shall I?"

Aidan waved a hand. He couldn't care less. He'd go in and convince them to give him more money. That was what he was good at. Rain came down in sheets outside the window, and men hurried past with black umbrellas over their heads.

Another tap at the door. "Now what?"

The door opened. "The conference room can't be ready yet," he said, rounding on Pryce with an angry retort. But it wasn't Pryce. It was Jenny, wet hair streaming down her cheeks and mouth flattened in a tight, angry line.

"What the devil?"

She stomped in, trailing water with her soggy hem. Her dress was cream and clung to her body. The sleeves and the upper part of the bodice were almost sheer, showing patches of skin beneath. "How dare ye?" she spat.

Aidan finally closed his mouth and ceased gawking. He crossed the room in two strides, took her arm, and brought her close to the hearth. Her skin was cold. "You'll catch your death," he said.

She gave him a weary look. "A bit of water never killed me before." She yanked her arm away from him. "Don't change the subject. I want to know 'ow ye did it. 'Ow did ye convince 'im to leave?"

She wasn't making any sense. "Pryce!" he bellowed. "Pryce! I need a blanket and tea."

"I told ye, I'm fine," she said, giving him a shove to prove it. "But ye'll soon be missing parts of yer anatomy if ye don't go tell Roland 'e can stay."

"Tell Roland he can stay?" Aidan repeated slowly.

"Sir?" Pryce was at the door. His eyes widened when he spotted Jenny dripping on the floor. "Shall I dispense with this…person?"

"Ye go ahead and try it!" Jenny said, taking a menacing step toward Pryce, whose steel gray hair seemed to turn white as Aidan watched.

"Pryce, hot tea and a blanket, please," Aidan said. He wasn't certain if his secretary's eyes widened this time because of the request or the *please* he added at the end. But there was no denying that his mood had improved as soon as Jenny had entered.

"Yes, sir." Pryce turned on his heel and walked away. Aidan crossed to the door, closed it, and turned back to Jenny.

"Do you want to tell me what this is about? If you wanted to see me, you could have sent a note. I would have come to you and spared you the trek in this weather."

She put her hands on her hips. "I'm not some 'elpless lady who sits in 'er drawing room all day fretting about a bit of a drizzle."

Aidan glanced at the window through which he could see nothing due to the heavy rain pouring down.

"And don't pretend ye don't know why I'm 'ere."

"All right." He clenched his hands, wishing he had the blanket already so he could wrap it about her shoulders. He didn't care what she said, she was cold. He could see her shivering, and her lips looked decidedly blue. "The truth is,

I'm not pretending. I didn't think I'd see you again after you kicked me out of your bed a few days ago."

"So ye decided to punish me by sending Roland away."

"I didn't send Lord Chamberlayne anywhere. I haven't seen or spoken to him in days."

Her eyes narrowed.

"The most I've done is send a note with the contents of the larder. In the note, I requested he send me an inventory and appraisal of the contents of the trunk before he made it public."

There was another tap at the door and Pryce entered carrying a blanket, followed by a clerk with the tea tray. "Pryce," Aidan said. "What did the note I had you send to Viscount Chamberlayne say? Can you paraphrase it here?"

"Of course, sir."

While Pryce recited the note, saying almost exactly what Aidan had related a moment before, he took the blanket and wrapped it around Jenny's shoulders. She batted his hands away but held on to the blanket and sniffed.

"Is there anything else, sir?" Pryce asked.

"No, you may go."

"Sir, the Bainbridge investors will be here in a quarter hour," Pryce said, glancing at Jenny.

"Tell them we'll reschedule."

"Very good, sir. And your lunch with the Chancellor of the Exchequer?"

"Cancel it," Aidan said sharply. "Cancel everything."

Pryce stared at him for a long moment, obviously not believing his ears.

"That will be all, Pryce," Aidan said. "You." He pointed to the clerk who shrank back. "Leave the tea cart."

Pryce ushered the clerk out and closed the door again. Aidan went to the tea cart, poured a generous cup of tea for Jenny then looked at her. "I have no idea how you take it."

"Black." She crossed to his desk and sat behind it. Aidan frowned at her presumption but thought it better not to argue. He set the tea on the corner of his desk and watched her lift it and cradle it in her cold hands. He sat down across from her, in the chair reserved for guests.

"Now what's this about Chamberlayne leaving? I thought you were to be married."

She waved a hand as though dismissing the idea. " 'E won't marry me."

Aidan knew he should try to express some sympathy, but the vise around his lungs—the tightness he hadn't even known was there—suddenly loosened, and he could breathe for the first time in days.

"I can see ye smiling. Ye might as well stop trying to 'ide it."

He cleared his throat and used the excuse to put a hand over his mouth. "I am sorry. Why won't he marry you?"

"Because 'e says I'm in love with ye. But I'm not."

Aidan clutched the arms of his chair and tried to catch his breath. He felt as though all the air had been knocked out of him, and he hadn't felt that way since…since the first time she'd told him she loved him.

"And he doesn't believe you don't love me," Aidan said, when he was able to breathe again.

" 'E thinks 'e's being lofty by calling off the wedding. Says 'e doesn't want me to make a mistake. But if we call off the wedding, 'e and Oscar 'ave to leave the country. They're sailing to the Continent."

"Jenny, I'm sorry," Aidan said and meant it. "I had nothing to do with this. If there's some way to help—"

"The way to 'elp was for me to marry 'im. Now I may never see 'im again. Thanks to ye!"

Aidan sat back surprised at the venom in her voice. But then Chamberlayne was probably her only true friend. He was like a brother to her, and now she was losing him. He couldn't imagine her grief. "Maybe if I talk to him. He could go to one of my country houses, stay out of Society for a few months—"

"I think ye've done enough." She tossed the blanket off and stood. "I'll thank ye to stay out of this."

Aidan jumped up, reaching the door before she did. He'd walked out of her life once before and thought he would never see her again. Now she was walking out of his life. He couldn't let this happen without saying something, without trying to convince her to stay.

"Get out of my way."

"I will, but I want to say something first. Have you considered that Chamberlayne is doing this because he cares about you? Because he wants the best for you?"

"That's what 'e said. And ye know wot?" She glared at Aidan. "I'm tired of everyone else thinking they know wot's best for me."

"Fine. Then I won't tell you what I think. I'll tell you what I feel."

She went still at those words, her gray eyes becoming steely. It wasn't exactly the most encouraging expression, but Aidan plowed onward. "I still love you, Jenny. Yes, I left you, but I did as I promised. I came back for you. I searched for you for weeks. I tried everything I could to find you. I thought you were dead." His voice broke, and he thought her expression softened slightly.

"You were safe with Chamberlayne by that time. But I didn't know that. I thought I'd never see you again, but now that I have, I can't let you go again. These past days without you, I've been miserable. I know you think the only thing I love is money, but if you give me a chance, I'll show you that I love you more."

She said nothing. Did nothing. Aidan got on one knee. He was nothing if not a risk-taker. "Jenny Tate, will you do me the honor of becoming my wife?"

She stared at him, and he thought he might have seen the shimmer of tears in her eyes. And then she gazed into his eyes and said, "No."

She swept past him, opened the door, and gave a small gasp. Aidan had expected her to stomp away, but instead he turned to see Pryce standing outside, his hand on the shoulder of a small child. "I'm dreadfully sorry to interrupt, sir," Pryce said, showing no reaction to the fact that Aidan was kneeling on the ground. Aidan rose slowly. "But this person says it needs to see you, and nothing we have said or done will dissuade it."

"Wot's this then?" Jenny asked instantly moving closer to the wet child in rags. "Wot ye need 'im for?" She jerked a thumb back at Aidan.

"I'm 'ere to collect me money," the child said.

Jenny looked at Aidan, who shook his head.

"Shall I try throwing it out? Again?" Pryce asked.

"Oy! Not until I get me money. Ye promised." The child—a girl, Aidan thought—pointed at him. "Name is 'Arley. Ye owe me."

Thirteen

Jenny gasped. " 'Arley?" she said. "Yer 'Arley?"

"Who wants to know?" the girl said, sounding suspicious.

"Sir?" the gray-haired man who worked for Aidan said again. "What shall I do with it?"

"Bring her inside and fetch refreshments," Jenny said, using her lady's tone and accent. "And be quick about it. We'll need another blanket."

Aidan seemed to understand what she had planned because he opened the door wider, showing the fire and tea tray. "Won't you come in and warm yourself?"

"I just want me blunt," Harley said.

"I'll have to send for it. I don't have ten pounds in my pocket."

Jenny doubted that. He probably had twice that lying about, but she didn't argue. Instead, she entered the room first and moved closer to the fire. She was cold and shivering, and she'd never admit as much to Aidan, but she wouldn't mind more tea and a cake or two.

"It were twenty pounds," Harley said, following her into the room and moving close to the fire. "Not ten."

Jenny nodded. "That's right. It was twenty."

Aidan gave her a narrow look. "I said ten."

She shrugged. "I said twenty, and she's 'ere now."

The girl looked up at her. "Ye one of them or one of us? Ye keep changing yer voice."

Jenny wasn't quite sure how to respond to that as she was a bit of both. "I'm somewhere in-between, I suppose. I used to be like ye and now I'm a little more like 'im."

Aidan made a strangled sound, but she ignored him.

"I didn't want to come," the girl said. "Everyone told me it were a trick. Is it a trick?"

Jenny considered. "It is in a way. 'E will give ye the money, but we wanted to talk to ye too."

"Is this about the orphanage? That nob FitzRoy with the pretty wife is always trying to catch me and put me there." She wiped her nose, which was running. " 'Is wife is a nice lady, but I'm not going to no orphanage."

"Sit down and 'ave a cup of tea," Jenny said, indicating a chair close to the fire. "I'm freezing and a body can't think when it's shivering."

Harley looked at the chair and then at Jenny. "I'll ruin it. I'm wet and dirty."

"Oh, that's alright," Jenny said cheerfully. " 'E can buy another." She shepherded Harley to the chair and ignored the glare Aidan gave her as Harley plopped her soggy behind on the expensive upholstery. Jenny poured a cup of tea and handed it to the girl, but she looked at it suspiciously.

" 'Ow do I know ye didn't put something unnatural in it?"

"Suspicious little creature," Aidan muttered.

"Fine. I'll drink it too." Jenny poured herself a cup, sipped, then nodded at Harley. But the girl narrowed her eyes.

" 'Ow do I know ye really drank it? Maybe it's a trick."

Jenny had to give the girl credit. She had street smarts and would not be an easy mark. Jenny moved closer to the child and fought not to wrinkle her nose. She smelled of the streets, which was a scent Jenny remembered well and did not like to revisit. She made a show of drinking the tea so that Harley could see it enter her mouth and then she swallowed it. When Harley frowned, Jenny rolled her eyes and opened her mouth to show it was empty.

That seemed to be all the encouragement Harley needed. She drank the tea and then held out the cup for more. Jenny looked at Aidan, who gave a pained expression and filled the teacup again. "Anything else?" he asked. Either Harley didn't note the sarcastic tone of his voice or she didn't care because she pointed to the tea tray.

"One of them sandwiches."

Fearing a mutiny on Aidan's part, Jenny rose and brought the plate of cakes and sandwiches to Harley. The girl took it but then looked at Jenny. "Do ye want me to take a nibble of each?" Jenny asked.

"Just..." She took her time deciding. "This one." She pointed to a small biscuit, and Jenny lifted it, took a bite, and smiled. Harley downed the rest of her tea, set the cup aside, and started inhaling the food. Jenny stepped away to stand next to Aidan. In unspoken agreement, they moved away from Harley, toward the rain-streaked window.

"Wot do ye think we should do next?"

"With her?" He shrugged. "Take her to the orphanage. Let's get that done so we can finish our discussion."

"Wot discussion? Ye asked me to marry ye and I said no. 'Ow many times do ye want me to reject ye?" She didn't want to admit that his admission that he'd gone back for her had affected her. He hadn't forgotten her. He'd kept his promise to come back. Clenching her fists, Jenny reminded himself that none of that mattered. He'd left her once, and she wouldn't let him do it again.

His look was steely. "None. That's why we need to talk."

"I said all I 'ave to say. And if we take her to the orphanage, she'll just run away. We'll be right back where we started."

"No, we won't. FitzRoy will see I tried, and that will be the end of it."

"I thought 'e was yer friend. This is 'ow ye treat yer friends?"

Aidan closed his eyes briefly. "Fine. What do you suggest?"

"Well." She straightened her shoulders. "Since ye asked."

"I won't like this. I can already tell."

"I suggest we take 'er 'ome."

"Whose home?" His brow furrowed. "Not *my* home." The look on his face was one of complete and utter abhorrence, and Jenny had to bite the inside of her cheek to keep from laughing. Oh, she was even more determined to bring the child to his home now. It served him right for all that he'd done to her. She had everything planned out, everything just right, until he'd come along. Now her only friends were forced to leave England, not only leaving her alone but jeopardizing her income. Could she really manage the business on her own? Roland had always taken the lead in that area, and now thanks to Aidan, she would soon have the entire weight of it on her shoulders.

"Ye 'ave enough room," she said. "Why not?"

"Why not?" He seemed to be searching for a reason, and she could almost see when he snatched one out of the air. "I can't have a young girl in my house unchaperoned."

"She's 'ardly a girl. She's a street urchin."

"Which makes her even more vulnerable. She should go to your home."

"Oh no, ye don't. This is *yer* problem. I won't solve it for ye."

Aidan looked like he wanted to argue, but he swallowed instead and nodded. "Fine." Taking a deep breath, he approached Harley, who had almost finished with the tray of food. "Miss Harley."

"I ain't no miss. Just 'Arley."

"Very well, Just Harley."

The girl gave a small smile at his quip.

"You said you do not want to go to the orphanage. I understand your suspicion of orphanages. I'd like to you to see it before you decide. What would you think of coming home with me and touring the orphanage tomorrow?"

"Nope. I just want me twenty quid."

A look came into Aidan's eyes that Jenny knew well. It was what she assumed his business adversaries saw when they sat across the table from him. "I'll give you ten now and ten after you tour the orphanage."

"That weren't the deal," she said, standing and glaring at him. "I was to come 'ere, and I got twenty quid."

Aidan lifted a shoulder. "I'm changing the deal." He moved around the desk, opened a drawer, and withdrew a stack of notes. He took his time flipping through them as Harley's eyes widened. Jenny could see her counting the money, just as Jenny would have done in her place. Finally, he took a ten-pound note from the stack, put the money back, and closed the drawer.

"I thought ye said ye didn't 'ave the money with ye."

"I said I didn't have it in my pocket." He held out the ten pounds. "As you see, I don't."

Harley snatched the note and stuffed it in her dirty shirt.

"Now," Aidan said, "you can take that money and go or tour the orphanage and receive another ten pounds."

" 'Ow do I know this isn't a trick?"

"You don't, but if you know anything about me—and I assume you did your research before you came calling—you know I can be trusted to keep my word. I do business with the richest men in London. In the world. They wouldn't even look at me if I couldn't be trusted."

Harley seemed to consider then looked at Jenny. "That true?"

Jenny considered. Aidan had always kept his word to her—except the once. And then he had tried to keep it, in his own way. She saw that now. "Yes. That's true."

"I ain't going to 'is 'ome alone. I'll go if ye come with me."

"Capital idea," Aidan said. Jenny glared at him then gave a loud sigh.

"I'll go and 'elp ye settle in."

Harley shook her head. "Ye 'ave to stay as long as I do. I 'eard of girls being taken off the street and sold to brothels or worse."

Jenny looked at Harley who was as skinny as a lamp post and just as flat-chested. She seemed an unlikely candidate to be sold to a brothel, but then there were men who lusted after children. Harley was not wrong to be careful. What she didn't know was that by asking Jenny to stay with her at Aidan's, she was putting Jenny at risk—not physically, no. But it would be easier to protect her heart from Aidan if she wasn't under the same roof.

Jenny gritted her teeth. "Fine. I'll stay as long as ye stay," she grumbled.

"And ye promise not to let 'im force me into the orphanage?"

"I promise," Jenny said. "Let the devil dance on my grave if I'm lying."

Harley seemed to consider just as Aidan's secretary tapped on the door then entered with more tea and a stack of blankets. Jenny took them and draped one over Harley and took one for herself. Her fingers were no longer blue, but she was still shivering. Harley reached for the plate of food. "I'll take that."

The secretary made a sound, but Aidan flicked his hand, and the secretary closed his lips. "Anything else, sir?" he said through a clenched jaw.

"Call for my carriage, Pryce. I'm to escort these two ladies home."

***

Aidan watched Harley look out his window with her mouth agape. He imagined she looked something like Jenny would have looked if she'd been given a ride in a carriage like this at the age of ten, which was the age he guessed Harley to be.

He tried not to think about what stains she might be leaving on the expensive velvet squabs, but fortunately the blanket was between most of her and the upholstery. Still, he would have to have the entire vehicle cleaned and aired out. He'd already decided the child must have a bath as soon as they arrived home, and he knew it would be an issue. One thing he'd learned living in the rookeries was that baths were a luxury, and some were suspicious of bathing.

Jenny hadn't been. Whenever they found clean water, she would dip a rag and wash her face and neck and hands. But clean water was hard to come by and they were usually so dirty by the time they did come across some that it seemed hopeless, and they chose to drink it instead.

"Will there be more of them tea cakes at yer 'ouse?" Harley asked.

"There might be," Aidan said. "But you'll have to wash and change before I allow you to sit on any of my furniture."

Harley looked down at herself. "Why? The rain washed away most of the grime."

"Not enough of it. You'll have to bathe, and we'll burn those clothes."

"Oh no, ye won't!"

"We'll find ye something else to wear first," Jenny said, her voice calm and soothing, though her gray eyes flashed silver lightning in his direction. "Will ye wear a dress or do ye prefer trousers?"

"She'll wear a dress," Aidan said. Jenny flashed those eyes at him again. Perhaps he said it just so she would.

"I've worn a dress before," Harley said. " 'Ard to climb in and out of windows in skirts, though."

"And why might you need to climb in and out of windows?" Aidan asked.

Harley raised a brow. "No reason."

"Fine. We'll get ye skirts and trousers. Then ye can choose," Jenny said.

Aidan added skirts and trousers to the long list of things he would need to make sure were either produced or procured before he could pull Jenny aside and speak to her alone. The one thing about Harley that pleased him was the child had given him more time with Jenny.

He should be annoyed that his meetings for the day were cancelled, and he was dragged away from his offices. But truth be told, he didn't mind. He was with Jenny, and that was more important than any business ventures he'd had planned.

The thought shocked him. He couldn't remember when anything had been more important to him than making money. But at this moment, there was nowhere in the world he'd rather be.

"Oooh! Look at that big 'ouse!" Harley said.

"Just wait," Jenny muttered.

"Harley," Aidan said. "That's an unusual name. Is it your given name?"

"Sure. Given to me 'cause no one 'arley sees me." She made a swaying sort of slithery motion with her body. "In and out of the dark like a shadow. That's me."

Aidan frowned. "But you can't see a shadow in the dark. You need light for that."

"Exactly." Harley pointed at him.

Aidan decided the argument was pointless. "Harley was the name given to you in the rookeries. What name did your parents give you?"

"Wot's it matter?"

"I'd like to know."

She crossed her arms. "Well, I don't remember. Never had much use fer me parents anyway."

Jenny exchanged a look with Aidan, and he nodded. The girl was lying, but they'd not force the information out of her. They'd have to gain her trust, and Jenny was more likely to accomplish that than he. He added another two tasks to his mental list: discover Harley's real name and find out what happened to her parents.

Harley had a predictable reaction when she was admitted into his home. Her jaw dropped to her knees, and she wanted to know how much everything cost. Aidan could have told her, precisely, how much everything in the house cost, but instead he sent Jenny and a maid with her to bathe. He gave his housekeeper the task of finding something for Harley and Jenny to wear. Then he went into his library, sat at his desk, and opened letters that had arrived earlier that day. But he couldn't read a single one. The words just swam in front of his face as though the rain still slapping against the windows outside had blurred the ink on the paper.

His gaze strayed to the windows where Jenny's desk had been. It was gone now as were the pigeons, and though he'd always relished his solitude, he wished both were back. He wished Jenny were here. He wished the two of them could sit in companionable silence again—well, at least he had been silent. She was forever exclaiming over something in the journals. Aidan wondered what would happen to the find from his larder now that Chamberlayne and his lover were to travel abroad. Would it be returned to him? Had anything of value been discovered?

It showed just how much Jenny had distracted him that these issues had not occurred to him before. He was never one to allow an opportunity to make a profit to go unexplored. Jenny had done what he didn't think was possible: distracted him from business and profit. It was nothing new. She'd always been able to make him forget that he was hungry or cold or miserable. She'd made poverty bearable. Now Aidan realized it was more than that. She'd made his miserable existence bearable, worthwhile even.

Now his existence was far from miserable, but these past few days without her in his life, it had lacked any color or flavor or meaning. He needed her. Before she'd come back into his life, he'd been an empty shell of a man, but he hadn't known it or perhaps he'd only sensed it. Now he knew he was nothing without her. And he was about to lose her and face a lifetime of nothingness.

"That was an ordeal," a familiar voice said, and Aidan looked up from the yawning maw of blackness that was his future. It was Jenny, of course, and she was dressed in the simple garb of a servant, the black color of the dress making her look pale and wan. Her dark hair had been pulled back and secured at the nape of her neck, showing the fine bones of her cheeks and jaw.

He could hear the fire in the hearth crackle and pop softly and realized the rain must have eased to a drizzle. Aidan rose hastily to his feet. "Where is Harley?"

"In the nursery."

"I have a nursery?"

"It's not furnished as such—in fact, it's not furnished at all—but yer 'ousekeeper said it was the chamber best suited to that purpose and asked yer footmen to move two beds inside."

"Two?"

"One for me and one for 'Arley."

For a moment the tightness in his chest eased. "You're staying then?"

"One night." She held up a single finger. "I promised 'Arley I would. Just until she gets a look at the orphanage."

Aidan moved around his desk. "I need to find out her real name and discover what's happened to her parents."

Jenny leaned against the door, not seeming inclined to come any further into the room or any closer to him. "Then find it out. That's yer problem, not mine. I left 'er eating from a tray of vittles stacked to the ceiling. If ye offer 'er sweets, she'll probably tell ye anything."

"I think you're more likely to get answers from her than I."

"Thanks to ye, I 'ave a business to run and no time for games." She cocked her head. "Wot's that?"

Aidan had heard the clicking sound as well. "Rain on the windows."

She started across the room, toward the windows her desk had once overlooked. "I don't think so." She reached the curtains and opened the drapes. Aidan saw nothing but darkness, but Jenny turned the latch and opened the window.

"What are you—"

A pigeon hopped inside, a small sack on its back.

"Peggy!" Jenny looked outside, presumably for more birds, then closed the window. "Clever girl," she said, stroking the pigeon.

Aidan looked at the window then the bird. "Why is there a bird tapping on my windowpane?"

"Roland must have trained 'er," Jenny said, opening the sack on the bird's back and removing a slip of damp paper.

"Trained her to do what?"

"To see this as 'ome. She's a 'oming pigeon. She always returns to 'er 'ome." She drew in a sudden breath.

"What is it?"

" 'E 'as tickets on a ship leaving in two days."

"Who? Chamberlayne?" Aidan moved behind her, looking at the paper over her shoulder. He shouldn't enjoy this closeness. She was obviously distraught. He should be comforting her, not thinking of how he might seduce her.

" 'E wants my permission to spread it about that I ended the betrothal."

"That's good of him," Aidan said. "It spares you any questions about your character."

She rounded on him. "And creates a dozen about 'im! Now everyone will ask why I ended it. What if the rumors about Oscar surface again?"

"Ah. Good point." She glared at him, and he took a step back and raised his hands. "I admit I don't know everything about the mechanisms of Society, but I have friends. I'll ask their advice."

"No."

"No?"

"Ye can't tell them the truth about Roland."

"Give me *some* credit."

She bit her lip then slowly nodded her head. "Ye'll go tonight?"

"In this weather?" He gestured toward the window.

"Oh! Yer so fine now ye can't get a bit of water on yerself?" She put her hands on her hips.

"That's not it." At least that wasn't all of it. "I don't want to leave you and Harley."

She took his arm and tugged him toward the door to the library. "We'll be 'ere when ye return."

Aidan dug his heels in. "And you'll try to discover her name?"

"Always trying to make a deal. Fine. I'll see if I can find out 'er name. Ye tell yer friends we 'ave 'er and ask 'ow to save Roland. But don't ask it that way, if ye know what I mean. Be subtle."

Aidan took her shoulders and looked down at her. "I know what to do. You'll wait up for me?"

She narrowed her eyes. "Just to talk."

"Of course." He tried to look innocent. Tried to look as though he wasn't mentally stripping that maid's uniform off her, but the way her eyes narrowed further made him think he didn't quite succeed.

She gave him a push. "Go then."

And Aidan, who took orders from no one, went.

***

At the Draven Club he didn't find Neil Wraxall, who was married to Lady Juliana, daughter of the Earl St. Maur. Lady Juliana was benefactress of the Sunnybrooke Home for Boys, where Colin FitzRoy had tried to persuade Harley to go. Aidan sat at a table to write a note to Neil, informing him of his plans to visit, just as the Duke of Mayne stepped into the room. Aidan looked up in time to see the duke try to retreat without being noticed.

"Too late," Aidan said.

Mayne's shoulders slumped. "Listen, Sterling. The Lords just adjourned, and it's been a long night. All I want is a drink and quiet. I don't want to discuss tariffs or taxes or shipping insurance."

"Fine," Aidan said. "I give you my word, I won't mention anything to do with business."

"Forgive me if I have my doubts," the duke said.

Aidan sat back. "I really have been an arse, haven't I? Lately, every time I see you—any of you"—he gestured to the empty reading room—"I have an agenda."

Phineas moved closer to the chair Aidan occupied. "That does seem to be the case of late."

"No wonder you tried to avoid me."

"I wouldn't say we avoid you."

Aidan gave him a look, and Phineas smiled. He had boyish good looks, and when he smiled, he looked particularly mischievous. "Alright, we avoid you. These past few months, you've been…obsessed." He sat opposite Aidan and gestured to the paper on the small side table between their armchairs. "What's that? Your plan to take over the Continent?"

"A note to Neil. I found that little orphan Colin's been looking for, and I'm taking her for a tour of the orphanage tomorrow."

Porter entered just then with a tray and a bottle of wine.

"Is that the '89?" Mayne asked.

"Yes, Your Grace," Porter answered. "I took the liberty of bringing two glasses in case Mr. Sterling might also like to sample it."

Aidan hadn't intended to have anything stronger than coffee, but in the past, he'd found Phineas an excellent judge of wine. "Very well," he said and took a glass. When the wine had been poured and sampled—it was indeed very good—Mayne peered at him over the rim of the glass.

"What's happened to you?"

"What do you mean?"

"You aren't prodding me about tariffs, you rescued an orphan, and you're here, rather than at your office."

"Nothing has happened. I came because—" He looked at Mayne. A duke would certainly know everything there was to know about Society's rules. "I had a question."

"For whom?"

"You'll do."

Phineas sipped his wine. "I'm honored, as usual."

"Here is the situation, a lady and gentleman wish to call off their engagement. The lady is concerned about casting the gentleman in a bad light. But the gentleman insists on the lady calling off the betrothal to spare her reputation. Is there any way she might also spare his?"

"That's the most cordial ending of a betrothal I've ever heard. Perhaps they shouldn't call it off at all."

"It's done. Now there's just the scandal rags to manage."

Mayne sipped his wine again. "The gentleman is right to allow the lady to jilt him. If he jilts her, she'll be deemed unmarriageable. I don't see why her calling it off should be any blight on him, though. Everyone thinks ladies are fickle and indecisive. No one will blame a man for a female's capricious whims."

Aidan sat back. "It's a good thing no women are about to hear you say that. We'd both lose our heads."

Phineas smiled. "I didn't say *I* thought that about women. My wife is the cleverest person I know. She's more decisive and logical than I ever have been, but we're not talking about how my wife would react. We're speaking of the *ton* as a body."

"Agreed. And let us say, for argument's sake, that there is a need to protect the gentleman from unseemly rumors. How might that be accomplished?"

"That's easy enough. The lady should make the reason for the break public in advance of the announcement. If the reason is something benign, then in all likelihood, that will be the end of the rumors."

"You could have done very well in business," Aidan said.

Mayne shrugged. "My ancestors would turn in their graves if I ever did a day's labor for wages. I do agree that it takes the same sort of cunning to survive in Society as to negotiate the purchase of a company. It's all about making the other party believe the truth as you see it."

"Agreed." Aidan rose. "I should have this letter sent and return home."

"Of course. It was good to have a drink with you, Aidan," Mayne said. "Let's do it again soon."

"Of course." He started away, surprised at the pleasant feeling flowing through him at the duke's compliment.

"And let me know when I'll be introduced."

Aidan turned back. "Introduced to whom?" he asked the duke.

"To the lady breaking her betrothal for you."

Fourteen

Jenny was not sleepy. Harley had fallen asleep almost as soon as she'd been put to bed. The child was clean, warm, dry, and fed. It was no surprise that she was fast asleep. Jenny hoped she felt safe enough to sleep soundly the entire night. For years after leaving the rookeries, Jenny had problems sleeping. Even though she had known she was finally safe, her mind had not accepted that fact right away.

But fear was not keeping her awake tonight. The nursery was cozy and her bed comfortable, but the rain pattered on the window and the fire crackled and cast shadows on the unfamiliar walls. And, of course, she couldn't seem to stop her ears from straining to hear when Aidan returned. It seemed he had been gone for hours when the clock on the mantel had only chimed midnight a short while earlier.

She thought she heard the clip-clop of horse hooves on the road outside, and she sat, listening closely. The rain had kept all but the most dedicated revelers home this evening, and she'd not heard another carriage in a while. Below, she

365

heard the murmur of voices and the sound of a door closing. Jenny's heart beat faster. Aidan was home.

She forced herself to lie back down. It did not matter that he was home. He'd ruined her entire life. She had everything planned. She'd planned to marry Roland and take a lover and continue appraising antiquities. Now nothing would go as she'd expected. She was nothing if not adaptable, but it rankled that Aidan should make her adapt again. He'd turned her life upside down once before. How could she believe that though he proposed marriage, he wouldn't just leave her again?

He said he loved her. Still. But anyone who spent a quarter hour with him knew his one true love was money. He surrounded himself with luxury and had had two or three of everything. He'd never have enough to truly feel secure.

She'd never be enough to give him security.

She heard footsteps outside the door, and knew they were Aidan's. He'd asked her to wait up for him. She could pretend to be asleep, postpone the conversation until the morning. But when the door opened, and Aidan's silhouette was clear, she sat, put a finger to her lips and crept out of bed, wrapping her robe securely around the thick nightgown she'd been given. Jenny had never been able to resist him. She didn't know why she thought she would have the strength now.

Once outside the bedchamber, Aidan drew her away from the door. "Is she sleeping?" he whispered. His dark hair was wet from the rain, and he'd slicked it back from his face, outlining the strong cheekbones and square jaw already dabbled with stubble. His dark eyes were especially dark tonight.

"She fell asleep as soon as 'er 'ead 'it the pillow," Jenny whispered back. "And no, I didn't find out 'er real name. I'll need more than a few 'ours for that."

"Let's speak somewhere in private," Aidan said. "I have an idea for how to handle the betrothal." He looked about. "Shall we go to the library?"

She was sick of that library and all the arguments they'd had there. "I don't want to traipse about in my nightwear for all the footmen to gawk at."

"My bedchamber then? It's on the other side of the landing. We can use the sitting room."

She remembered his chamber did have a grouping of chairs away from the bed. She imagined the idea had been to host close friends or family in an informal setting. Still, spending time in his bed chamber had its perils. The bed would be right there. Tempting her.

"Fine," she said. "Let's make this quick."

Inside the bedchamber, Aidan lit several lamps and Jenny took a seat in a large armchair that all but swallowed her. She left the more ornamental one for Aidan. He went to a side table and offered her a glass of wine. She took it, hoping it would help her sleep.

"Ye aren't 'aving a glass?" she asked.

"Not right now. I spoke with a friend of mine, the Duke of Mayne."

"Never 'eard of 'im."

"He's rich and a duke, which serves our purposes." He explained the duke's suggestion, and Jenny nodded.

"Smart fellow, this duke. Easiest to say something in front of the servants and start the news flowing that way. And we can mention it in front of Lady Juliana at the orphanage tomorrow."

"And what reason will you give for calling off the wedding?"

"Let's say 'e went to join an excavation in Venice, and I didn't want to postpone the wedding or live in Italy. That's the sort of thing Society will believe."

"It is, yes." He'd rested a hand on the side table, and now his fingers traced the carvings in the wood absently. Jenny couldn't seem to stop looking at those fingers and imagining him tracing her body. "Now that you're a free woman—or will be soon—would you reconsider my proposal?"

She pulled her gaze away from his fingers. "I didn't say no because of Roland."

"You said no because you were angry." His fingers stopped their movements, and he looked directly at her.

"I said no because I don't want to marry ye."

"Because I left you all those years ago?" He came toward her, and she wished she had chosen the ornamental chair. It would have made extricating herself easier now.

"Exactly. Ye left me once and will do it again. Money is wot ye love." She gestured to the expansive chamber and all the luxuries.

He knelt before her, effectively blocking her escape. "*You* are what I love. These past few days, I came to realize that all of this means nothing without you."

"It'll come to mean plenty again if ye 'ave me. Ye only want me because I said no. Ye 'ate not getting wot ye want."

"That's true enough, but I will always want you, Jenny. I will never leave you again." He took her hands in his. "I think you want me too. You're just afraid."

"I'm not afraid of the likes of ye."

"No, but you're afraid of love. You don't trust it. You're afraid to risk your heart."

"Ye assume I 'ave a 'eart."

He smiled, and oh that smile was her undoing. Such a crooked, smoldering smile. "You have a heart. Somewhere in there." His hand brushed her chest, and she grasped it and held it for a moment before she moved it over her breast.

"This is lust between us. Nothing more."

"You keep telling yourself that," he said, fondling her breast until her nipple was hard and aching for his tongue.

"Ye talk too much," she said, grasping the back of his neck and pulling his mouth to hers. She kissed him fiercely, possessively, tasting the rain on his lips and the wine he must have drunk at his club on his tongue. His arms came around her, circling her and pulling her out of the chair and into his arms. She always felt so safe in his arms, and she hated wanting that feeling. Needing that feeling.

And so she kissed him deeper, felt his breathing grow more rapid as her hands slid down his chest and to the bulge in his trousers. He groaned, and his mouth went to her neck, delicately nibbling on the skin there while his hands loosed her robe's sash. The robe slid to the floor, and then his hands were cupping her buttocks through the thin muslin of the nightdress. He pulled her against his erection, and she was the one who moaned.

"Are you sure you want this?" he said, making sure she felt his hard length. "You want me?"

"One last time," she panted. "I swear, this is the end of it."

He chuckled against her ear, and she was too aroused to hit him for having the gall to doubt her. She'd hit him later. Right now, she wanted him naked and inside her. But he had other ideas. He lifted her in his arms, cradling her like she was a small child, and carried her to his bed.

He laid her down and came down over her, kissing her gently on the forehead, the eyes, the tip of her nose.

Tenderness. She didn't want tenderness from him. She didn't want this to mean anything. When he finally reached her lips, she bit him and raked her nails over his back. Even though she doubted he could feel much through his shirt and coat, he caught her hands and pushed them above her head, while he retaliated in kind, running his teeth down her exposed neck until he took the ribbon of the nightdress in his mouth and pulled it free. The garment was little more than a shift, the neck just an O held together by the ribbon, and once that was free, Aidan tugged the material down with his free hand.

She arched her back when his mouth closed over her breast, gasped when he took one nipple and then the other into his mouth, then gave a small cry of need when he lifted his head to look down at her. She opened her eyes and peered at him through a haze of burning need.

"I'll never leave you."

"Ye will," she countered.

"I love you, Jenny," he said without wavering.

She shook her head. She wanted none of this. "No, ye don't. Ye just think ye do."

"You think you're so unloveable." He kissed her lips quickly, avoiding her teeth. "But I love everything about you."

"Stop talking and take yer clothes off."

"I love how you're bossy." Instead of taking his clothes off, he pushed her shift down, baring more of her body to him. "I love your independence." His hand trailed from the valley between her breasts down her belly. "I love your clever mind and your hard exterior." He reached the triangle of dark hair between her legs. "You had to be hard to survive."

She tried to ignore his words and focus on what he was doing with his fingers. Her body had started writhing under his ministrations.

"You don't have to be hard with me, love. I know what's underneath that tough exterior."

"And wot's that?" she challenged. "There's nothing but iron."

"Let's see what happens when that iron heats."

"No," she said as he released her hands and moved between her legs, parting them so he could press his mouth there. She wanted to grasp his hair and yank his head away. Jenny needed him inside her, not making her senseless with his tongue. But she fisted her hands in his hair and allowed her weakness to get the better of her as he teased and sucked and flicked his tongue against her.

She held off as long as she could. She made him work, but he didn't give up. He continued his torment until she couldn't hold back, until the pleasure tore through her and she had to bite her lip to cut off a scream. "Aidan!" she cried. "Yes, yes, yes."

He rose to his knees and tugged off his coat. "Is that a yes to marrying me?"

"No," she said weakly, her body feeling as though it belonged to someone else. How did he make her feel like this? No one had ever made her feel like he could. His shirt came off, and her gaze focused, sliding down to the fall of his breeches, which he flicked open to reveal his hard cock. Jenny wet her lips.

He pushed off the bed, shrugged out of the rest of his clothes, then reached for the packet with the French letters. He extracted one, and while he tied it on, she murmured, "I thought you were determined to marry me."

Instead of ignoring the slight, he moved back onto the bed, parted her legs, and paused with his cock at the entrance of her sex. Jenny was breathing hard now, fighting not to use her legs to urge him forward.

"I am determined to marry you, but I'm not so pathetic as to force a child on you to have my way." His cock nudged her entrance. "You'll marry me because you want to." He entered her just a fraction, and she closed her eyes in pleasure.

"No, I won't."

He slid deeper. "You will. You just don't want to admit you love me yet."

She moaned as he pushed deeper into her and angled upward so her already sensitive center throbbed again with need. "Yes," she murmured, pulling him closer, wanting to feel his skin against hers. "Stop talking and make me come again."

He grasped her hands, locked his fingers with hers, and looked down at her as he moved inside her. She tried to look away, but his eyes kept pulling her gaze back. She saw lust in his eyes, definitely lust, but that wasn't all. In this moment, as she climbed higher and higher, she wanted to believe what she saw was real. "Aidan?" she asked, suddenly afraid of what she was feeling, what might happen if she allowed herself to be vulnerable.

"I'm here, Jenny."

Yes, he was. And she was so close. She didn't even try to fight it, didn't even try to make it last. She tipped over the edge, her hands closing tight on his as her body pressed closer and closer to his.

"God, you're beautiful," he said before groaning and thrusting hard as his own pleasure crested. His weight was a pleasant heaviness on top of her, and then he moved away briefly and came back, pulling the covers around them both. He gathered her close, and Jenny tried to pretend she didn't want this, didn't need it. But he was whispering that he loved her in her ear, telling her he would always love her, that he wanted her for his wife.

"That was the last time," she said, still trying to catch her breath.

"That's not even the last time tonight," he promised, and she hated that a frisson of pleasure coursed through her at his rumbled words.

"I'm not marrying you," she said defiantly.

"Not today," he agreed. "But you will. You love me, Jenny."

"I don't," she said, already feeling herself drifting off to sleep.

"Not even a little?" he murmured.

"No," she mumbled.

"A very little?"

"Maybe a *very* little."

She slept, vaguely aware of his arms around her and the ping of the rain on the roof. At some point, his lips teased behind her ear and his hands slid down between her legs and stroked her. She moaned and thought about rejecting him, but his fingers were making it hard to think, and he was whispering how hot and wet she was, and that was only making her want him more. But instead of turning her toward him, he rose to his knees and pulled her to hers, taking her from behind with a thrust that left her breathless. He hadn't bothered with the French letter, and the feel of his skin stroking inside her, was almost more than she could bear. He took her hard and fast as she held on to the headboard and shamelessly gave herself up to his whims. He brought her to a sharp climax that left her practically sobbing as he withdrew and spent himself on a nearby piece of linen.

She collapsed on her belly, and the bed beside her sagged with his weight. His arm went around her, his mouth in her hair as he whispered that he loved her again and again until she slept deeply and did not dream.

***

Aidan sat up at the sound. It was familiar and yet alien. Jenny stirred beside him, pushing her hair out of her eyes, then throwing her feet over the edge of the bed.

"Wait," he said. "Stay here."

"It's 'Arley," she said. "She's probably 'aving a nightmare."

She was right. He could tell the sound was a child screaming now.

"I shouldn't 'ave left 'er."

Jenny was dressed quickly and had his bedchamber door open before he could even think where his clothing might be. A moment later, he heard her voice, probably giving an order to one of his servants, and then another moment later, the screaming ceased.

"Sir?" Pierpont was at his door, his eyes carefully averted. "Miss Tate has asked for warm milk for the…child. Shall I have a maid fetch it?"

Aidan understood exactly what the man was saying. Jenny had no authority here. Pierpont didn't want to take orders from her. But he'd have to get used to it when Aidan married her. "Do whatever she says, Pierpont. Her wishes are mine."

"Yes, sir." Pierpont began to move away then paused. "Shall I rouse your valet, sir? He—er, retired to the servant's wing so as not to disturb you."

"I can bloody well dress myself," Aidan said. When the butler left, he half doubted his own words. Finally, he pulled on his breeches and a robe and padded barefoot to the nursery to find Jenny sitting on Harley's bed, stroking the child's hair. It was a motherly sort of thing to do, and not the kind of behavior he expected from Jenny. He doubted her own mother had ever soothed her fears after a nightmare. The little girl was talking about her dream, about a man with a stick who'd been chasing her, and Jenny murmured that she was safe.

Aidan moved aside as a maid brought the warm milk. Jenny gave him a look and made a shooing motion with her hands. He supposed his presence wasn't helping, so he went back to bed. But he didn't sleep. He missed Jenny beside him and knew she'd stay with Harley now until morning. It was the perfect escape, and he'd given her plenty to escape from. She wasn't lying when she said she didn't want to marry him. He knew she didn't want to risk her heart.

And the only way to make her risk her heart was to break down her outer defenses. That wouldn't be easy. She had layers and layers of them. She had defenses he probably didn't even know about. He'd made it past the first few layers last night. She'd even grudgingly admitted she loved him a *very little*, but she'd try to keep him from getting any closer to her heart. And one of these times when she threatened it was the last, she'd make sure that was so.

He made halfhearted attempts to go back to sleep, and when sleep eluded him, he finally rang for his poor valet, washed, shaved, and dressed then went to his library to work.

So he was awake when Harley tried to sneak out of the house. He heard her step on the stairs and went to the library door, leaning against the jamb and crossing his arms as she crept across the marble foyer.

"And where are you off to this early?" he asked.

She jumped. It would have been almost comic if she didn't then hide the spoon in her hand behind her back.

"Stealing my silver?" he asked, raising a brow.

"It's me compensation," she said, facing him head on. This child was no coward. She also looked much more like a little girl this morning. The weak early morning light illuminated her small, clean face, and her brown hair reached just past her shoulders, which were garbed in a plain dress. God knew where his servants had found it.

"Because you've only been paid ten of the twenty pounds you were promised," he said.

"Exactly."

"I hardly think that spoon—is that from the milk last night?"

She nodded.

"That spoon is not worth ten pounds."

"I know." She gave a sheepish look then reached under her skirts and extracted a candlestick—no, two candlesticks, a tray, and a…

"Is that a door latch?"

"Looks expensive," she said.

"How the devil did you manage to stuff all of that under your skirts?"

She shrugged. "Practice."

"Yes, well, hand it over." He held out his hand and she reluctantly trudged toward him and gave him the tray, the candlesticks, and the latch. "The spoon too."

"Aw, give me something."

"I'll give you ten pounds after you visit the orphanage with Miss Tate and me."

"I told ye. I ain't being locked up in an orphanage."

"And I told you that no one will make you stay if you don't want."

"And 'ow can I trust ye'll keep yer word?" she asked.

"I'll vouch for 'im."

He looked up to see Jenny on the stairs. She was still wearing her nightgown and robe, her black hair a tousled mess that framed her face. Her cheeks were pink, and he could see the faintest traces of pink where he'd bitten her neck. Her gray eyes flicked to him, and her cheeks reddened. That was interesting. He didn't think he'd ever seen her blush before. Of course, she didn't always behave as wantonly as she had last night. He had a distinct memory of her begging him to thrust harder.

Aidan merely raised a brow at Jenny's pronouncement.

"Wot's that mean?" Harley asked, her tone suspicious.

"It means, I give ye my word, 'e's telling the truth."

Aidan thought Harley might ask how she knew Jenny was telling the truth, but the child didn't question her. Instead, she sighed and handed Aidan the spoon. "Fine, let's go."

"Although I believe Mr. Wraxall and Lady Juliana wake rather early," he said, "I think this is still a bit too early for a social call."

Harley frowned and looked at Jenny. "Wot's 'e talking about?"

"I think 'e's suggesting we eat before we go," Jenny said.

Harley seemed to brighten at the idea of food. "Eat wot?"

"Whatever ye like," Jenny said. "A 'ouse like this—ye'll have porridge and scones and kippers and more."

Harley's eyes went round. "Where is it?"

"I'll take her," Aidan said before Jenny could start for the dining room. He doubted Cook had breakfast prepared yet, but the child could have a cup of chocolate while they waited for the rest. "You should dress," he told Jenny. "I took the liberty of sending a footman to collect a few things from your flat. Your maidservant was there and sent a dress or two."

Jenny gave him a murderous glare. "It's all going right back," she said, apparently seeing right through his ploy to bring as many of her things here as he could. "When 'Arley goes, so do I." She stomped up the stairs, and Aidan gestured to the dining room. Harley followed him inside, climbed into a chair, and happily accepted the chocolate. Her eyes went round after she tasted it.

"Where's the rest of the lot?" she asked.

Aidan flicked his wrist at the footman. "Tell Cook to send whatever is ready."

The footman hurried away, and Aidan sipped his coffee and opened the *Times*, which was always on the table each morning along with several other papers.

"Why don't she like ye?" Harley asked. Aidan lowered his paper. He wasn't used to being interrupted.

"Why *doesn't* she like me."

"That's wot I said."

Aidan decided to forego the grammar lesson. "She *does* like me, Miss Harley. The problem is that she doesn't *want* to like me."

"I can understand that," the child declared.

"Can you?"

"I don't want to like ye either. And yet, I almost do."

"I'm not quite sure how to take that." He raised his paper again and tried to ignore the sound of slurping.

"Oy! Wot is this?"

Aidan lowered his paper again. He glanced at the cup the child held. "Chocolate."

"I want more."

"Finish that cup, and you shall have more."

As she proceeded to do just that, he laid the paper back on the table. He couldn't remember the last time he had dined with anyone so informally. His meals were always taken alone or were part of a business negotiation. Moreover, this dining room had rarely been used by anyone other than he. He hosted the obligatory dinner parties, but usually he breakfasted alone. It was nice to have someone across from him.

Harley was not what he would call an attractive child. Her face was too thin, her brown eyes too big in her small face. Once all the dirt and grime had been washed out of it, her hair had turned out to be a dark blond. Her table manners were atrocious, of course, but Jenny's had been as well. He remembered teaching her to chew with her mouth closed and how to hold a knife and fork. They'd had to practice with sticks as they didn't have a knife and fork in Spitalfields.

"More." Harley held out her empty cup.

"Please."

She wrinkled her brow, and from the doorway, Jenny said, " 'E wants ye to say *please*."

Aidan glanced at her and smiled at how pretty she looked in the simple blue dress with her hair pulled back in a loose bun at her nape.

"Why?"

"It's polite," Jenny explained. "Say, *May I have more, please?*"

"May I 'ave more, please?" Harley said, almost perfectly imitating Jenny's upper-class accent.

Jenny looked at Aidan and so did Harley, and he realized he was expected to pour. He rose and did so, offering it to Jenny as well, but she waved it away and took a cup of tea instead. By then the footman had returned with another and placed trays full of pastries and typical breakfast fare, and Jenny brought Harley to the sideboard and helped her fill her plate.

Aidan rarely ate breakfast, but he also had no desire to open the paper again, even though he'd heard there would be news about a large tea import company. He was enjoying watching Jenny and Harley, enjoying the sound of voices and laughter filling the usually tomblike quiet of the house.

Finally, after three plates of food, Harley announced she couldn't eat another bite and Jenny said it was time to go to the orphanage. She looked at Aidan, who had half a mind to tell them all to forego the orphanage. He liked having Harley here. He liked having Jenny here. But she already knew that. She just didn't believe he would continue to feel that way. And yet, he couldn't imagine going back to life before Jenny had come back into it. It seemed as though he'd been a shadow, moving through a dark world, and she had come in and pulled open the drapes to allow the sun in.

"Do we get to go in that fancy carriage again?" Harley was asking.

"Of course," Jenny said.

Aidan quietly ordered the custom carriage he'd had made with the seat that pulled out into a bed. "Actually, we'll take my other carriage," he announced.

"Aww!" Harley said loudly.

"And this one is even better," he said.

Jenny smiled at Harley's whoop of joy.

***

Sunnybrooke Home for Boys was located in a new building that had only recently been constructed. The original structure had stood in Spitalfields and been destroyed by fire. Neil Wraxall, who had been Aidan's commander during the war, had moved the dozen or so orphans to the Earl St. Maur's town house until the new building was ready. Now he and Lady Juliana met Aidan, Jenny, and Harley in a sunny courtyard accessed through a tall iron gate that would provide privacy from passersby and yet allow some view of the outside world.

Lady Juliana's nephew was toddling about, pulling leaves off bushes as she followed him, and Neil stood speaking with Colin FitzRoy and his wife, the lovely Lady Daphne. Jenny stopped midstride when she saw the foursome, and Aidan could hardly blame her. Lady Juliana was short and voluptuous with coppery red hair. Lady Daphne was taller with blue eyes and silvery blond hair. She was a typical English beauty, and her eyes lit up as soon as she spotted Harley. She'd obviously been looking for them as she was the first to see them.

"Harley!" She lifted her skirts and practically ran to greet them. To Aidan's surprise, Harley didn't turn and run the other way. She stopped, smiled, and consented to being hugged and fawned over by the duke's daughter.

The others gathered around, and Aidan bowed to Colin, Neil, and Lady Juliana and introduced Miss Tate and Harley, though she seemed to need no introduction. Jenny hovered in the background, but soon Daphne had engaged her in a three-way conversation with Harley. And then Lady Juliana asked everyone to come inside for tea.

Aidan glanced at Harley, who he suspected would revolt as the idea of going inside the orphanage. Instead, she said, "Do ye 'ave that chocolate?"

"Of course," Lady Juliana said. "I have sweet currant buns as well."

"I'm not 'ungry," Harley said, crossing her arms over her little frame. "But I'll take that chocolate out 'ere."

"Harley, we had an agreement," Aidan said, but instead of giving in, she raised her chin and set her mouth in a mulish line. He was about to speak again, but Lady Juliana shook her head slightly.

"We can take our refreshments outside," she agreed, "but then you won't be able to meet Galatians, Ephesians, and Philippians."

"Wot are they?"

Aidan wondered the same thing. He watched as Major Wraxall caught the little boy and hoisted him into his arms, tickling him before the child could slip out the front gate. "Rats," Neil said. "Pet rats."

"Oh, I know rats," Harley said. "I've been bitten by them. Want to see?" She started to pull her skirts up to the knee, and Lady Daphne grasped her hands and pushed them back down again.

"But these rats are friendly. And they know tricks," Lady Juliana said.

"Wot sort of tricks?" Harley asked.

"Come and see."

The eight of them went into the orphanage, which was relatively quiet as Lady Juliana told him the boys were in class. While Neil and Juliana showed Harley and Jenny around, Colin and Lady Daphne cornered Aidan.

"Mr. Sterling, we are forever in your debt," Lady Daphne said.

"I was happy to be able to help."

Colin raised a brow at that but said nothing.

"My concern," Aidan went on, "Is that she won't want to stay."

"At least she knows where to go if she needs help," Lady Daphne said.

But Aidan had difficulty imagining allowing Harley to go back to the rookeries. He certainly wouldn't make her stay at the orphanage if she didn't want to, but he felt somewhat responsible for her now. Colin obviously felt the same because he pulled Aidan aside and asked where he'd found Harley.

Aidan explained how he'd arranged for Harley to come to him, and Colin was glad that at least Harley would have a bit of blunt.

"Whether or not she can hold onto it in the rookeries is another matter," Aidan said, though he thought Harley was about as cunning as they came.

The boys emerged from their classrooms in a loud cacophony and Lady Juliana told them they could have an hour of exercise since the day was so fair. A loud cheer just about deafened Aidan as the boys went back into the courtyard and began a complicated game of catch that Aidan had never seen before. Harley stood beside him and watched for a bit then when the ball rolled to her feet, she picked it up, threw it back, and joined in.

Jenny's hand closed on his arm, and he looked over at her. "She likes it 'ere," Jenny said.

"Chocolate, rats, games—what's not to like?"

She smiled up at him, and he had a hard time not pulling her into his arms and kissing her right there.

"I don't think she'll agree to stay." Jenny looked back at Harley who was now playing catch as though she had played it all her life. "She's not ready to trust yet."

Aidan refrained from pointing out that same statement could have been said of Jenny herself. "She doesn't have to decide today. She has all the time in the world."

Jenny looked back at him. "Do ye mean that? She can stay at your 'ouse again tonight?"

He hadn't exactly meant that. In fact, he'd been thinking about Jenny and himself when he'd said she had all the time in the world. But he realized he didn't mind having Harley come back home with him as well. Especially if Jenny also came.

The ball landed at Jenny's feet and Harley and several of the boys called for her to throw it back. She did and then surprised him by joining in the game as well. Her hair came loose but she ignored it and jostled among the boys as though she were one of them. And, of course, she was.

Neil moved beside Aidan. Lady Juliana's nephew, whose name was Davy, had his head on Neil's shoulder and his thumb in his mouth. "Where have you been hiding her?" Neil asked.

"I don't have to tell you everything, Major," Aidan said.

"You had us all fooled into thinking all you cared about was money. Clearly, there's more."

Aidan glanced at Jenny and remembered Phineas's advice. "I haven't said much because she's just broken an engagement to Viscount Chamberlayne."

Neil raised a brow.

Aidan pretended to be watching the game and spoke in a nonchalant tone. "He's a good man, but he's determined to live in Venice for the next year or so and work on an excavation. Miss Tate is not pleased with the notion of an extended visit to Italy and she was insulted when he suggested postponing the wedding."

Neil looked at Jenny then at him. "Is that the story I'm to tell my wife?"

"And Lady Daphne and as many others as will listen."

"And how do you know Miss Tate? You fell in love with her while she was appraising the trunks in your larder?"

You fell in love with her. Wraxall said it so casually, though the words jolted Aidan. He'd been in love with Jenny for years. "Maybe if she agrees to marry me, I'll tell you how I met her."

Neil clapped him on the shoulder. "It's good to see you happy, Sterling."

Aidan had the audacity to believe that happiness would last.

Fifteen

"The orphanage didn't seem so bad, did it?" Jenny asked as they climbed back into the carriage several hours later.

Harley made a non-committal sound and Aidan blew out a breath. Jenny had never seen him with the men he'd fought with during the war, and she'd found that watching him with Wraxall and FitzRoy showed her a different side of him—a side that wasn't the pauper boy or the money-hungry businessman. She'd seen a man who was a friend—someone who could be counted on and trusted. Those men had trusted each other with their lives. They'd seen horrors she did not want to imagine, and they'd come home with the scars on their souls, if not their bodies. Clearly, even though Aidan had left her in the rookeries, he hadn't gone to live in luxury. He'd been a soldier and fought in a war.

"Do you know what I think?" Aidan said. Jenny looked at him as did Harley. "I think we need to go shopping for new clothes."

"For 'er?" Harley asked.

"For you," Aidan said.

"I don't need no clothes," Harley said, crossing her arms over her chest. "Just be stolen anyway."

Jenny watched Aidan's jaw tense as he resisted pointing out that if she were living in the orphanage, nothing would be stolen.

"I want to buy you clothing," Aidan said. "Indulge me."

"When do I get me ten quid?" Harley asked. "I went to the orphanage. I want me blunt."

With another sigh, Aidan reached into his pocket, withdrew a note, and handed it to Harley.

"You can let me off 'ere," Harley said. "No use for dresses and the like."

"What's your hurry to get back to living on the streets?" Aidan asked. "You had a clean, dry bed last night, and a full belly.

"Too good to last," Harley said. "I like to get out before things go sour."

Aidan exchanged a look with Jenny. She knew they could both understand that thinking. And she knew Aidan needed help.

"Ye can always sell the dresses," Jenny said. Aidan scowled at her. Apparently, that wasn't the help he wanted. "If things go sour and ye need to go."

She seemed to be considering when he straightened suddenly as though with inspiration. "If you come with us, I'll buy you ices at Gunter's Tea Shop afterward. Have you ever had ices?"

Harley's eyes had widened slightly before she quickly masked her expression. "I could try them."

"Good. Then we'll start on Bond Street." He tapped the roof with his walking stick and gave his coachman the instruction.

Jenny cleared her throat. "I'm afraid ye'll 'ave to go without me. I need to speak with Viscount Chamberlayne."

"You're leaving me to shop for dresses alone?"

She smiled. "I think ye'll do just fine."

But Aidan looked terrified when he finally stepped out of the coach and took Harley's hand. The gesture was so sweet that she pulled the curtains aside and watched them walk away as the coach started for Roland's town house. Her heart ached a bit when she saw Harley look up to ask Aidan something and he leaned down to give her his full attention. No parent had ever held her hand or given her anything more than a smack. Aidan was a good man, and he'd apologized for leaving her. It was time to let go of her anger about the past.

Time to let go of her anger about the present as well, she thought as she neared Roland's home. She wished she had been able to marry Roland and keep Oscar and him close. She wished things could have gone on as they always had, and it rankled that they had to bend to fit into Society's strictures. But Roland and Oscar would be safer abroad, and Roland was leaving because he wanted the best for her. She did love Aidan, as much as she tried to stop herself. And she could never really be with Aidan if she were Roland's wife. A scandalous affair between the richest man in England and the Viscountess Chamberlayne would not do Roland any favors.

And so she stepped down from the carriage and entered Roland's house, moving aside as two servants carried a vase from one room to another. Indeed, all the servants were hastening about, and Jenny swallowed when she saw the crates, the straw, and the piles of burlap and linen used to cushion belongings that would travel with them and cover the furnishings that would stay behind.

She heard Roland's voice in the drawing room, and climbed the steps, pausing outside to watch as he directed a footman to carefully pack a painting that had been hanging on the wall.

"Yer not taking that, are ye?" she asked from the doorway.

Roland swung around. "Jenny." He smiled, his blue eyes crinkling. "I was beginning to think I wouldn't see you. We leave tonight, and none of my notes or birds reached you."

"One did," she said.

"Ah. The one I sent to Sterling's house?"

"That's the one."

He threw the Holland cover partially off a couch and sat, patting the cushion next to him. She sat beside him, looking about the half-empty room. "I'll miss ye," she said.

"We'll be back."

"I don't even know where yer going. Italy, I assume." Oscar always talked about wanting to travel to Italy.

"We thought we'd start in Venice. I've always loved Venice, and Oscar has never been."

Jenny wrinkled her nose, and Roland laughed. "I know you've never liked Venice."

"It stinks in the summer."

"So does London." He took her hand. "Listen, dear girl, my house is always open to you. I haven't touched the parlor where you like to work, and if you need funds, my solicitor—"

"I don't need yer blunt."

"Yes, but if you do, don't hesitate to ask."

Jenny nodded and felt her eyes sting with tears. She bit the inside of her cheek to keep from crying. She hadn't cried when Aidan left her, hadn't cried when her mother beat her, she wasn't going to cry now. Roland would be back. Once upon a time, she wouldn't have believed that. But she trusted Roland. He'd come back, and if he didn't, she'd go to visit him.

"You must come down and say good-bye to Oscar."

She followed Roland downstairs and found Oscar in the dining room packing china. Oscar was not shy about weeping, and he burst into tears and Jenny found herself comforting him. When he'd recovered, Roland held out a folder tied closed with twine.

"What's this?" she asked.

"My notes on the Sterling find," he said.

She didn't take the offered folder. "But I thought you'd want to write it up and present the paper."

"You do it," he said.

"Me?

"Why not?"

"I don't 'ave—*h*ave the qualifications."

"Rubbish. I taught you everything I know. You can present this as well as anyone."

"But I'm no writer."

"Then make Sterling spend some of his riches and hire you an editor. With a bit of help, you'll publish a fine paper. Just don't forget to put my name on it."

She laughed. "Determined to 'ave yer credit."

"That's right. Now, if you have a bit of time, would you mind seeing if there is anything in the parlor we might pack? I didn't want to touch it, but since you are here—"

"Of course." Jenny and Roland stepped into the parlor where they'd worked for a decade for perhaps the last time.

***

Several hours later, Sterling's carriage came for her. There were more tearful good-byes from Oscar, but Roland just took her hand, kissed it, and said, "I'm proud of you, Miss Tate."

She looked as though she might cry then, but his brave girl lifted her chin, took a breath, and squeezed his hand. She walked to the carriage, back straight and head held high.

He watched the coach drive away then went back inside. The packing was far along now, and the foyer echoed and seemed empty. "Not to pat myself on the back," he said to Oscar, who was still sniffling, "but I did a good job with her."

"She's a true lady now," Oscar agreed.

"It's a shame we'll miss the wedding."

Oscar gave him a look. "Jumping ahead as usual."

Roland shrugged. "She loves him, and if I know my Jenny, she won't let anything she loves elude her ever again."

"Advice to live by," Oscar said, putting his arms around Roland from behind and resting his chin on his shoulder.

Roland looked about the room. "I think we're just about done here."

"You still haven't told me what you plan to do with the pigeons. I don't like to trust them to the servants."

"Oh, the pigeons will be fine," Roland said with a smile. "I expect they'll have a new home soon, and it will be even better than this." He turned his head, kissed Oscar. "Now, you and I have our own adventure."

"Italy!" Oscar practically shook with excitement. "It's a dream!"

"Yes," Roland agreed, smiling at Oscar. It was a dream, and it was coming true.

***

" 'Ow did ye convince 'er to stay?" Jenny asked while the maids took Harley up for a bath and to change into her nightclothes.

Aidan lifted his wine glass and propped his feet on the footrest in the drawing room. He rarely used this room, but he thought he should do so more. Perhaps he would have the music room furnished as well. "I bribed her with another trip to Gunter's tomorrow. She wants to try all the flavors. As long as Gunter keeps changing flavors, I can persuade her."

"I'm sure the five-course dinner 'elped too."

Aidan studied Jenny. She stood by the window, looking out.

"You didn't eat much."

"I don't feel 'ungry."

"Has the ship sailed yet, do you think?" he asked. He wanted to go to her, take her in his arms, and hold her. He knew her thoughts were on Roland, knew the man was the only family she'd ever had. Aidan wanted to be her family now, but she wasn't quite ready for that. And she would not welcome his sympathy or his embrace right now. He could see that by the stiffness in her shoulders.

"Yes. They're gone." She sounded so forlorn that Aidan had to rise and go to her. But she moved before he could reach her and lifted a folder from a side table, holding it out between them. "He gave me this."

"What is it?" Aidan tugged at the twine, let it fall, and opened the folder.

"Notes about his findings."

Aidan flipped through the pages. "Have you looked at them?"

"Roland believes the items are from before the Great Fire."

"Really? Do you agree?"

"Based on wot I read in the journals, yes. But the most important discovery is a journal with observations about the Great Fire. First-'and accounts are valuable. Ye could sell it for a tidy sum."

"I could. Or I could keep it."

"I didn't think ye were sentimental."

"I never was before." He continued looking through the notes then pulled out the last sheet. "What's this?"

Jenny came to stand beside him and peered down at the sketch. "Oh, no," she said.

"It looks like some sort of structure," he said.

"It is. It's for the pigeons."

"The pigeons?" He noted the street and number on the drawing. It was his house. This was a structure to be constructed on his roof. "He left me the pigeons?"

" 'E still thinks we'll marry."

"I'd ask you again if I thought you'd say yes."

"Save yer breath."

"That's what I thought."

"Miss Tate!" The high voice seemed to echo through the house.

"How does a child that small manage to make so much noise?" Aidan asked.

"Miss Tate!"

"I think that's my cue to tuck 'er in."

Aidan followed her, partly because he thought he knew more about tucking children in than Jenny but also because he didn't really want this day to end.

Harley didn't seem to mind that he'd come, and she allowed him to tuck her in and even to read her a chapter from one of the books they'd bought this afternoon. He was almost to the end of the chapter when Jenny put her hand on his and said quietly, "I think she's asleep."

Aidan looked up. "I think you're right."

"Not asleep," Harley said, her voice thick.

"Sweet dreams." Aidan gave her a kiss on the cheek. "Sleep well, Harley."

"Name's not 'Arley," she said, voice still slow as syrup.

Aidan looked up at Jenny.

"Wot is yer name then?"

Aidan held his breath as time seemed to slow and stretch and become infinite. Finally, she answered. "Rosaleen. Call me Rosaleen."

"Good night, Rosaleen," Jenny said.

"Sleep well, sweet Rosaleen," Aidan said. He went to the door. "The night is still young," he said to Jenny.

"Then I 'ope ye 'ave a book to keep ye company."

He had work, Aidan thought, as he went down to his library. He'd neglected it the entire day. Pryce had brought him ledgers and invoices just before dinner, and Aidan had sent it all to his library. Now he sat at his desk but didn't bother to touch it.

He'd most likely lost money today, but he didn't care. The money only mattered if he could use it to buy Harley—Rosaleen—pretty dresses and books and toys. Jenny didn't need him for that. All he could offer her was himself. And as the hours ticked by, it was clear, she would not come to him. If last night truly was the last time they were together, he would have to accept it, but he hadn't gotten as far as he had in this world without having a few cards up his sleeve. Aidan never cheated exactly, but he definitely liked the odds in his favor. And now he made a plan to tip them that way. It was his last chance.

Sixteen

She hadn't gone to Aidan that night, but that didn't mean she'd slept. She'd lain awake most of the night, listening to Rosaleen's quiet breathing and wondering if Aidan was asleep. Half a dozen times, she sat up and almost climbed out of bed, but then she laid down again and forced herself to stay where she was. If she went to him, her heart would be his.

It had been easy to go to bed with him when it was only about physical attraction or their shared history. But the last few days she had seen a side of him that stole her breath away. She could picture him as a father, perhaps even the father of their children. The way he treated Rosaleen, as though she were the most important person in the room. The way he looked at *her*, as though she was the most important person in the world. A few weeks ago, he'd been preoccupied with work every time she saw him. Now he hadn't mentioned it all day.

She was beginning to believe he really did love her. And she had no doubt if she went to him tonight, he would prove it with slow kisses and soft touches and words that would make him impossible to resist.

And Jenny Tate, who had shivered and starved and fought off arch rogues for seventeen years of her life without a second thought, was scared. She hadn't believed anyone could ever love her. Her mother hadn't. Her father hadn't. When Aidan left, she told herself he hadn't.

But he had. He'd loved her enough to leave her. He'd loved her enough to go back for her. Now he loved her enough to pursue her. He loved her enough to keep proposing, even when she had told him no and walked away. She'd thought that would make her feel powerful. Finally, *she* was the one who'd walked away from him. But she'd just felt confused and sad.

She'd loved Aidan since she was thirteen. She loved him still.

But she wasn't any good at saying those sorts of words. And what if he'd changed his mind overnight?

She must have finally slept because she was shaken awake by Rosaleen the next morning. "Wot is it? Wot's wrong?" she asked.

"I'm 'ungry."

"Then go eat." Jenny turned over and put the pillow over her head.

"Ye 'ave to come with me."

Jenny moved the pillow enough to see the girl. "Ye don't still think Mr. Sterling will snatch ye and send ye to the orphanage."

"I don't trust no one."

"Ye trust me."

"More than 'im." She shook Jenny again. "Come on. I can smell the food!"

Jenny rose, dressed, and tried to do something with her hair, but Rosaleen pulled her away before she could do more than secure it in a tail down her back. She was aware she looked more like the girl Aidan had left than the lady she'd tried to be when she sat down to dine across from him that morning. He didn't seem to mind. His dark eyes met hers with a heat that made fire ignite low in her belly.

So perhaps he hadn't stopped loving her overnight.

"Shall I help you fill your plate, Rosaleen?" Aidan asked.

The girl started at the use of her real name, but then she nodded. "I can fill this one. Ye fill the other."

Aidan didn't comment on the fact that she was filling two plates. He did as he was bade and then sat down again and sipped tea while Rosaleen ate as though she hadn't seen food in days.

"Sir, Pryce is here to see you. Shall I send him to the library?" The butler stood in the doorway, his gaze anywhere but on the urchin with the two plates piled high.

Aidan's gaze met Jenny's. "Go ahead," she said. "We'll eat while ye see to yer business."

"This actually isn't just about my business," he said. "It has to do with Rosaleen."

The girl stopped shoveling food in her mouth and looked up. "Me?" she said, her words garbled from the food stuffed in her mouth.

"Bring him here, Pierpont."

"Yes, sir."

Aidan pushed his tea aside. "Last night I sent word to my secretary with your real name," he told Rosaleen. "He'd already been looking for the parents of a girl named Harley. Now he was looking for those of a Rosaleen."

"Ye didn't 'ave to do that," Rosaleen said. "I could 'ave told ye they were dead."

"I did ask."

Rosaleen shrugged. "Didn't know ye very well then." She took a bite of a scone. "Died of the cholera."

Just then Pryce walked into the room. Jenny recognized him from Aidan's offices.

"Is that right, Pryce? Miss Rosaleen tells us her parents died of cholera."

"To the best of my knowledge, sir, that is correct," Pryce said, seeming not to mind that his efforts were for naught. "They were a Molly and Tom Baker. They died in the outbreak about six years ago." He handed a folder to Aidan who opened it and perused the contents.

"You're ten," he said to Rosaleen.

She screwed up her face. "Sounds right."

"Born Rosaleen Jane Baker."

"That's me."

Aidan looked at his secretary. "That will be all for now, Pryce."

"Yes, sir. Will you be in today, sir?"

"I don't know, Pryce. I trust you can handle things without me, yes?"

"I can sir, but—"

"Then you are in charge."

"*Me*, sir?"

"Yes. And I imagine that means you have a lot to do. Best to hurry, Pryce."

"Yes, sir!"

Jenny rose from her seat and went to kneel by Rosaleen's chair. " 'Ow are ye feeling?"

"Same as before," she said. "I knew I was an orphan." She pointed a fork at Aidan. "Not that I'm agreeing to go to that orphanage."

"You don't have to go, if you don't want," Aidan said.

"I don't?"

"Are ye sending her back to live on the streets?" Jenny asked, surprised at how angry the thought made her.

"I don't mind," Rosaleen said. "I 'ave me twenty quid now."

"I'm not sending her back to live on the streets." Aidan stood. "In fact, I wanted to ask you a question—both of you, actually."

Jenny knew that look in his eyes, and she took a shaky breath.

"Rosaleen, I wondered if you might like to live here, with me."

Rosaleen's eyes narrowed. "Wot do I 'ave to do?"

"A great many things, actually," Aidan said, pacing across the room. "You'll have to go to school or learn from a tutor. There will be lessons in reading, arithmetic, and writing. Plus, dancing, piano, and drawing."

"Will I get to eat whatever I want?"

"You'll never be hungry," he said.

"What about ices?" she asked.

"I'll buy you ices and toys and dresses—as many as you like."

She opened her mouth, presumably to agree, and then looked at Jenny. "Wot about 'er?"

"I'm hoping she will agree to live here too."

"Well, ye 'ave to ask 'er."

"Jenny," he said, coming to stand above her. He held out a hand and she took it and allowed him to pull her up. "Miss Tate. I know I will never deserve you, and I know you probably don't believe I love you, but I do love you. More importantly, I will never leave you. I don't want to spend another minute without you at my side. I—"

"Oh, shut yer potato 'ole," she said.

Even Rosaleen gasped.

"I love ye too," she said and threw herself into his arms.

He caught her, swung her around, and kissed her.

"Oy! None of that now!" Rosaleen objected.

Aidan smiled and looked down at her. "Later," he said.

She nodded. "After we go shopping."

"Shopping?"

"For a ring!" Rosaleen said, pushing herself between them.

"Of course!" Aidan lifted Rosaleen into his arms, and the two of them held her as the warm summer sun streamed in behind them.

Epilogue

Aidan opened the door to the roof and stepped out into the cool air of early fall. The summer had been long and hot, but it hadn't stopped Jenny and him from meeting here. She waited for him now, a light shawl wrapped about her shoulders. The cooing from the pigeons, now safe in their aviary for the night, blocked out the sound of costermongers and carriage wheels on the streets below.

She turned to look at him, and he took a breath. It was still difficult to believe she was Mrs. Sterling, his wife. Sometimes he woke in the morning and found her watching him. On those days, he pulled her into his arms and promised her he'd never leave her and would always love her. She needed the words, and he never tired of giving them to her.

"Is she asleep?" Jenny asked.

"Finally," he said, sinking down on a chair near the pigeon aviary. Damn Chamberlayne for giving Jenny all his birds. Aidan had to hire workers to build them a palace on his roof, complete with shade and all sorts of trees. Winter would

413

be here in a few months, and how was he to keep the trees alive and the pigeons warm? "It took me two chapters," he said.

Jenny sat beside him. "That's yer fault for reading *Waverly* to 'er. It's so exciting, no wonder she wants ye to keep reading."

"As soon as you finish writing your paper for the archaeological society, you can take over," he said.

"Oh, no." She shook her head. "Ye've proven yerself more than capable. I couldn't possibly take over."

He reached over and poked her in the ribs, causing her to jump and laugh. She'd always been a little ticklish there.

"Stop," she said, still laughing, "Or I won't tell ye wot Roland said in 'is letter."

"I hope it's that he's found another home for these pigeons."

"Of course not!" She withdrew a paper from her pocket. " 'E says 'e and Oscar 'ave settled in a lovely palazzo on the Grand Canal *and* he invites us to come and visit." She looked up at him. "Wot do ye think?"

"I'll go wherever you go," he said.

"I think Italy in the spring," she said.

"Rosaleen will love it."

"I love ye," she said. She was saying it more often now, but every time still made his heart clench. He pulled her onto his lap and kissed her. "I love you. Then." He kissed her again. "Now." Another kiss. "Forever."

About Shana Galen

Shana Galen is three-time Rita award nominee and the bestselling author of passionate Regency romps. Kirkus said of her books: "The road to happily-ever-after is intense, conflicted, suspenseful and fun." *RT Bookreviews* described her writing as "lighthearted yet poignant, humorous yet touching." She taught English at the middle and high school level for eleven years. Most of those years were spent working in Houston's inner city. Now she writes full time, surrounded by three cats and one spoiled dog. She's happily married and has a daughter who is most definitely a romance heroine in the making.

Would you like exclusive content, book news, and a chance to win early copies of Shana's books? Sign up for monthly emails for exclusive news and giveaways.

Want more Aidan and the other Survivors? Keep reading for an excerpt from Her Royal Payne, Rowden's story, on sale now!

The German was enormous, and his right hook was deadly, but he'd been hit in the head one too many times. He was as dim as the stars shining in the London fog. That didn't mean Rowden wasn't dancing in the ring. He didn't want a ham-sized fist plowing into his face. But the German had no strategy. Rowden had lasted four rounds with the brute, and he could see the man was tiring. If Rowden could survive one round more, the German would be tired enough that Rowden could get in a few jabs and take him down.

Rowden danced back, twisted, felt the swipe of the German's fist a fraction from his ear. The crowd yelled and cheered, and Rowden flashed them a grin. Some of them had bet against him of course, but most of them were smart enough to bet against the German. Rowden wasn't known as The Royal Payne for nothing. He glanced at his manager, standing with arms crossed on one side of the ring. Chibale narrowed his eyes, reminding Rowden to focus. They'd be called to their corners soon.

Then he'd get a drink, take a breath, and start his attack. In another quarter hour, the prize money would be his. Fifty pounds wasn't a fortune, but it was nothing to scoff at. Once Rowden would have considered fifty pounds nominal. But that was before his father had disavowed him.

Younger sons of dukes didn't have many useful, practical skills. Rowden had tried the army, but he hadn't liked taking orders. Now he made his way in the fashion he preferred—with his fists.

He ducked as the German swung at him, then skipped behind the man and jabbed him in the lower back. The German grunted and swung around. That punch was easy to evade as the German hadn't even aimed it. Sweat poured from the giant's forehead, and his blue eyes were red-rimmed. Rowden could feel the fifty quid in his pocket already. Well, thirty-five quid. He'd have to pay Chibale fifteen pounds.

Rowden glanced at Chibale who nodded and raised a hand level to the ground. Hold steady.

Suddenly a loud bell rang out and a voice shouted above the men lining the ring. "Woe to ye, sinners! Repent and God will forgive thy sins!"

It was a woman's voice, and Rowden tried to ignore it, but the bell had been loud and unexpected and thrown him off balance.

"Flee this den of iniquity!"

Den of iniquity? It was a tavern with an area roped off for boxing in the back. A bit of drink and sport was hardly wicked.

"Flee now afore the fires of hell descend!" The bell rang again, and a burst of fire seemed to leap into the crowd. The men on the side of the ring closest to the fire moved aside, and Rowden couldn't stop himself from looking. Even as his mind screamed, *No!*, his head turned to glance at the spectacle.

It only took an instant for him to see the woman's companion held a torch. No one was in any real danger. Except for Rowden, in the ring with the German. That was the instant he should have turned back to his opponent. He should have ducked. He should have done anything other than lock eyes with the woman dressed in black. Her gown was severe with its high neck and coarse cloth. Her hair was covered by a white cap.

But her eyes.

Her eyes were the most beautiful shade of hazel he'd ever seen. Truly, they were remarkable. He stared at her, and she stared at him, and then she winced.

Like an idiot he turned to look at what had caught her attention, and pain struck the side of his head like a boulder smashing down on it.

And then he was down, and for a moment the world was gray and all but silent. Rowden felt as though he had fallen into a lake and was struggling to swim to the top of the water. Everything was murky and muted, but finally he broke through to the surface and a dark brown face was right above him.

"You lost," Chibale said.

Rowden shook his head. "No. I can still fight. Give me a minute." He tried to sit, but his head felt too heavy.

Chibale shook his head. "You've been lying on the ground for two minutes. It's over."

Rowden growled. He was suddenly hungry and thirsty, and his pockets were not fifty pounds fuller. "Goddamn it."

"I think that is exactly what happened, my friend." He offered a hand, and Rowden took it, allowing Chibale to pull him to his feet. "Those zealots came in and ruined everything."

"I shouldn't have let myself become distracted."

Chibale put an arm around Rowden, led him to a table, and signaled to a server to bring him a drink. "It's not like you to lose focus."

Rowden closed his eyes. He opened them again when he heard a cheer from the other room, then scowled when he saw the German and his friends raising their pints in celebration.

"Get me another match with him," Rowden said.

"And how am I supposed to do that? He knocked you on your unfocused, white arse. No one is interested in a rematch."

"Make them interested. That's what I pay you for."

Chibale sat back, crossed his arms, and looked up at the ceiling. "Neither of us made any blunt tonight. And we could have used it after your holiday a few months ago."

Rowden blew out a breath. "I was helping a friend, not on holiday." He'd spent most of October in the countryside at the home of his friend Nash Pope. Pope's father, the Earl of Beaufort, had offered to pay Rowden for his time, but Rowden hadn't felt right about taking the money. Now that Nash was planning a wedding and threatening to invite Rowden, he wondered if he should have accepted the money.

"I was hoping to buy a new waistcoat," Chibale complained.

Rowden rolled his eyes and then winced. His head was still ringing. "You're already the best-dressed man east of Mayfair. The last thing you need is another waistcoat."

Chibale nodded at the server who brought his ale and drank. "You could use a new waistcoat." He handed Rowden his shirt so he could pull it over his head and bare chest. "And a few new shirts, come to think of it."

Rowden drank his ale down. "Only get blood on them," he said. Rowden stared at his empty glass. "Besides I have no one to impress." He glanced at Chibale. "How is your sister's gown coming along?"

"It's finished," Chibale said, looking annoyed.

"And the modiste still hasn't succumbed to your charms?"

A few months ago, Chibale had drank a bit too much wine when they'd been celebrating one of Rowden's wins, and he'd confessed he was half in love with a French modiste named Madame Renauld. But the dressmaker refused all of Chibale's efforts to court her, so he'd finally brought his sister to her to have a dress made. Apparently, that effort had not gone as planned.

"How's your head?"

Rowden turned to see where the voice had come from and immediately regretted the quick movement. Aiden

Sterling grabbed a chair and sat, laughing. "That bad?" He signaled to the server to bring another tray of drinks. "That German knocked you flat. I haven't seen you lose that badly since you fought that Spaniard in Portugal."

"Spaniard in Portugal?" Chibale asked.

"When we were in the army," Aiden said. "Before you started calling Rowden The Royal Payne and charging to watch him fight."

"Ah." Chibale nodded. "When you fought for free." His tone held a trace of contempt.

"It was those goddamn Methodists or Puritans or whatever the hell they were this time," Rowden said. "They threw my concentration." That wasn't exactly true. It was the woman who had distracted him. Those eyes. He'd never seen eyes like that before. Nothing else about her was remarkable. He couldn't even remember her face. She had seemed a black, shapeless thing yelling about sin and hell. Usually, the religious zealots stood on the street corners by the whores and harangued the men soliciting the prostitutes. Lately, they'd become bolder, entering taverns to preach about the evils of drink and sport. This was the second time they'd interrupted one of his mills, though he'd heard of other fights that had been disrupted by them. Last time he'd considered it a nuisance. This time he was angry. And bruised.

"A sect of Methodists, I think," Chibale said.

"You cost me five pounds," Aidan said.

"Only five pounds?" Rowden asked. "That's all you wagered on me?"

"No, I wagered ten."

"Then how did you lose only five?" Chibale asked, passing out drinks from the server.

Rowden glared at his friend. "Because he wagered five on the German."

Aidan smiled and lifted his ale. "You know me too well."

Rowden brought the ale to his lips then set it down again. His belly roiled and his head hurt like the dickens. "I'm done for tonight." He stood, wobbling a bit.

Chibale stood too. "I'll go with you."

Rowden waved him off. "Your rooms are nearby. It would be out of your way." Rowden caught the look Chibale and Aidan exchanged.

"I'll go," Aiden said. "I haven't eaten yet. I'll stop in at the Draven Club and see what Porter is serving tonight."

"I don't need a chaperone," Rowden said. But he didn't argue very forcefully. He'd rather Aidan go with him, hail the hackney, and haul him up to his flat. Rowden's head hurt too much to think about anything practical.

"Tomorrow at Mostyn's," Chibale said as the two men started away. "I made notes for improvement."

Rowden blew out a breath and leaned on Aidan as they stepped out into the frigid February night. Aiden raised a hand, and a jarvey just down the street called to his horse and started their way.

"I thought you didn't like taking orders," Aidan said.

"He works for me."

Aidan raised his brows but didn't speak. Rowden didn't like taking orders, but he also wasn't an idiot. That's why he'd hired Chibale. The man knew boxing, and he knew what Rowden needed to do to win. It was Chibale who had come up with the name The Royal Payne, and it was largely due to Chibale that the name was becoming known not only within London but throughout England.

So Rowden might not like having to go to the boxing studio tomorrow, but he'd do it.

And next time, no goddamn zealot would throw off his concentration.

***

Modesty Brown stood on the corner and watched as the fighter—they called themselves *milling coves*—climbed into a hackney with his friend. She heaved a sigh of relief. He had been hit so hard, and when he'd fallen it seemed the entire floor shook. She'd known it was her fault. He'd been looking at her when the other man hit him. She'd wanted to warn him, but she was supposed to be there to disrupt the sinful activities, not take part in them.

Beside her, her father called out Bible verses to men and women passing by. No one seemed to pay him any attention. She held her wooden sign higher. It read, REPENT! THE END IS NEAR!

The torch one of the other congregants held lit the words on the sign. The older woman with the torch would take over preaching when her father's voice tired. It was only half past ten, and they would probably be here until midnight at least. She did not like staying out that late. The later it became, the more intoxicated the people. The Fancy—what the men who liked to watch fights called themselves—were especially rude. Men and women alike yelled foul things and made vulgar gestures. Modesty always tried to look away. When she'd been younger, her father had covered her eyes. But now that she was almost four and twenty, she had seen just about everything the underground of London had to offer. A boxing match between two grown men seemed relatively tame to her, but she had not argued when her father instructed the small group of parishioners to follow him and disrupt the match.

Modesty never argued. Her mother had not argued. She had been an example of perfect womanhood—obedient, submissive, soft-spoken, and pious. Modesty wanted to be everything her mother had been. She wanted her father to love her the way he'd loved her mother.

And her mother would not have countenanced her staring at the pugilist as she was. Modesty averted her eyes from the hackney and tried not to think about the man. She'd seen bare-chested men before on other occasions when she had been in the party that disrupted a boxing match. She saw bare buttocks even more frequently. All she had to do was look down the alley to her right to see prostitutes pushed up against a wall and men with their breeches about their knees. She did not concern herself with matters of the flesh. It was the spirit inside the flesh that mattered.

But she had been sorely tempted tonight because the flesh encasing the pugilist's spirit was rather enticing. She'd have to ask for forgiveness later because she had looked far too long at his bare chest. And then she'd looked even longer at his almost-handsome face and his green eyes.

"Beware the serpent!" her father called out, and Modesty nodded in agreement. She did need to be wary.

"Beware the fires of—" Her father broke off and the other parishioners looked at him with alarm. He cleared his throat and continued. "The fires of hell!'

Modesty frowned. Something was not right. Her father did not sound like himself. "Excuse me. Brother John, please take my place for a moment."

"Father!" Modesty grabbed his arm. "Are you well?"

"The Lord is my shepherd," Brother John began.

Her father gave her a tight smile and wiped a bead of sweat from his cheek. Like the rest of the party, he was dressed in all black. His black hat obscured his face in the dim light, and she could not see his eyes.

"Yes, child. All is well. I see someone I must speak with. I will return in a moment."

He walked away, and Modesty rose on tiptoes to watch where he went. He passed several buildings then stopped in front of a younger man dressed in plain brown trousers and the sort of coat farmers wore. He removed his hat, and the two men stepped around the corner and out of sight.

Modesty felt her belly tighten with unease. Her father had never done such a thing before. He never left his preaching like this. The only time he left off was when someone passing by asked for a blessing or to pray with him. But if that man had wanted a blessing, then why had he not asked in front of all of them? Why had her father gone off with him in private? London was dangerous, and it made her nervous to think of her father alone and undefended.

But presently, he returned. She waited for him to explain himself, but he said nothing, just took over for Brother John. Modesty glanced down the street where her father had gone to meet the man and noted he was still standing on the corner. He still held his hat and he seemed to be watching her. Modesty looked away, feeling self-conscious. And when she looked back, he was gone.

Printed in Great Britain
by Amazon